This is a work of fiction. Unless otherwise indicated, all the names, characters, places, events, and incidents in this book are either the product of the author's imagination or used in a fictitious manner. Any resemblance to actual persons, living or dead, or actual events is purely coincidental. For full content warning, please see the author's note located in the back of this book.

Copyright October 2023 Vanessa Kramer
Second Edition published October 2024
Virtue Publishing

ISBN 979-8-9916277-1-9 (paperback)

<u>Life</u>

1

"Dearly beloved, we are gathered here today to celebrate the joining in marriage of these two people."

I look at my dad standing next to me and smiling. I am holding a beautiful bouquet of white and red roses. The church is filled with people who are watching me. My brother and mom are sitting in the front row.

"Who here gives this bride away?" the priest asks.

"Her mother and I do," my dad replies, tearing up.

He kisses my cheek and walks away. I turn to my groom and feel myself beaming. I am marrying Matt Kinsley, the lead singer of the Broken Chandeliers, my favorite band. I had every single album they ever made and thought he was one of the most handsome men I had ever seen. And now I am getting to marry him! I remove the veil from my face and pull it over my head. Matt smiles at me, and I can see every one of his blinding white teeth. Every hair on his head is ideally in place; a change from his normally tousled mane. His black tuxedo is crisp and free of dandruff and wrinkles. He is wearing a red tie that matches the roses in my bouquet.

My white dress is covered in lace and has little beading details. A train flowing in the back of my dress lays on the stairs leading up to the altar. I look back at my mom, who is wearing a lavender dress. I always loved lavender on her. She dabs at her eyes with her handkerchief. My dad smiles at me. My little brother wears a lavender dress shirt that matches my mom's dress. He's also smiling at me, but his smile looks much happier than my dad's. I turn back towards the priest.

"Do you, Emma, take this man as your husband? To love and cherish forever?"

"I do," I grinned.

"And do you, Matt, take Emma as your wife?"

"Nooooo," he groaned.

My smile faded.

"To love and cherish forever?" the priest asked.

"No!" Matt yelled.

I stirred in my sleep.

"NO!"

I sat up quickly.

"Ouch, shit."

I rubbed my head where I had hit it as I tried to sit up. I reached out in the dark and looked around for my phone. I pushed a button to light up the screen and looked around the room. The soft

4

glow from my phone landed on clothes, textbooks, various sports balls, and a poster of one of those first-person shooter video games.

"You okay?" I heard a sleepy voice ask.

"I'm fine," I muttered. "Go back to sleep."

"Are you going back to your room?"

"Yeah, Simon," I sighed. "I'm sorry, but I can't sleep in here all night. You'll be fine without me, I promise."

"What if I get scared again or have another bad dream?"

"Only you can control your dreams," I explained as I stood up. "If your dream gets too scary, change it to something else."

I blamed video games for his bad dreams. Simon didn't have nightmares until he started playing more graphic games. He would beg my mom and dad to get him something with zombies or aliens or maniac killers, and they would finally give in. He'd promise that they weren't too scary or violent. And then I'd wind up sleeping on the bottom bunk with the wadded-up clean clothes and forgotten stuffed animals. I leaned in and touched my little brother's hand with mine.

"Goodnight, Simon. Love you."

"Love you, Emma," Simon mumbled and turned over.

I slowly walked through the dark hallway, stopping only when the stupid cat scared me by batting at my toes.

"Jesus, Cheeseball, you scared the crap out of me!" I whispered loudly, kicking a foot at her.

Cheeseball slinked down the hall to Simon's room. She was probably mad at me for shutting her out of his room earlier, but I didn't feel like waking up with my eyes swollen shut. We got her several years ago because my parents, not knowing I was allergic to cats, thought that having a pet would help me cope with my disease. I decided to let Simon name the cat since I couldn't be around her. I honestly think he did it on purpose. I'm allergic to cats and dairy, so why not name the fucking cat after a dairy product?

I walked through my bedroom, into the bathroom, and sat on the toilet. I know this is way too much information, but this was my ninth time going to the bathroom that day. Pretty good, considering I usually go ten or eleven times a day. I had been trying to force myself to hold it as long as possible. My first year of college started in a couple of months, and I didn't want to be known as the girl who took a shit every two hours. Maybe I'd even have a boyfriend this year.

"As if," I chuckled to myself.

I have Crohn's disease. I was diagnosed with it when I was twelve years old. I've always had digestive issues and abdominal pain; for as long as I can remember, it's been a pain in the ass. I'm lactose intolerant and have allergies to peanuts, soy, bananas, shellfish, strawberries, eggs, dogs, cats, and a handful of seasonal bullshit. After a few teachers my kindergarten year accidentally letting me have milk or candy with peanuts in it, not remembering how to use my epinephrine pen (although my mom probably had shown them a thousand times), and getting in trouble for using the bathroom too much during class time, my mom pulled me out of public school and home-schooled me for a year. My parents needed two incomes, however, so my mom started working again and put me back in public school for second grade.

I continued to be the center of my parents' world until Simon came along. He wasn't planned. I was already enough for them to have to deal with. I had so much wrong with me and they were bringing another baby into the world, so I know they were scared. But he was perfect. He only ever cried if he was hungry or needed his diaper changed. He was always a perfectly happy, perfectly healthy kid. Our age difference caused a little bit of a wedge in our relationship. Simon was a toddler and I was going into middle school. I wanted to be as normal as possible, even though I was always in pain. I tried really hard not to let my stomach issues bother me so my mom wouldn't worry so much. She could still tell though. My parents finally decided to take me to a specialist that ran test after test until they diagnosed me with Crohn's disease.

I made the mistake of telling a couple of kids at school about it; all they did was make fun of me. So, I learned to keep it a secret, wear cool clothes, and make incredible friends. I wasn't one of *the* popular kids by any means, but I wasn't a loser. I was on the newspaper and yearbook staff, so I knew everything about everyone. Everyone wanted to be my friend so they could get their picture in the school newspaper. I was never interested in taking posed photos of people. I can't stand that fake shit. I wanted to be a wildlife photographer. I wanted to take pictures of concerts for bands. I wanted to travel the world and take photos that told stories. I've had so many different dreams. Thinking about how big my dreams were throughout my life made me feel so small. Instead of traveling the world, I was doubled over on my toilet, looking at the chipped nail polish on my toenails.

After going to the bathroom, I tiptoed through my room and found my senior yearbook. I opened up the page where my senior story was written and skimmed through it before tucking myself back into bed. I graduated with honors for my newspaper stories and even won awards for some of them. I was going to be a journalist. I'd start small, probably having to write locally at first. However, I was going to make my way to New York and get into entertainment journalism. I wanted to write about upcoming bands, concerts, and albums for entertainment magazines. I closed my yearbook and tossed it onto the floor.

I wanted to go off to college with my best friends. I wanted to live in a dorm, attend classes, join a sorority, and have a typical college experience. I wanted to live my dream. Instead, I was 21, living with my parents and 10-year-old brother. I was stuck in our dumpy little town, surrounded by everyone else who was stuck.

I woke up the following day and went downstairs for breakfast. Simon and my dad were already sitting at the table eating while my mom pranced around the kitchen in her robe.

"Hey, Sweetpea," my dad smiled at me behind his reading glasses.

"Hey, hey," I grinned. "What are you reading?"

"This boring book about war," Simon rolled his eyes.

"It's not just about war," My dad started.

"Oh, here we go," my mom laughed.

"It's about getting left behind by your brothers in arms so that their lives could be spared while yours is about to end and looking death in the eye and saying, 'Not today, you son of a-'"

"Carl!" my mom threw a piece of toast at my dad, and he stopped. Simon and I laughed.

"I like the sound of it," I said. "Can I borrow it when you're done with it?"

"Sure," my dad said.

9

"Emma," my mom added. "Wouldn't you enjoy getting out and doing something more exciting? Summer is almost over, and school will start before you know it."

"I know," I sighed. "And I can't wait for it. It can't get here soon enough. It's so boring here."

"Ugh," Simon scoffed. "Why do you have to wish summer away? Just because most of your friends went out of town for the summer doesn't mean you have to wish mine away. I still haven't beaten all the video games I got for Christmas."

"That's because they keep you up all night and make you too scared to sleep," I said to him.

"That's not what scares me," he said, looking down at his soggy cereal.

"Well, what does then?" I asked.

"You dying."

I looked at my dad, who looked at my mom, who then looked at me. I went over to Simon and put my head on his shoulder, wrapping my arms around his skinny body.

"Simon, why would you say that?" my mom asked. Simon shrugged.

"You don't have to worry about that," I said quietly. "I'm not going anywhere for a long time. Besides, I'm probably going to outlive you. All you do is sit around eating and playing video games. You're probably going to form a blood clot. You're a toothpick. You're not that healthy of a kid."

He looked at me and smiled.

"At least I can eat ice cream without farting and gassing up the whole house."

"You're so funny," I said sarcastically. My parents both laughed.

"Now that the tension has gone down, I think I *will* go out and do something today," I stood up. "Maybe I'll ride my bike into town and walk around a bit."

"Make sure you take your medicine with you if you decide to eat while you're out," my mom reminded me. "Also, don't overdo it with the walking. I don't want you to get out of breath in case you need to run to a bathroom,"

"Mom," I said sternly. "Stop, please."

"Sorry," she replied loudly as I went upstairs. "You know I worry about you."

I hopped in the shower and then got dressed, wearing a pair of blue shorts and a red and white tank top. I had planned to wear the outfit to my friend Whitney's 4th of July party, but she ended up canceling it to go out with her new boyfriend. I was the only single one in our group of friends besides Maddi, but that was only because there were no other gay girls in our town, and Maddi rarely had a chance to meet anyone at her private Christian school. Her parents didn't know she was gay because Maddi feared they'd stop financially supporting her. She was at some young adults retreat for the summer (fully paid for by Daddy) and wasn't even allowed to have her cell phone while she was there. I guess it was one of those "off-the-grid" kind of things with zero distractions.

We planned to move into a dorm together when we graduated high school. The three of us had been accepted to State, and everything was going great. Until my parents and I sat down and figured out how much tuition would be. With the ever-piling medical bills, my parents weren't exactly in the best place to take on college tuition. So instead, I started working while Whitney and Maddi moved in together at State. After a while, though, Maddi started partying too much. Her parents didn't want to waste anymore of their money so they made her leave. Since then, she's been mostly working as a server in various restaurants. Whitney, however, quit college to go to cosmetology school. That also didn't last long. She left that to start working as a receptionist at the tattoo shop her then-boyfriend worked at. Luckily, I've talked both of them into starting school with me this fall, so I won't have to be completely alone.

Maddi and I will get an apartment on campus together this year. Whitney was also going to live with us, but that was before she met Sam, her current boyfriend. Sam started working at the same tattoo shop Whitney, and her now-ex worked at. Whitney cheated on her ex with Sam, and her ex quit. Sam's kind of an idiot but nice all the same. And he seems just as crazy about Whitney as she is about him. I wish my life were half as exciting as my friends' lives. The highlight of my week was doing a new art project with the kiddos at the daycare that I work at.

I was riding my bike through town, taking everything in. The banners on the lamp posts advertising the summer fair, the purple and yellow petunias planted along the sidewalks, the small children holding their mother's hands on their way to the park, the older women sitting around gossiping outside the bakery. I loved my small town, sure, but I dreamt of visiting big, far-off cities. Still, I liked the comfort of home. I could make my way through town with my eyes closed. I knew the best place to get breakfast. I knew that a man named Bo opened a stand on the corner every Friday and sold delicious homemade ice cream for only one dollar. I knew the high school baseball field dugouts were covered in the names of graduated seniors, including my dad's. I knew the best place to stargaze, watch fireworks, read, or just watch the town was on the roof of the old dog food warehouse (a quick trip through the hole in the back fence and up the building's side ladder).

But still. I knew my life had to be more than this small, almost *invisible* town. As safe and familiar as it was, my hometown also felt like a cage. I was like an animal in a zoo exhibit. I was safe and content, but I belonged on the outside. I was a smart enough person to stay out of harm's way, but a little excitement and danger was something I wanted- something I longed for. And it felt just out of reach. I hoped and even prayed that something thrilling would happen to me.

I pictured myself in a convertible, with the sun shining on my face, driving up the coast in California. I was wearing a tight-fitted black dress, dark sunglasses, and red lipstick. I had a Golden Retriever, named Frans (after the famous photographer, Frans Lanting), who had his head out over the side of the car. His tail was wagging and his big slobbery tongue was waving in the wind. The car radio blasted pop hits and I sang along to every one of them. Frans leaned over and licked my cheek. I laughed and petted him as I drove alongside the ocean.

I was daydreaming when someone in a parked car opened the driver's side door right in front of me. I gasped and squeezed the breaks as hard as possible, turning my wheels, but hit the car door, and my bike started tumbling with me shortly after. I landed hard but didn't hurt my head, luckily. I heard people moving toward me, sounding worried.

"Oh my god," I heard a voice say. The sun was in my eyes, so I couldn't see who was standing above me.

2

"Are you okay?" the voice said. "I'm so sorry I didn't see you!"

"Obviously," I muttered and put my hands as a visor over my eyes.

Leaning over me was a guy about my age. He had hazel eyes, full lips, and ashy blonde hair. He smiled at me, and I swear, his teeth nearly blinded me; they were so white. I sat up slowly and looked down at my hands and knees.

"Yeah, you're skinned up pretty bad," he said. "Do you need a ride home?"

"No, I'm fine," I said as I hobbled to stand up. "I'll just ride my bike back home."

I turned around and looked at my bike, which looked like it had been beaten with a crowbar. The chain guard was busted, and the back tire was bent.

"Shit," I breathed.

"Sorry again," the boy said. "I can throw your bike in the back of my car and give you a ride home."

I picked up my bent bike, ignoring him, and started pulling it along. A few locals asked if I was okay. I smiled and nodded, refusing to look around in case the hot idiot was following me.

Well, I thought. *There goes my relaxing outing.*

About five minutes later, the same guy pulled up next to me in his car, creeping alongside me while I walked. I tried to ignore him, but it was hard, especially since he had his music turned up loud.

"What are you doing?" I finally asked, frowning.

"I wanted to make sure you got home safely," he smiled. "I thought since you were too stubborn to let me give you a ride home-"

"You thought it'd be better to be creepy and follow me there?"

He laid his foot on the brake pedal. I kept walking.

"Please just let me take you home," he called. "Your leg looks pretty bad."

I looked back at him with furrowed brows. He was smiling this big, cheesy smile with little beads of sweat on his forehead. I opened his back door, shoved my broken bike in, and got in the front seat.

"My name is Alastor," he said, sticking his hand out at me. I just looked at him.

"This is when you put your hand out and tell me your name."

"Emma," I said as I fastened my seat belt. "I don't shake hands."

Alastor shrugged and started driving.

"How come I've never seen you around before?" I asked. "You don't live here, do you?"

"Just in town for the day, checking out the area," he explained. "I was going to Holden County Community College to get my associate's degree, but Smith County offers classes that Holden doesn't that I wanted to take. I wanted to move out from my mom's place, but I need to find a job first. I was hoping to run into someone who's also going to Smith County to see what jobs are in the area."

"That's where I'm going," I said, sounding a little more enthusiastic than I meant to.

"Oh well, awesome!" he smiled. "What are you studying?"

"Oh, um, I'm just working on getting my general associate's degree. I'll probably figure out my major once I get the hang of things."

"Is this your first year of college?" he asked.

I blushed before answering.

"Are you only eighteen?"

"No, if you must know," I snapped. "I'm twenty-one. I couldn't decide on a college when I graduated high school, so I worked until the timing was right."

"I didn't mean to offend you."

I looked out the window until the silence started bothering me.

"Alastor?" I asked. "What kind of name is that?"

He laughed, and it bothered me.

"My mom used to be really into Greek mythology. Alastor was the god of vengeance and

17

familial bloodshed. He started many fights between family members to the point they'd kill each other. Alastor is also the name of Hades' black horse."

I tilted my head slightly and gave him a weird look.

"My name means 'scoundrel,'" he continued.

"How charming," I said sarcastically.

"I'd like to think I'm pretty charming."

"Do you have a girlfriend?"

Alastor looked at me and smiled.

"I'm just wondering," I added quickly. "I'm not asking for me. I thought a name like that might make dating a little difficult for you. I have a boyfriend."

"Oh yeah?" Alastor chuckled. "What's he like?"

"Tall, handsome, athletic, funny, and drives a nice car."

"Damn, I knew it," he shook his head. "The exact opposite of me. What's his name?"

We drove past Benjamin's Boat and Fishing Surplus.

"Ben," I answered.

"Ben, what?"

"Why do you care?" I asked.

"Just wondering," he winked. "I'm not asking for me or anything."

"Ben..." I paused. "Um, Forest."

Alastor started laughing.

"What?" I asked.

"Seriously? *Forest?* As in the name of the street we just passed? You're not very quick on your feet, are you?"

I tried not to smile, but the harder I tried, the harder I laughed.

"No, by the way," Alastor said. "I don't have a girlfriend."

"I don't have a boyfriend either," I smirked.

"You don't say?"

We pulled up to my house, and Alastor got out to come over to my side and opened the door for me. I looked up at him.

"Really?" I asked.

"What can I say? I'm a gentleman. One might say that I'm even *charming*."

I rolled my eyes.

"Hey," he said. "Your words. Not mine."

I hobbled through the door, and Alastor followed with my bike. My dad was sitting in his chair reading his book but got up suddenly when he saw me.

"What happened?" he asked as he walked over to me.

"I just had a little accident," I smiled. "I'm fine, I promise."

My dad looked at Alastor over the top of his glasses.

"Dad, this is Alastor. Alastor, this is my dad."

"Alastor King. Nice to meet you, Carl," Alastor stuck his hand out. My dad looked at him.

"How did you-"

"Saw the name badge on the table when we came in," Alastor smiled. "So, you work down at the new warehouse?"

"Oh! Yes, I do," my dad laughed.

"I passed it on my way into town this morning and recognized the symbol on your badge."

"So, Alastor, huh?" my dad grinned. "Mind if I call you, Al?"

"Yes, I do," Alastor said sternly. My dad's grin quickly disappeared. "I don't do nicknames. Besides, I like my name too well to have a nickname."

"Fair enough," my dad replied. "Why don't we head into the kitchen?"

We all moved into the kitchen, where my mom was peeling potatoes. She stopped when she saw us come in.

"Who's this?" my mom wiped her hands on her apron and stuck her hand out.

"Hi, I'm Alastor. Alastor King."

"Hi, Alastor. I'm Sue."

Her eyes moved to my cuts and scrapes.

"Emma Rose! What happened?"

"Emma tried to run over my car with her bike."

I rolled my eyes.

I cleaned and bandaged myself up while my dad and Alastor talked. I kept thinking Alastor would find some excuse to leave, but he stayed. Even when my mom had made dinner and invited Alastor to eat, he not only endured but helped my mom out in the kitchen. I was surprised by how well he got along with my family. Everyone except for Cheeseball. She hissed at Alastor the second she saw him and hid under Simon's bed until Alastor left. Dinner went well; everyone laughed and shared stories. It felt like Alastor had been a part of our family for years. At one point, Alastor took an ink pen out of his pocket and drew a heart on the bandage that covered my scraped hand. My mom cooed over how sweet the gesture was, and I scrunched my nose at her. After dinner, Alastor and I sat on the back porch swing and looked up at the sky in silence. I could feel Alastor's eyes shift from the stars to my face. My cheeks were warm, and I looked at him.

"What?" I asked finally through gritted teeth.

"I think you're beautiful."

"Oh please," I laughed off.

"You are."

"Don't."

"What?" he asked.

"Just don't," I said a little more sternly. "You hit me with your car door. I was having an ordinary day, and you came out of nowhere and hit me with your car door. Then, you give me a ride home and stay for dinner, and it's just too perfect."

I started laughing awkwardly.

"And you're perfect. You're nice and handsome and get along with my family. It's too obvious, like a written story. And that's not how life works. Or at least not my life. Nothing good-"

"Emma, stop," he said. "I know what I want when I see it, and I want you. Something brought us together today. I would have preferred it to be something better than hitting you with my car door, but I'm still glad it happened. I had a great time with your family tonight and hope to do it again. You're scared. I'm not sure why, but I can see it. Don't be. I'm not a bad guy. I'll spend every day trying to convince you that we should be together."

"You've known me for like, what, a day?" I said. "Do you know how borderline creepy you sound right now? I don't know hardly anything about you, and you suddenly want me to be your girlfriend?"

"You're right," he sighed. "No, you're right. I'm sorry. I was just worried that if I didn't ask you to be my girlfriend right away, school would start, you'd get busy with your friends, and other guys would have a chance to ask you out."

"We can still be friends. It'll be nice to know someone new at school if we run into each other and who knows, we may have a class together. I just can't commit to a boyfriend that easily. It'll be my first year in college, and I need all my focus. I can't do the official titles and such."

"So, we'll be friends?" Alastor repeated. "Then, when you fall madly in love with me, we'll be more."

I shook my head and giggled. Alastor took an old receipt and pen out of his pocket.

"Here," he said after writing down a phone number. "In case you need a study buddy at school or something."

I took the receipt, tore it, and wrote down my number on the blank piece.

"Don't expect me to text you a lot," I said. "I have a pretty busy work schedule."

"Oh, I probably won't text you at all," he said sarcastically. "I'll be pretty busy with stuff too. You know, not thinking about you every second of the day."

We both smiled at each other again.

"Well, I better get going. I have a bit of a drive to make it back home."

"Goodnight, Alastor."

"Goodnight, Emma."

I sat and watched Alastor walk to his car. A chill ran up my back as he ran his hand through his messy hair. I shook it off and stood up, waving goodbye to him again. I walked through the front door, not realizing how big the grin was on my face until I looked at my mother, father, and brother.

"Ooooh, Emma has a boyfriend!" Simon said.

"Oh shush," I replied. "He's just a friend."

"I don't think he thinks so," my mom smirked. "Did you see how he fell all over himself trying to impress us? I like him. He's adorable."

"Mom, come on," I said. "I just met the guy today. I don't know anything about him, and he doesn't know anything about me. Well, besides all the embarrassing things you insisted on telling him. What if he's a psychotic serial killer?"

"Hardly seems the type," my mom replied.

"If you guys like him so much, you can go out with him. I'm going to bed now. Goodnight."

"I thought he was rather dreamy," my dad winked. "Goodnight, honey."

I stomped up to my room and got ready for bed. I got into my pajamas and laid down. I looked at my phone to check the time and saw that I had a text message from Alastor.

Hey, friend. It was nice meeting you.

I wasn't going to respond, at least not immediately. I didn't want to look desperate. I tossed and turned, not being able to turn my mind off. I huffed, threw the blanket off me, and looked at my hand. The moonlight through my window shone on the tiny drawn heart. I started thinking about Alastor. His hair, eyes, smile, and lips. I slowly ran my hands over my breasts and closed my eyes. I pictured Alastor touching me and slowly ran my hand over my underwear. Suddenly, someone knocked on my door, and I jumped.

"Goodnight!" Simon said from the other side.

"Night!" I answered, jumping.

I looked at my phone and saw there was another message from Alastor.

Sweet dreams.

I tucked my hand back under my pillow and eventually fell asleep.

All around me are the sounds of people screaming. I hear men, women, and even children around me shrieking and crying. I can hear them being tortured and ripped apart, begging and pleading. Some of the screams are cut off with gasps or gurgling. I can hear moans and thuds of something falling around me. It is pitch black wherever I am and I can't see anything, only hear the awful sounds of people in pain, the crackling of burning, and crunching.

I can smell smoke and sulfur. Suddenly, something warm and thick begins to fall on me. It is a small amount, dripping at first, but it turns into a downpour. It is difficult to breathe through whatever is pouring down on me, especially when some gets into my mouth. I had tasted it before. It was that metallic-like taste when you get a bloody lip or bite the inside of your cheek. It is raining blood. I try to run but keep slipping on the blood and bumping into things. The screaming is getting so loud I can hardly stand it. I cover my ears with my hands as I try to run. The lumps of things I keep running into are gooey and have hair in some places and limbs reaching out. I can guess what's lying around me as my arms brush outreached fingers and feet. I'm glad I can't see the mangled bodies around me, but I can only think about how to get away. I feel a hand grab my clothes, and I try to let out a scream, only to choke on the blood raining down. Another hand grabs my leg while yet another one grabs my hair. I flail my hands around, reaching out to anything that would free me from their grip. Suddenly, there is a bright, fiery explosion and for a brief second I can see everything around me before I wake up screaming.

3

"Emma!"

I opened my eyes and looked around. It was morning, and my dad was standing over me, shaking me.

"Oh my god, honey, are you okay? You're bleeding."

I looked at my hand where the heart bandage had been. The bandage was gone, and the scab was opened, trickling blood down to my elbow. There was smeared blood on my bed sheet and pajama shirt.

"You must have scratched off the bandage and scab in your sleep," my dad explained. "I'll get a warm, wet washcloth and clean you up. You have some blood on your face too."

I nodded and watched as my dad left the room. I could hear him talking to my mom down the hallway.

"Is she okay?" my mom asked.

"Yeah," my dad sighed. "I think she just had a bad dream. She scratched off the scab on her hand and got blood on the bed, but she's okay."

I took the blanket off and looked down at my leg. My eyes got wide, and I let out a gasp. There was a burn mark that almost resembled a handprint. It was right where the hand had grabbed my leg in my nightmare. My dad returned

27

to my room with the washcloth, and I looked at him.

"What?" he asked. "What's wrong?"

"Dad, what do you think this is?" I asked, pointing to my leg.

"Oh," he said. "Most likely road rash. Got yourself pretty banged up, huh, kiddo?"

I kept looking at the mark on my leg.

"You want to tell me about your dream?" he asked, wiping my face and hand.

I looked at him. I thought about the brief moment when I saw everything around me before waking up. I saw a field of mangled bodies, screaming people falling from the sky, and blood rain.

"I don't remember it," I lied.

"Probably for the best," he smiled. "Well, whatever it was, it's over now. You ready to get up for church?"

I nodded. My dad leaned forward and kissed my forehead before leaving the room. I got up slowly and made my way around my room, getting my clothes on, and my hair brushed, trying to erase my nightmare from my memory. When we got to church, I blessed myself with holy water and sat down between my mom and dad while Simon sat on the other side of my dad. Typically, our family is loud, crazy, obnoxious, and all-around goofy, but for an hour and a half every other Sunday, we get all serious and listen to our priest while he talks about the bible and sin and blah, blah, blah. Thank goodness my dad has to work every other Sunday, or else I'd have to endure Mass once a week instead of every other week.

Don't get me wrong, I believe in God and love God, but I honestly do not see the point in all of this. Getting dressed up, going to a building, confessing to a stranger about stupid shit you've done, and saying some prayers that make up for the shit you've done. Then, sitting for an hour listening to the only guy in the room that knows everyone's secrets as he tries to make everyone feel even more guilty. And yet again the feeling of guilt when the offering plate comes around. Then, eating an extremely dry cracker that's supposed to be flesh, drinking cheap wine that's supposed to be blood, and listening to a group of old people sing slow and boring songs.

I honestly think my parents only go to church because of me. Maybe if they suck up to God, my illnesses will magically go away. No such luck.

"That was a wonderful Mass," my mom chirped on the way home.

"That's an oxymoron if I've ever heard one," I rolled my eyes.

"Are you calling Mom a moron?" Simon gasped. "Mom, Emma just called you a moron."

"Shut up," I said before punching Simon on the arm. He reached across the back seat and hit me back.

"Ow, you little pervert! You just punched me in the boob!"

"Okay, enough!" My dad yelled. "We just left the church, and you two are already starting. Christ on a cracker!"

The car was silent. My mom glanced over at my dad and started giggling, which got him laughing. Soon, we were all laughing and changing the subject to something lighter. That's just how our family was. One minute we were punching and yelling at each other; the next, we were laughing and joking around.

"Someone's got a visitor," my dad said, pointing at the driveway as we pulled up to the house.

"Holy crap," I whispered.

I got out of the car and smiled at Alastor as he walked toward me.

"I thought I recognized that death machine of a car," I said.

"Oh, come on, you're not still mad about that, are you?" he winked at me. "At least you still have all of your limbs."

"You're a monster," I said playfully. Alastor just smiled at me.

"By the way," he added. " I have something for you."

"Like, a present?" I asked, blushing.

"Well, it's something that's already yours. I just...borrowed it for a bit."

He opened the back seat of his car and pulled out my bike. No dents, no scratches, and freshly painted. It looked brand new.

"Is that my bike?" I asked.

"Yeah," Alastor nodded. "I asked your dad if I could pick it up and take it to the bike shop to get fixed up. I feel bad for what happened yesterday and wanted to make it up to you."

"Wow," I said, running my hand on it. "I don't know what to say."

"Take a walk with me?"

I looked at him and frowned.

"Are you asking me or telling me?"

"Just take a walk with me."

Alastor grabbed my hand and started leading the way. My hand started getting sweaty, so I pulled away from Alastor, pretending to fix my hair and adjust my shirt. I crossed my arms for the rest of the walk, worried that Alastor would notice and say something. We walked around my neighborhood and talked for a long time. We talked about music, movies, food, and anything else we could think of to get to know each other. After a while, my stomach started hurting.

"We should probably start heading towards my house," I said.

"Why? Are you not having a good time?" Alastor asked.

"No, I am," I explained. "I just, I don't feel very well."

"Well, maybe if you just sit for a moment-"

"I need to go home," I said more sternly.

"Okay," Alastor said. "I'll walk you home."

When we got to my house, Alastor looked at me, waiting for me to say something.

"Sorry I had to cut our walking date short," I apologized. "I just really don't feel good."

"Date?" he asked.

"Not a *date*," I said quickly.

"Don't apologize," he smiled. "Can I call you later?"

I nodded and said goodbye before going inside. I ran up the stairs and got in the bathroom just in time. When I was finished, I saw blood in the toilet.

"God damn it," I whispered.

It had happened before when I was in high school. My parents freaked out, and I spent some time in the hospital. The timing of this was terrible. I was about to move in with Maddi and start school. There was no way I was going to tell my parents. They would lose their minds, and my plans would go down the drain.

A couple of hours later, I was watching tv in the living room when my phone rang.

"Is that Alastor?" my dad asked, smiling.

I gave him a dirty look and went upstairs to my room. Meanwhile, Simon ran full speed for the television to change the channel.

"Hello?" I said.

"Good evening, Emma," I heard Alastor say. His voice sounded so silky over the phone. I was glad he couldn't see me blushing and smiling.

"Aren't you sick of me yet?" I said.

"Nope," he answered. "I was sitting at home, thinking about you, so I thought I'd call and see how you were feeling."

"Fine," I said shortly. "I'm fine. Thanks."

Silence.

"Sorry again about that."

"You apologize way too much."

"Sorry."

Alastor laughed, which made me start laughing. We talked on the phone for a couple of hours before my mom came in to tell me goodnight.

"I've got to go," I said. "I've got to get up early tomorrow for work. I guess I'll talk to you later?"

"Yeah, I'll talk to you later," Alastor replied. "Goodnight. Sweet dreams."

"Goodnight," I said before hanging up.

The next three days of work dragged by. I worked as a teacher in a toddler classroom at a local daycare. All of the local kids went there from infancy to the time they started kindergarten at the elementary school. A few of the people I went to high school with had young kids at the daycare. Seeing other people my age, married or with kids, was weird. That wasn't on my agenda for quite some time. I didn't even know if I ever wanted kids.

Every chance I got to check my phone, I grew more disappointed. By the third day of work, I started coming to terms with the fact that I wouldn't be hearing back from Alastor. Maybe I had done something wrong, or he caught on to just how boring of a person I was. When I finally decided that Alastor was done with me, he sent me a text message from a new number, apologizing for not getting in touch with me. He asked if he could call. I paced my bedroom floor and thought briefly about not responding for another week and then decided how immature that was. I replied, "Yes." My phone rang.

"Hello?" I answered, plopping down on my bed.

"Emma, I am so sorry," Alastor said, tired. "My phone was stolen, and I had to get a new one. I had to get a new number and everything. It's been a huge mess, and I'm sorry I didn't let you know sooner."

"It's okay," I lied. "I wasn't that worried about it. I've been pretty busy with things, so it's not a big deal."

"Oh," he said. "Well, that's good. I was afraid you would be mad at me. How have you been?"

"Fine. I've been going through my bedroom and packing some stuff. Next month I will move to an apartment on campus right before school starts."

"I bet you're getting excited," Alastor said. "I'm ready for school to start already. The best part will be seeing you around."

"Mm-hmm," I smiled.

We talked on the phone for a while until it started getting a little late.

"I have to get up early tomorrow," I said. "I'm helping my mom and grandma bake pies for the end of summer fair."

"Yeah, I should probably get some sleep too. Can I see you at some point tomorrow?"

"Yeah," I smiled. "I'll see you tomorrow."

"Emma Rose?"

"Yeah?"

"Goodnight."

"Goodnight, Alastor."

I went to sleep quickly and slept soundly straight through the night. I woke up to the smell of pie and saw my grandma moving around my room.

"I'm sorry, honey, did I wake you up?" she smiled. "I came over early to get started on the baking and didn't want to wake you. You looked so beautiful sleeping there. I just wanted to grab some laundry while I was up here."

"Hey, Grandma," I yawned. "Has anyone made coffee?"

"Your mom made a pot when she woke up. You shouldn't drink coffee; it'll stunt your growth."

I looked down at my boobs and long legs.

"I'm pretty sure I'm as grown as I'm going to be."

I got up and went downstairs with my grandma and a big pile of my dirty laundry. I looked into Simon's room and saw Cheeseball hiding under his bed. After dropping my clothes off in the laundry room, I walked into the kitchen where my mom was working on the pies. With Alastor.

"Good morning, sunshine," Alastor smiled at me. "Coffee?"

"Holy shit," I gasped and crossed my arms over my chest. "What are you doing here?"

"Emma!" my grandma glared at me. "You should not use that kind of language."

"I'm guessing you forgot to tell her that Alastor was here," my mom said to my grandma.

"If you all will excuse me, I'm going to go get ready," I said before walking back upstairs.

The sudden stress of Alastor being in my house with my family made me have to urgently use the bathroom. I prayed that they were making enough noise downstairs that they wouldn't be able to hear the particularly loud noises my body was making as it emptied all its contents into the toilet. I was having unusually painful cramping; enough that I started sweating and doubling over, clenching my teeth. I noticed more blood in the toilet. I knew eventually I would have to say something to my parents if it didn't stop. But now was definitely not the time.

Before returning to the kitchen, I got dressed and put my hair in a bun. The four of us worked on baking pies all morning. It amazed me how well Alastor got along with my family. My grandma seemed to like him, just like everyone else. She was even playfully flirting with him, and when Alastor responded with his Alastor-like charm, my grandma would giggle and blush like a schoolgirl. At lunchtime, my mom gave us money to pick up food for everyone before we returned to the pies. We were driving to get food when Alastor reached over and held my hand. I looked at him.

"What?" I asked.

"Your mom told me," he said.

"About what?"

"Your disease."

Shit.

"Seriously?" I said, throwing my hands up in the air. "Okay, before you say another word, let me explain a few things."

Alastor pulled his hand away.

"It doesn't change anything about me," I said reassuringly. "It doesn't make me a different person. I'm not fragile or scared or careful because of it. I have a crappy digestive system and feel sick almost every time I eat, and I poop a lot. I mean, *a lot*. I have ulcers, suffer from fissures, and generally feel like shit. However, I can push through it and live normally, unlike my mother. She treats me like I'm dying. I'm not. I haven't had any major surgeries or complications. I don't know why she insists on telling people my business."

"Were you going to tell me?" Alastor asked.

"Why would it even need to be brought up?" I asked. "It's not like I'm deathly allergic to peanuts and didn't tell you before you brought me an economy-sized jar of peanut butter. That reminds me, I'm severely allergic to peanuts, along with a bunch of other crap."

"God damn, Emma," Alastor said. "That's some serious shit. Is that why you don't want to date me? Because you're afraid I'll be grossed out by your disease or what?"

"No!" I was getting frustrated. "I told you. Right now just isn't a good time for me to start dating. I don't want to date *anyone* at the moment. I have other things to focus on."

I paused for a moment.

"Why, *does* my disease gross you out?" I asked.

"No, of course not!"

Alastor pulled up to order food.

"Emma," he sighed. "I've never met a girl- a woman- like you before. Everyone pretends to be someone they're not because they think they have to impress people. They have to keep everyone's interest. Not you. You're this blazing wildfire that cuts through everyone's bullshit. You have this strange and intimidating power that could destroy anything and everything in your path. But instead, your warmth and glow bring this sense of comfort that makes me want to give you all of me and make me yours. It's a scary and safe feeling at the same time. You think of yourself as plain or ordinary, and you're anything but that. You're extraordinary. You're someone anyone would be lucky to know."

"Can I take your order?" the voice said through the speaker. Alastor smiled at me and began to order our lunch. That is the exact moment when I fell in love with him.

The rest of the day was spent in the kitchen, the four of us laughing and sharing stories and baking. It was great getting to spend so much quality time with my family and Alastor. My mom invited him to stay for dinner, but he insisted on getting back home. I walked out to the front porch with Alastor to say goodbye. I crossed my arms as I always did in my standoffish, defensive manner. I looked out at our yard and saw lightning bugs twinkling. Alastor never took his eyes off of me.

"You want to go to the fair with me?" he asked.

"Yeah," I smiled.

"Can we officially call it a date?"

I nodded and then let out a small laugh.

"Okay," he smirked. "I better go before we get eaten up by mosquitoes. I'll pick you up tomorrow at sundown."

"I'll see you then," I replied. "Goodnight."

"Goodnight, Emma Rose."

4

I dug through my whole room, trying to find something cute to wear to the fair. Everything was either too casual or too dressy. Too plain or not plain enough. Too old or not worn in enough. I sat down on my bedroom floor and pouted. I knew I looked dumb, but this was an official first date. It was important to me and could've been my only chance to have a boyfriend during my first year of college. My first real boyfriend ever. This was something I was longing for and terrified of at the same time. I felt so mad looking through my clothes. Everything I owned was either meant to be worn for church or work. My stomach made a low gurgle sound. I was getting myself stressed out over clothes. There was a knock on my door, and Simon came in and plopped on the bed covered in clothes.

"Are we getting ready to have another garage sale?" he asked.

"No! Why?" I asked.

"What's with the huge mess then?"

"None of your business."

"Fine. Just wondering."

I looked at him and sighed.

"Okay, Alastor asked if I would go to the fair with him on an actual date."

"That's a surprise," Simon rolled his eyes. "He's been wanting to ask you."

"How do you know?" I asked.

"Dad and I have talked to him a couple of times without you being around. But don't worry, I made sure Dad didn't embarrass you or talk about your Crohn's."

"That's okay. Mom told him this morning."

"Of course she did," Simon smiled at me, and then the smile faded. "What will I do when you move away for college?"

"What do you mean?" I asked. "I won't be that far away. Besides, you'll have Mom and Dad all to yourself. You'll see what it's like to be an only child."

"I don't want to be an only child," he smiled. "I like having you for a sister."

I couldn't say anything because I was worried I'd start crying. Simon walked out of the room and went to his room. A few moments later, Simon returned to my room with a shoe box. He handed it to me.

"What's this?" I asked.

"You can have it. Consider it an early Christmas present."

"You never give me Christmas presents," I laughed and opened the box. It was full of money.

"Simon-"

42

"It's from mowing yards and helping Grandma do some housework. I was saving it up to buy a new video game console."

"I can't take this," I said, trying to hand it back to him. "I have a job, you know."

"It's okay," he pushed the box back. "I accidentally snooped in Mom and Dad's room and saw the console I wanted in their closet. It ruins my birthday surprise, but I'll still act surprised. Besides, you need money from your job for your apartment," Simon paused and glanced around the room, "and looking around at your clothing options, you need this."

I stood up and gave Simon a big hug.

"Love you, stinker," I smiled.

"Love you too, butthead," Simon replied.

"Aw, I love it when you two are so loving," my mom said from the hallway.

We pulled away, and Simon dramatically brushed his clothes off before walking out the door.

"Hey," I called down the hallway. "Do you want to go with me to pick out something?"

"You mean we go shopping together?" Simon scrunched his nose at me.

"Yeah, you're right," I said before shutting my door.

I counted all the money in Simon's box, and there was a little over a hundred dollars. That would cover a cute outfit, plus give me some extra cash in case Alastor didn't pay for me at the fair. I was not expecting him not to pay for me, but a person could never be too prepared.

I rode my bike into town and went store to store, looking at options. I spent most of the day trying on different things and taking pictures of myself in them so I could compare notes at the end of the day. I stopped long enough to get a quick lunch before returning to the dressing rooms. I thought about wearing a dress or skirt but then worried about the wind blowing up and showing off my underwear. I was afraid that the pants would be too hot and then worried about the shorts being too cold. I was starting to get frustrated when I decided that the next outfit would be my last. If I couldn't pick from any of the clothes I had already tried on, I would wear something I had already. I put the outfit on and looked in the mirror, smiling.

"I'll take these," I said, handing the clothes to the cashier.

"Cute outfit!" the girl behind the cash register smiled. I recognized her from school but couldn't remember her name. I hoped she wouldn't recognize me.

"Are you wearing this to the fair tonight?" she asked. I nodded.

"Well, have a great time!" she said. "Thanks for stopping by!"

I rushed home, took a shower, changed, did my hair, and did my make-up. I looked at myself in the mirror. I had on a pair of black shorts with pink and red roses printed all over them and a black crop top. I tried on the pink, open-front cardigan in case I got cold and then took it off to cram it into my hobo bag. I slid on my black tennis shoes and raced down the stairs to see if anyone noticed me. My mom immediately saw me and gasped.

"Oh, Emma, you look so adorable!"

"Uh, thanks, Mom," I said.

"Is your stomach supposed to show?" my dad asked.

"Yeah, it's a crop top, Dad," I laughed.

"Oh, stop it. I used to wear stuff like that all the time," my mom said. "And you thought I looked amazing."

"I remember exactly what I thought about when you wore stuff like that," my dad grumbled. "That's what worries me."

There was a knock at the door, and I jumped. Everyone looked at me.

"I'll get it," I said.

I opened the door and saw Alastor. He had a handful of daisies and a smile on his face.

"Wow," he said. "You look amazing."

"Thanks," I smiled, taking the flowers. "I'll leave these here so my mom can put them in water."

I looked back at my mom, who rushed over to take them from me.

"You two have fun," she smiled. "Be sure to stop by our pie booth to say hi. Your grandma is there already, and we're about to load up the last batch."

"Okay, Mom," I gritted my teeth. "Bye."

We rode in Alastor's car to the fair and parked in the grass by the stage. The performances usually included old guys playing country music, some kid from the high school doing a trumpet solo, and the Baptist church's choir performing some religious songs before the mayor made a speech. The stage was the last place to be seen because nothing extraordinary ever happened there. Everyone my age hung out at the games and rides while the parents and grandparents enjoyed the craft booths. Alastor held my hand the entire time and paid for everything I wanted to play, ride, and eat. He was charming and so much fun to be with. At one point, three older teenage girls walked by us, all staring and smiling at Alastor. He immediately put his arm around my waist as we walked by. I avoided asking to ride the Ferris wheel because everyone knew that only teenagers who wanted to make out with other teenagers rode the Ferris wheel. It's almost like a rite of passage in my town. You weren't serious with someone until you made out with them on the Ferris wheel at the end of the summer fair. And I wasn't sure I was ready for that. Or if Alastor was.

"You want to ride the Ferris wheel?" Alastor asked, eating the last bite of cotton candy. I choked on my lemonade.

"Or not," he added.

"Sorry," I sputtered. "I, um, sure. We can ride it, but only if you want to."

"It's pretty much the only thing we haven't done unless you want to go do some square dancing."

I laughed nervously as we approached the guy who was taking tickets. I looked at the people already seated. Besides one little girl with her mom, everyone else was a boy and girl sitting together, cozied up close. The ticket guy caught my eye, gave Alastor and me a thumbs up, and winked. I blushed as we got into our seats. The lap bar came down, and I started shivering from nervousness more than the cold night air. Alastor put his arm around me.

"Is that better?" he asked. I nodded. *Great,* I thought. *He probably thought I did that on purpose so he would put his arm around me. Now I feel like a dumb ass.*

The ride started along with a cheesy '80s song about being in love. I was so afraid of looking at Alastor. I looked everywhere but at him. The Ferris wheel slowly went around a few times without anything awkward happening. On the fourth time around, our seat stopped at the top. Like clockwork, fireworks started going off at the fair, and we looked up as the sky lit up with reds, blues, and greens. I was smiling at the fireworks when I felt Alastor's hand on my chin. He turned my face towards his and kissed me. It was perfect. The chill of the night air left me, and I felt warm down to my toes.

It felt like time stood still as Alastor ran his fingers through my hair, and I put my hand on his waist. We pulled away briefly to catch our breath. Alastor placed my hand in his lap, and I was surprised to feel how hard he was through his jeans. He moved his hand from my hair and reached up under my shirt. I couldn't believe this was happening in a public place. The Ferris wheel started moving again, and we quickly stopped. When we got off the ride, my knees were shaking so badly that I felt like I couldn't stand up straight. Alastor put his arm around me and kissed my forehead before we started walking again.

After we were done at the fair, Alastor took me home. He turned his car off, and we started making out again. My head was pushed against the passenger side window while Alastor kissed my neck. I wanted to go further, but I knew doing anything serious on the first date would have made me look awful. Even though I was usually a proud and modest virgin, Alastor made me want to be anything but one. The windows fogged up, and the radio was on, but I still didn't want my first time to be on a first date in a car parked in front of my house. I wanted it to be more special than that.

"We better stop," Alastor said like clockwork. "I don't want you to get the wrong idea about me."

Could he seriously be any more perfect?

"I agree," I panted. "I should get inside. My parents might come out any second."

"Can I call you tomorrow?" he asked before taking my hand and kissing it.

"Of course," I smiled and opened the car door.

"Emma Rose?"

I looked back at Alastor.

"Would you...want to be my girlfriend? You know, official titles and such."

A huge, goofy grin ran across my face.

"I know, that sounded lame considering we're both adults. And I know you told me you're not ready for a serious relationship. I just really, really like you. I haven't stopped thinking about you once since I hit you with my car door. Not the most romantic thing you can say to someone you are really into. I want you to be mine. So, what do you say?"

"Yeah, okay," was all I managed to get out before shutting the door and running up to the house, giggling.

I went inside and ran up to my bedroom. I was so tired from the night that I fell asleep on top of the blankets in the clothes I had worn that night. I slept so profoundly that my nightmare couldn't even wake me up.

I am in a darkly lit room, chained to a cold steel board and wearing a white nightgown. My hands and feet are chained to each corner of the board. A figure walks into the room, breathing heavily. I try to speak, but nothing comes out. The figure comes closer, and all I can make out are razor-sharp teeth and black eyes, and I can see that the creature is entirely naked. It walks up to me and rips my clothes off. I try screaming but again, no noise comes out. I start crying as the creature pushes against me. I close my eyes, waiting for it to be over. I feel a cold hand wrap around my throat as lips softly kiss my cheek. I look up, and the creature has turned into Alastor. I initially seem confused and try to pull away, but after a while, I start enjoying it.
Alastor tightens the chains, and I feel myself getting more and more into what he's doing to me, even though some part of me knows it's wrong. I see blood running down my legs, but I don't seem to mind. Snakes start slithering up our bodies and wrapping themselves around us. Several of the snakes start biting me, and it seems only to be adding to the pleasure I'm feeling. As Alastor

finishes, he takes a large knife and runs it across my throat.

That's when I woke up screaming.

5

"Emma, please wake up!"

I swung my arms around and knocked into someone. I heard an "oof" and then a thud on the floor. I opened my eyes full of tears and saw Simon on the floor next to me. He quickly got up and leaned over me.

"Are you okay?" he asked frantically. "I couldn't get you to wake up, and you just kept screaming. It was freaking me out."

"I'm okay, "I said, trembling. "I'm okay."

"Mom's down in the car. She wants to take us shopping for school clothes. Do you want me to tell her you're staying home?"

"No, I'll go with you guys," I answered, wiping my face.

"You sure?" Simon asked. "I'll make sure she doesn't buy you anything super ugly."

"I'm sure," I smiled. "Give me about five minutes."

Simon nodded and walked out, closing the door behind him. As I got dressed, I noticed a few bruises on my inner left thigh. I placed my right hand over the bruises and saw that they almost resembled fingerprints. I pulled my jeans up and tried to take my mind off them. Also, my stomach felt a little odd. I thought it was something I may have eaten at the fair.

Shopping with my mom and Simon wasn't exactly thrilling, but it was nice to spend time with them. My mom was always much less fun when my dad wasn't around. Something about him made her less uptight and more easygoing. I always worried about something happening to my dad and my mom becoming this miserable, awful person for the rest of her life. She would sometimes joke with my dad that she would marry a wealthy guy so she wouldn't have to work anymore. But we all know my mom wouldn't know how to function without my dad, let alone remarry.

"Did you want to try on any dresses?" My mom asked. "So far, you've only picked out pairs of pants."

"Yeah, because it'll be cooler weather soon and dresses are for warmer weather," I explained.

"Not if you wear leggings or a sweater with it."

"I don't want any dresses," I said.

"Will you just try a couple for me?" she asked.

"I don't want any dresses," I repeated. I was getting irritated.

"Dresses are fun and girly, though," she smiled.

"Obviously, you're not getting it," I snapped. "I don't feel like wearing any dresses. If the time comes that I feel like wearing a dress, I will go out with my own money and buy my own fucking dress."

"Emma!"

"Emma," Simon pouted. "Don't get an attitude. We're all having fun."

"It's easy for you, Simon," I said. "You have no other choice besides pants. If I want to wear pants, I'll wear some god damn pants!"

Suddenly, my stomach hurt so bad that I doubled over and gasped.

"Emma?" My mom grabbed me. "Are you okay?"

"My stomach," I breathed. "It hurts really bad."

"Like, how bad?" Simon asked. "Like when we ate at that crappy Chinese place and your Crohn's flared up?"

"Worse than that. I feel like there's a rock in my stomach."

"Do you want to go to the doctor?" My mom asked.

"No," I said, wiping the sweat off my forehead. "I just want to go to the car and lay down. You and Simon keep shopping without me."

"Are you sure?" My mom asked. "We can go home if you want to."

"No, seriously, it's all right," I smiled. "I'll just go lay down for a bit."

I took my mom's car key and slowly headed to the parking lot. My stomach hurt so bad that I wanted to drop to the ground and crawl to the car. I stopped for a moment and leaned on my knees. The pain was radiating all over my abdomen. I felt like I was going to pass out. And then I did.

When I came to, I was lying down in the backseat of my mom's car. I could see Simon sitting in the front, looking back at me. I leaned over the seat and threw up.

"Mom," Simon said. "She's throwing up."

"It's okay, Simon," she responded. "We just need to try and stay calm....for her. We don't want to do anything to upset her."

"It looks like there's blood in it," Simon muttered.

I laid back down and closed my eyes. The car soon stopped, and my mom jumped out of the vehicle while Simon came around to help me. A couple of guys returned with my mom and a stretcher and helped me into the hospital. They got me set up in a room and quickly started taking vitals. I was in and out of consciousness while everything was happening around me. I was in so much pain that I could barely comprehend what was happening. The doctor started me on an IV because I was so dehydrated. They took blood samples and ran tests. Finally, after hours of waiting, the doctor returned to talk to us. My dad woke me up so I could hear what the doctor had to say.

"Good evening, everyone," he smiled. "My name is Dr. Steinbeck. I specialize in gastroenterology. I understand you have been struggling with Crohn's disease for some years now, correct?"

I nodded.

"How long have you been experiencing the bleeding?" he asked.

I looked at my parents. They waited for me to answer.

"For a little while now," I said softly.

"What!" my mom yelled.

"Emma!" my dad said. "How could you not tell us that you were bleeding?"

"I don't know!" I panicked. "It wasn't hurting me! I didn't think anything of it."

"Actually, it *has* been hurting you," the doctor said. "Looking at the colonoscopy we did and other tests, it seems as though you have a tear in your intestine. It's been getting bigger as time has passed, so who knows how long it's been there. We'll have to do surgery to try and fix it."

"What if you can't fix it?" my mom asked.

"We will be able to fix the actual tear regardless. Unfortunately, if too much damage has been done to the area, we might need to remove a part of the intestine. If we have to go that route, there is a possible chance of having to add a colostomy bag."

My heart sank. Having a digestive problem, I knew there was always a slight possibility that I'd need a colostomy bag. It's the one thing I've always been afraid of, even over cancer. A colostomy is where a doctor cuts a hole in your abdomen, and a tiny piece of your intestine sticks out, called a stoma. It looks like a reddish, purplish belly button, except grosser. A colostomy bag is placed over the stoma with adhesive, and you poop out of the stoma and into the bag. Yeah, you heard me right. I might have to start shitting out of my stomach and into a bag. Awesome.

"Screw that," I said. "I'm not getting a colostomy bag."

"Emma," my mom scolded. "The doctor will do everything he can to ensure you won't have to."

"That's right," Dr. Steinbeck said. "I will do everything I can to ensure you won't have one. Also, your mom said that school would be starting for you soon. You'll need the recovery time before school begins, so I suggest we start prepping for surgery as soon as possible."

I looked at my parents, and they nodded. The next couple of days flew by as doctors and nurses prepped me for surgery. I asked my mom several times to call Alastor to let him know about the surgery, but he didn't answer or return her call every time she called. I spent a lot of time hanging out with Simon or watching television. When it was finally time to go, the only one who cried was

Simon. He held my hand until the doctors told him he couldn't go any further. When we arrived at the operating room, the people around were telling me what would happen in a step-by-step manner. I blocked them out and closed my eyes, waiting for the anesthesia to kick in.

What happened next was the strangest thing that had ever happened to me. I wasn't dreaming and knew I wasn't dead because part of me could still feel the slightest pain. I sat up from the operating table and noticed that everyone was frozen. No one moved or blinked or breathed. I got off the table, my bare feet slapping against the cold tile, and my hospital gown swished as I walked. I walked past waiting rooms and people until I reached the front door. A blinding white light made me cover my eyes.

"Emma," I heard a soft voice say.

"Who's there?"

"Emma," the voice said again. "Don't be afraid."

"Who are you?" I asked, trying to look around. I couldn't see anything.

"Someone that cares for you very much," the voice said. "You will wake up from this surgery safe and healthy. But you must be careful."

"About what?" I asked.

"Whom you let into your heart. Don't let the darkness in."

"What do you mean?"

"You are so innocent and pure. Be careful. There isn't much time. It will be here soon. I must go."

"I don't understand," I said, trying to feel my way around the brightness. "Who will be here soon?"

"Emma," the voice sounded further away. "Be careful...."

"Wait!" I yelled. "Where are you going?"

"Emma...."

I could barely hear the voice now. The brightness quickly fades to a dark blue, almost black. I look around and gasp. Everything around me is burned up or rotting away. The wind is fierce and kicks up dust all around me. I make my way around to look for the source of the voice but find nothing.

"Emma," a new voice says. This voice is very different from the first. The first voice was soft, warm, and inviting. I could almost taste honey in that voice. This voice, however, is nothing like that. This voice sounds hoarse and cold and almost like an animalistic growl. It sends shivers down my spine like nails on a chalkboard. The voice makes me scared and sad and lonely. I start running away from where the voice is coming from.

"Emma!" The raspy whisper is right behind me.

"Stay away from me!" I shriek. "Leave me alone!"

A hand grabs my arm and pulls me back. I feel like I am right on the line between light and darkness. I stretch my arms towards the light, but it seems to move away as I reach for it. I can only see the hand of what was holding onto me, nothing else. A gray, webbed hand with long, dirty nails is grabbing my arm so tightly that it hurts. The hand feels cold and dead, and if it gets too far into the light, its hand starts burning. I fight with the creature until finally, I can free myself and am in the blinding white light again. I am back in the hospital. I look ahead at the wall in front of me. It is opening wider and wider, revealing the darkness. I back up, tripping over my feet and falling back onto the cold tile. I watch as the darkness extends towards me, and the hand reaches out again for me. I keep scooting backward across the floor, trying to escape the darkness until I back up to a wall.

By now, the creature is fully visible to me. It is a slender reptilian monster. It has shiny gray scales like a snake and crawls on all fours. Its face is round, and its bulging yellow eyes never blink because it has no eyelids. It also has slits where a nose would be and a mouth full of long, needle-like teeth. It hisses at me as I try to scream and the creature starts crawling toward me faster.

"Stay away!" I repeat. I cover my head with my arms and feel the hot breath of the monster above me.

"Emma."

There was a third voice but a more familiar voice this time. I tried opening my eyes, but they felt too heavy. A hand gently brushed through my hair.

"Emma, sweetie," my mom repeated. "Can you hear me? You were mumbling something."

My eyes fluttered open, and I could see my mom sitting in a chair next to me. I could see my dad and brother on the other side of the room.

"Thirsty," I whispered.

"I'll get you some water after I let the doctor know that you're waking up," my mom smiled at me with tearful eyes.

"Mom?" I said. She looked at me.

"Sorry for yelling at you in the store. And for throwing up all over your car."

She smiled without saying a word, her red eyes filling with tears. As soon as my mom stood up to leave the room, my dad and brother came closer to me.

"How are you feeling, kid?" my dad asked, gently touching my hand.

"Can't complain," I closed my eyes.

"The doctor said your surgery went well," he grinned weakly.

My mom came back in with the doctor.

"How are you feeling, Emma?" Dr. Steinbeck asked.

"Fine, I guess," I said. "I'm thirsty, and my mouth tastes like a butthole."

"Emma!" my mom said sternly. Dr. Steinbeck laughed.

"Well, I'm glad to hear you still have your sense of humor. Now, we need to go over a couple of things."

My mom and dad looked at each other with worry. Simon was avoiding all eye contact with me. I knew the news wasn't good.

"We found inflamed pouches along the inner wall of your colon, which tells us you've suffered from diverticulitis. Because of the inflammation, tears have been made to the colon, which is what has caused the most damage. Now, I have good news and bad news."

I held my breath.

"We did have to give you a colostomy bag," Dr. Steinbeck added. "However, if your colon heals like it's supposed to, we should be able to reverse the colostomy, and it will only be temporary while we give your body time to heal."

I touched my stomach ever so gently. I could feel the bag attached under the blanket. Tears started rolling down my face.

"That's great news, Emma!" my mom cried. "At least it's only temporary. Also, the bleeding problem has been fixed. Isn't that wonderful?"

I glared at her and then at my doctor.

"You promised to try your best to ensure I didn't need this fucking thing!"

"Emma Rose!" My dad scolded me. "Dr. Steinbeck has done everything in his power to help you."

"I didn't want this stupid bag," I sobbed. "I didn't want to start school carrying my shit around in a bag all day. I can't believe this is happening to me! I wish I would have just died during surgery!"

"Don't say that," Simon said.

"I want everyone out of my room!" I yelled.

"Emma-" my mom started.

"OUT!" I screamed.

"We can talk out in the hallway," Dr. Steinbeck said calmly as he led my family outside.

I pulled the blanket down to my knees and lifted my hospital gown to see the bag. It was hideous and disgusting. I wanted to rip it off but knew that would piss my doctor off because he'd have to have a nurse put a new one on. Under my bag was all bandaged up, probably my surgical stitches. If I could get my hands on a sharp object, I could tear off the bandages and cut open the stitches. I would bleed to death before anyone came back in, and they would feel so bad for making me live like this.

There was a knock on the door. I didn't say anything. The door opened, and Alastor walked in. I immediately burst into tears. He ran over and hugged me tightly.

"I'm so sorry," he said softly. "I know this isn't what you were wanting."

"I can't believe they cut me up and mutilated me like this," I cried.

"It's only temporary, though," he smiled at me.

"If you don't want to deal with this, I'll understand," I blurted out.

"What are you talking about?"

"Eventually, someone at school is going to notice my bag. People are going to notice eventually. They'll stare, make fun of me, or even worse. People might start feeling sorry for me. People who didn't even know who I was before will want to be nice to me and be friends. It's cool to be friends with people who have disabilities or special needs, or abnormal medical conditions. I've been dealing with it my whole life. Either I was made fun of or got unwanted sympathy for being the weird girl with the stomach problems. I went to a birthday party in 9th grade. The girl's mom announced they would say a prayer for me before they cut the cake; I was mortified. All I've ever wanted was to be normal and blend in. And I don't want to be a burden to anyone. I don't want you to have to deal with me. So if you want to end this before school starts, I understand."

"Emma," he smiled, tucking my hair behind my ear. "You are an amazing young woman. You've captivated me and kept me interested. The late-night phone calls and text messages and time spent together... I'm too invested now. You know too much about me to just walk away now."

He playfully raised one eyebrow. I let out a laugh and wiped the tears on my face.

"I'm becoming addicted to you," Alastor said. "The more I'm around you, the more I want to be around you. No, you're not getting rid of me that easily. Not only can I handle the rude people you're going to face at school, but I will be right by your side helping you tell them to fuck off."

We both started laughing, and then Alastor kissed me. I kissed him back and wrapped my arms around his neck. He leaned further in and put his hand on my waist. I pulled back a little, and he looked at me.

"What's wrong?" He asked.

"Nothing," I muttered.

"What is it?"

"This thing doesn't make me feel pretty," I admitted. "I feel gross."

"Don't be silly," he grinned and kissed me. "You're beautiful, smart, sexy, and everything I would ever want in a girlfriend."

We kissed again until the doctor came back in with my family. I wanted them all to leave to be alone with Alastor more. A nurse came in to show me how to use my colostomy bag, how to clean it, and what to look for in case anything should go wrong. It was agonizing sitting through it, pretending to listen and pretending to care. I spent the rest of my time in the hospital healing and resting while the nurses and doctors kept an eye on my incisions. Finally, I could go home, just in time for school to start.

"The doctor said that if you're not ready to go to school yet, it's okay to stay home a bit more," my mom reminded me the night before I was planning to move in with Maddi.

"I want to go to school," I said with a full mouth of mashed potatoes.

"I just don't want you to overdo it too soon and end up back in the hospital," she said softly.

I banged my hand on the table.

"Stop," I spat. "Let it go and quit nagging me about it. I'm not a little kid anymore. I'm an adult, so stop trying to make decisions for me. I'm moving in with Maddi tomorrow. I'm going to school in a couple of days. I've been waiting for this ever since I graduated high school. I want as much normal as I can get. I can't take one more day of just sitting around with you hovering over me. Besides, all of my stuff is packed up."

I pushed my chair away from the table and excused myself. As soon as I got up to my room, I texted Alastor about my mom irritating me at dinner. He reminded me that she was just worried about me and to be thankful for such a loving mother. I rolled my eyes and asked how soon he could meet me.

66

Alastor and I had been meeting every night since I had been released from the hospital the past week. The first night we stayed up all night just sitting outside talking and looking up at the sky. Also, we made out. Like, a lot. The second night we snuck off and got ice cream (dairy-free for me) and made out with some extra stuff added. The third night was spent laying on a blanket on the soft grass and playing with each other. It was the first time I had ever let a guy touch me like that. It was incredible. He knew exactly what to do with his hands and was patient while I figured out what to do with mine. The hand stuff continued on night four. Last night we used our mouths instead of our hands. I didn't think it could get much better. I was wrong. We had to relocate further away from my house because I was afraid I was getting too loud. But I couldn't help it. It was the best thing that had ever happened to me.

So tonight, my last night at my parents' house, we were going to go all the way. We had been a couple for almost a month and were already planning what we would wear to the college homecoming dance in the fall. I was so in love with Alastor that I would have done anything for him. When all the lights in the house went off and everything went quiet, and still, I grabbed the blanket we had been using and climbed out my window. I slowly made my way down the ladder Alastor would bring and hid it in the bushes while we ran off. We usually headed down the street to the end of my neighborhood and cut through the backyard of the last house, which was unoccupied. However, this time Alastor took my hand through the backyard and up to the back door.

"What are you doing?" I whispered.

Alastor sat down the bag he had been carrying, bent down to lift the doormat on the ground, and looked. There was nothing there.

"Alastor!" I whispered again.

He looked around and spotted a ceramic frog on the ground. He lifted it, and something inside the frog moved. He reached inside the mouth and pulled out a key.

"Alastor, no!" I said quietly. "We'll get caught!"

He looked back at me and smiled.

"What if there's an alarm?"

He put the key in and turned the knob. The door opened and revealed a dark, quiet house. No alarm went off, but my heart was still pounding. We went in, and Alastor shut the door softly.

"Give me about five minutes and then come upstairs," Alastor said before gently kissing my cheek and taking the blanket from me.

As soon as he was upstairs and out of sight I ran around trying to find a mirror. I found one on the wall in the downstairs bathroom and used the light from my phone to check out how I looked. I pulled my clothes off and examined what I had been wearing underneath. I thought I was going to look silly in it when I bought it at the store, but now I felt sexy and mature and beautiful. I had on a light pink sheer babydoll nightgown with a matching thong. I ran my fingers through my hair and then touched my colostomy bag. For a second I thought about putting my clothes back on and telling Alastor I wanted to go home. But I wanted to feel normal. I wanted to experience what other young women my age experienced. I was going to push through my insecurities and get what I deserved. I deserved to feel loved and wanted. I messed with my hair again and saw something move behind me. I turned around and there was nothing there.

"You're supposed to be upstairs," I whispered. No response.

I tiptoed down the hallway and heard a floorboard creak ahead. I looked up and saw a shadow move across the wall from the other room.

"You want to ruin the surprise, don't you?" I giggled.

I went around the corner and shrieked. My reflection in the living room windows startled me. There was no one there. I looked around, suddenly feeling exposed and a little frightened.

I made my way up the stairs and saw small candles lighting the way to the bedroom at the end of the hallway. I nervously followed the candles and opened the door. The whole empty room was filled with rose petals and candles. Our blanket laid in the center of the room with Alastor on it and another blanket on top of him. He sat up and looked at me. He wasn't wearing a shirt so I could make out all of his muscles in the candle light.

"Whoa, Emma," he breathed.

"What?" I asked, crossing my arms over my stomach. "Do I look okay?"

He got up and walked over to me in his boxers.

"You look amazing," he smiled. I smiled back.

Alastor picked me up and carried me over to our blanket and laid me down gently. He kissed my neck and cleavage before removing my thong. I pulled his boxers down and I pulled him in closer to me. It didn't hurt like I thought it would, and after noticing that Alastor was trying to be gentle, I asked him to go faster. Although, it didn't last long after he started going faster.

I've heard people refer to sex as "making love," but it's usually in love songs or romantic comedies. It didn't really ever seem like a realistic view on sex. Some of my friends who had lost their virginity called it weird or awkward. However, my first time was definitely love making. Alastor was so delicate with me, like I was as fragile as a butterfly's wing. Afterwards, he wrapped me in his arms and kissed my forehead.

"I hope that was okay for you," he said in my ear.

"Are you kidding me?" I looked up at him. "It was amazing. You're amazing."

"Good. I'm glad it was good for you. You're beautiful, Emma. And you felt so good."

I stared at Alastor.

"What?" he asked.

"I love you," I said suddenly. "You don't have to say it back. I know we haven't been together very long-"

"I love you too," he smiled. "You're wonderful. And I'm so lucky."

"This is all so crazy to me," I said. "I've never been a believer of fate or divine intervention, but I feel like this is as close as it can get."

"I do too," Alastor said. "How could I look at you and *not* believe in miracles? You're perfect. I can look at you and see God's beauty in you. And you *are* beautiful, in every way."

"Do you believe in God?" I asked.

"Of course I do," he said. "Don't you?"

"I don't know," I sighed. "I mean, I go to church with my family, read parts of the Bible, and I've prayed before. But whether I believe in God or not doesn't change whether or not He exists. He's never done anything for me before."

"He's brought us together," Alastor said.

"But then doesn't that interfere with free will? He can't know every decision we make before

71

making it and gives us the chance to make choices. It just doesn't make sense. Or some of the things that are considered sins. You don't usually go to jail if you kill someone in self-defense. But it is still murder. So do you go to Hell for killing someone who was trying to kill you? Or do you let the person kill you and die a righteous Christian? But then letting the other person kill you without stopping them indirectly kills yourself, which is also a sin, which is also kind of silly. Why would God want a person to live and suffer when they could die sooner to feel closer to God?"

I looked at Alastor.

"I'm sorry," I blushed. "I probably sound like a crazy person."

"Not at all," he smiled. "You're still searching for answers. That's good. When people stop caring enough to ask questions about their faith, there's no faith left. I don't think you're crazy. I think you're brilliant. And sexy. And kind. And wonderful."

I started kissing his chest before climbing on top of him.

"So, how good did it feel?" I asked. "Good enough to go again?"

Alastor smiled and pulled me closer. After the second time, we were both exhausted. I must've fallen asleep because the next thing I knew, I was dreaming.

6

I'm flying through the air, moving through clouds and past tall buildings. I can feel the sun shining on my face, making me smile; I am flying over a lake and look down to see my reflection in the water beneath me. A flock of ducks flies by, and it makes me laugh. I am as free as they are. I wear a beautiful white dress, have no shoes, and have enormous white wings. The feathers of my wings are ruffled by the wind and stretch out much farther than my arms. I go up higher and higher until I am above the clouds. I look up, going higher still, and a beam of light forms ahead of me. I am getting closer and closer to the opening of the beam when suddenly something tugs on my ankle. I look down and see Alastor hanging from my leg, trying to pull himself up so he won't fall.

"Emma!" he cries. "Help me!"

I am attempting to fly us to the beam of light, but Alastor is weighing me down too much. I reach down and grab him, holding on tightly. Then, my wings catch fire, and we both start falling. My wings are now burnt and blackened, and my dress becomes torn and ragged. We are getting close to the ground, and I turn to look at Alastor, except I'm not holding onto him anymore. I look up and see him fly away with a pair of wings like mine right before I hit the ground and wake up.

"Emma," Alastor lightly shook me awake. I looked around the room and noticed it was light outside.

"What time is it?" I asked.

"9:00," he answered as he pulled his pants on.

"What!" I jumped up and got my clothes on.

I looked at my phone. I had ten missed calls from my mom and eight missed calls from my dad.

"Holy shit, my parents are going to kill me!"

It was no surprise that when Alastor and I walked up my driveway, my parents were standing on the porch still in their pajamas. They both looked very pissed off and tired. My mom looked like she had been crying, and my dad's coffee mug was shaking in his hand.

"I can explain-" Alastor started.

"Alastor, I think it would be in your best interest if you just went home now," my dad said in a low voice.

"But, sir, I-"

"Go home, Alastor," my mom said.

I looked at Alastor nervously and nodded. He gave me a short wave and turned to make his way to his car.

I looked at my parents. They didn't say a word, just turned and went inside the house. I followed behind them without talking. Even once we got inside, they didn't speak to me.

"I'm going upstairs to take a shower," I mumbled.

"You're not hanging out with him anymore," my dad said.

"What?" I asked.

"You heard me. Do you know how worried we were? We didn't know where you were! We didn't know if something had happened to you! What if something had happened to you?"

My mom started crying again.

"Dad, I-"

"No, you don't get to talk. You get to stand there in silence and listen!" he yelled. "I'd like to think that your mother and I do a fairly good job raising you and your brother. We're not too harsh on you guys and give in to pretty much whatever you want. But sneaking off in the middle of the night with a boy and being gone all night?"

"It was just this one time!" I said. "I usually sneak back into the house!"

"How long has this been going on?" my dad asked.

"You didn't sleep with him, did you?" my mom sobbed.

"Do not answer that question, young lady!" my dad said. "If you don't want me to beat the living shit out of him, you will not answer that question."

"We love each other," I cried. "I love him, Dad."

"You're too young, Emma," he sighed. "You don't fully understand what love is."

"Yes, yes I do! I'm an adult!" I raised my voice. "Just because we're young doesn't mean we're stupid! I might die before I have a chance to get married or have kids, but I know that I love Alastor, and he loves me too! Do you want me to die before I get to live at all? Do you want me to die your little girl instead of a-"

"Go to your room," he slammed his fist against the wall, his hand going through the drywall a little.

"OW! GOD DAMMIT!"

"Oh my god!" My mom ran over to my dad. "Are you all right?"

"JUST LEAVE ME ALONE!" he bellowed. My mom backed away from him and looked at me.

"You can come out when it's time to head out to the apartment," my dad spat. "But for now, I don't want to see you otherwise."

"Dad-"

"GO!"

I ran up to my room and slammed the door before locking it. I hurried up and grabbed my phone to call Alastor. I told him what my dad had said and cried hysterically. Alastor told me that things would get better, especially once school started. He thought my dad would come around, and things would return to normal.

"He makes you sound so evil," I sniffled.

"Yeah, well," Alastor said quietly. "He's just protecting his baby."

"I'm not a kid anymore, though. I wish my parents would understand that. Just because I've been living with them doesn't mean they can control what I do. I follow their rules as much as I can without going insane. I'm an adult. And they never treat me like one."

"Well, we'll figure something out. It'll get better, I promise."

"I'm so sorry everything got so messed up," I apologized. "We had such a wonderful night."

"What happened with your parents didn't take away from last night. It was still wonderful."

I spent the rest of the morning boxing up the last few things left around my room. I played music loud enough to drown out whatever was going on downstairs. Occasionally, I could hear my dad yell but couldn't make out what he was saying. Nor did I care. I couldn't wait to get out of my parents' house. Whatever was left of me feeling sad about leaving was gone.

I got the last of my things together and started taking everything out to my parents' car. When Whitney and Maddi showed up, I told them what had happened.

"They'll get over it," Whitney said. "You should have seen my dad's face when I started hooking up with one of his old high school buddies. I was pretty sure he would never speak to me again. Or when I started dating one of my teachers. He said he was going to stop paying for my schooling. That didn't happen. You should have seen his face when he saw my tattoo! Ha!"

"I still can't get over the fact that you and your boyfriend got matching tattoos," Maddi laughed. "That's going to be on your ankle forever now."

"It's a wolf. It's not like I got his name tattooed on me anywhere," she smiled. "Besides, wolves mate for life. It's symbolic of our relationship."

I rolled my eyes.

"I seriously can't wait to meet Alastor!" Whitney squealed. "The pictures you sent to me over the summer were pretty impressive. He's fucking hot."

"The pictures don't do him justice," I smiled. "I can't wait to see him today! Well, after my parents leave. I cannot wait to get this move over with."

The three of us talked while we moved boxes from the cars. I ignored my parents the entire time, which made my friends feel uneasy. Maddi tried making small talk with my mom and dad. However, after I had given her several dirty looks, she finally gave up and stopped talking to them. There wasn't much to move into the apartment. I was bringing my bed, dresser, t.v., and clothes. My grandma gave us one of her recliners and a set of dishes. Maddi's parents bought us a used couch and a small dining room table. My mom helped me put clothes on hangers and hang them in my closet.

"Dad and I were thinking we could take you girls out for dinner tonight since you don't have any food in the fridge yet."

I didn't respond.

"We could go get pizza. You, Whitney, and Maddi always liked it when we'd take you three to Al's for pizza and arcade games."

"No thanks," I muttered. "Whitney and I already made plans with our boyfriends. And Maddi has dinner plans."

"Well, maybe the boyfriends would like to join us for pizza?"

"Yeah, because I want Alastor around you and Dad right now."

"Honey, I'm sorry for how your father and I reacted. But you have to understand how upsetting the situation is for us. You're our only daughter. Even though you're an adult, you're still our little girl. You won't understand that until you have a child of your own. You think you're going to be a certain type of parent, and you end up being completely different. You say, 'When I become a mom, I'll never do this or that.' You want your child to be safe, happy, and...healthy."

My mom started crying. I stopped and looked at her.

"I'm sorry," she said, wiping her nose. "I can't do anything about your health, but I can still contribute to your happiness. I want so much for you, and I want you to experience so many things. I don't want you to regret anything. I don't want to regret anything either. You're an adult and a damn good one. From now on, I will support any decision you make. No pizza tonight, but we'll plan a get-together with you and Alastor soon."

I smiled and wiped a tear from my cheek. I respected and appreciated my mom, despite her acting like a psycho half the time. My mom and I talked very little for the rest of the day while I still ignored my dad. After everything was unpacked and somewhat put away, my parents left without saying much. Whitney and I got ready for our dinner date while Maddi and I discussed plans to decorate our apartment. She was also going on a date, although she wouldn't tell Whitney or me anything about it.

"Is it someone we know?" Whitney asked.

"Why does it matter?" Maddi asked. "You don't have to know every single little thing. Plus, it's not even *that* serious right now. Maybe once it gets more serious, if it does, you'll be lucky enough to meet the person."

"You're so damn cryptic," Whitney said.

"Emma is at least respectful about it," Maddi smiled.

"That's because she's too distracted with her perfectly chiseled hottie."

I blushed as I put mascara on in the mirror.

"If I were straight, I would be too," Maddi laughed. "Apparently, Alastor has been gifted by the gods with that dick of his."

"Maddi!" I spun around.

"WHAT!" Whitney squealed. "Did you let him de-flower you?"

Whitney got behind me, grabbed my hips, and started pretending to hump me.

"You naughty girl!" She yelled. "One of us! One of us!"

Maddi and I started laughing.

"I'm so sorry," she said. "I thought you already told her."

"Can you see why I was holding it off?" I asked loudly over Whitney's fake moaning and animal noise.

"Okay, Whitney," Maddi said. "We get it. You're jealous."

"Of Alastor," Whitney winked at me and let go. "I'd kill to see how much of a freak you are."

"Ugh!" I scoffed. "I'm not a freak! It's not like that."

"Not yet, at least," Maddi muttered.

As if right on cue, there was a knock on the door.

"Speak of the devil!" Maddi giggled.

I ran to the door, Maddi and Whitney following after. I opened the door, and Alastor stood before me, grinning and holding flowers.

"Happy moving day," he said, handing the flowers to me.

"Thank you," I smiled. "They're beautiful."

Alastor leaned in and kissed me deeply.

"Well, shit," Whitney said. "I'm going to have some alone time after watching that."

I held up my middle finger, and Whitney and Maddi chuckled.

"I need to go pick up Sam," Whitney sighed. "Meet you guys at the bar? That is, of course, if you two will stop shoving your tongues down each other's throats."

I pulled away from Alastor. He put his arm around my waist.

"Yes, we will meet you there," I replied.

"I need to head out too for my date," Maddi said, making her way towards the door.

"Don't do anything I wouldn't do," she winked before closing the door behind her and Whitney.

Immediately, Alastor and I started undressing and heading back to my room. He gently pushed me backward onto the bed and crawled towards me. I grabbed him by the shoulders and pushed him down before climbing on top of him. Alastor looked surprised and sat up to kiss me as I wrapped my legs around him. While we were entangled in each other, Alastor started kissing my neck. I grabbed a handful of his hair and pulled his head back. He gasped and looked at me.

"Harder," I said softly.

Alastor started bouncing me on his lap harder and put his mouth on my nipple. My nails sank into his back, and he pushed me onto my back again.

"Harder," I said, wrapping my legs around his waist again.

Alastor took one of his hands to hold my wrist above my head and used the other one to pull my hair. He leaned in and started sucking on my neck. I orgasmed so hard that Alastor had to put his hand over my mouth to muffle my scream. He rolled next to me, breathing heavily. I looked at him and saw he was drenched in sweat.

"Well, my makeup is probably ruined now," I said, gently wiping my forehead.

"You look great," Alastor panted. "That was great."

"Yeah," I smiled.

"Seriously," Alastor looked at me. "That was amazing. I forgot how good sex is."

"We just did it last night," I said. "Unless you don't mean with me."

"Of course, I mean with you," he laughed. "Come on; we need to hurry up and get dressed. We're running late for dinner with Whitney and Sam."

I got up and got dressed, wondering if Alastor really was talking about just me. Or had he had sex with someone else before me? We never really discussed the subject before. I just assumed. After we were both dressed and ready, we made our way to the bar we were meeting Whitney and Sam at. The car ride was mostly silent, apart from the music and Alastor asking if the air conditioning was too cold. My mind was anything but silent, however. I couldn't help but feel like something was off about Alastor. I didn't like feeling like I had given in so quickly to the first boy who gave me attention. I had feelings for him, sure. But I never imagined myself falling so hard so fast for someone.

When we arrived, I tried to shake off my thoughts. I knew I was overthinking and getting myself worked up over nothing. Whitney and Sam were already sitting at the bar, sharing a basket of fries and drinking beers. I forced a smile.

"What took you guys so long?" Whitney asked as we approached them. She started giggling and poking my neck.

"Never mind," she snickered. "Judging by the size of that hickey, I guess I should be glad you showed up at all."

Sam started laughing. I put my hand up to my neck and gave Alastor a stern look. Whitney began to dig through her purse.

"Here," she pulled out a tube and handed it to me. "Go to the bathroom and put some concealer on it. Unless you want everyone to see it, I won't judge."

I handed it back to her.

"What the hell," I said. "I'm not in the company of saints."

"Cheers to that!" Sam exclaimed.

Surprisingly, Whitney's boyfriend, Sam, wasn't as big of a douche as I thought he'd be. He and Alastor got along well, and the four of us had a great time together. We drank a lot and shared stories about each other. For it being my first time going out and consuming a fair amount of alcohol, I felt I was handling myself pretty well.

"We should play Never Have I Ever!" Whitney clapped her hands. "If it's something you've done, you have to take a shot!"

"Shots?" I repeated. "Whitney…"

"Oh, come on!" she begged. "It'll be fun. Pleeease?"

I looked at Alastor, who just shrugged. I rolled my eyes and grunted.

"Yay!" Whitney exclaimed before stopping the bartender to order shots. "I'll go first! Never have I ever had a threesome."

As the bartender started sitting shot glasses down, Sam took one and drank it.

"Babe!" Whitney giggled. "Well, that's news to me."

Sam went next.

"Never have I ever slept with someone who was married."

We all looked at him.

"And not known they were married," he added.

No one moved.

"I'll go next," Alastor said. "Never have I ever gotten a tattoo."

Whitney and Sam looked at each other, laughing, and both took a shot.

"Never have I ever..." I started.

"Almost everything," Whitney laughed. I gave her a serious look.

"Sorry, but it's true," she chuckled. "No offense."

"Anyways," I said, irritated. "Never have I ever....met my significant other's parents."

Alastor and Whitney each took a shot. I thought I had gotten Whitney with that one.

"Wait, you've met Sam's parents?" I asked.

"Yeah, they stopped by his place to drop his laundry off, and I had been running late for work. So it wasn't planned or anything. But I'm glad I ran into them when I did, or else I don't know when I would have gotten to meet them!"

I looked at Alastor, who wouldn't look at me.

"Hey, Alastor," Sam said, breaking the silence. "Wanna go play pool? I'll bet you $10 on it."

"All I have is a twenty. But sure."

The guys got up and went to one of the pool tables at the back of the bar. Whitney got on her phone for a bit while I sat in my seat, sulking. Finally, I grabbed one of the shot glasses and drank it.

"So, I'm guessing it's bothering you that you haven't met Alastor's parents?" Whitney asked.

"It's just his mom," I answered. "Every time I bring it up, he changes the subject. I don't want to push him into anything he's not ready for, but he's been around my family a lot already, and he hasn't ever suggested that I meet his mom."

"Maybe he's embarrassed, or there's something wrong with her. Does he even ever talk about her?"

"Not really," I shrugged. "He's only mentioned her a couple of times, and it's just been about having to go help her with something."

I decided to let it go, even though it hung in the back of my mind for the rest of the evening. Sam and Alastor rejoined us at the table, and Alastor used the twenty dollars he had won to buy a round of drinks. We talked and drank and laughed. It was a fun night. Finally, Alastor mentioned how late it was, and the two of us returned to my new apartment. We stumbled through the door giggling and made our way to my bedroom. There were still boxes and bags everywhere, and I must have tripped over every single one. I laughed as Alastor shushed me until we finally collapsed onto my bed. I took Alastor's shirt off, and he started kissing me.

"Hey," I looked at him.

"Hey," he smiled and leaned in to kiss me again. I stopped him.

"No, I wanted to ask you something," I said.

"Okay."

"Why do you not want me to meet your mom?" I asked.

"I don't know. I didn't know it was that big of a deal."

"Well, you've hung out with my family a lot."

"I like your family," he shrugged.

"Do you think I won't like your mom?" I asked. "Or are you worried she won't like me?"

"Why is this an issue all of a sudden?"

"Why is it for *you*? And you didn't answer my question."

"Oh my god, why are you interrogating me about this? You were fine until tonight."

"It's something I've been thinking about for a while. I just haven't said anything about it."

Alastor stood up and put his shirt back on.

"What are you doing?" I asked.

"I think I better go home," he sighed.

"Which is where exactly?" I asked. "Seriously, I'm all for the sexy, mysterious thing you've got going on, but I don't know hardly anything about you! I've never been to your house or met your family or friends. I've never seen a childhood picture of you or known anything about your childhood. It's not fair how one-sided this relationship is!"

"This is ridiculous!" Alastor yelled at me. "You're drunk and making a bigger deal out of this than you need to! You wanna meet my white trash mother? Fine! You wanna see the shit hole house I grew up in? Fine! If you want to sit and listen about how hard it was raising me on her own, how tired she is from having to work so much, and how much of a pain in the ass I was growing up? FINE!"

My heart was racing, and my eyes filled with tears, both from Alastor yelling at me and the content of what he was yelling. He stared at me for a moment until he slowly sat back down on the edge of the bed. I watched him put his head in his hands and sigh.

"Look," he said, putting his head up but still not looking at me. "My mom- she doesn't necessarily like me. I've always been a constant reminder of my dad, who left her to care for a kid who wasn't planned. I was often told how much easier her life would have been without me. We've never been close, and I've always looked after myself. I made my own food, did my own laundry, and made sure I did whatever I could to make my mom's life easier. I was home alone a lot, and we always lived in sketchy places. Do you want to know why you've never seen kid pictures of me? I don't know if my mom even has any. And if she does, she keeps them boxed up somewhere. I finally had a chance to move out, but I can't find a job anywhere. I had a place lined up and everything. I had to let someone else take it because I couldn't find a job. And as happy as I am for you, it's still a little hard to watch you get your own place. I feel like such a failure. To my mom and you. You both deserve better."

"Alastor," I breathed. "You're not a failure. I'll ask around and find places that are hiring. At least you keep trying, and you're not giving up. Giving up is the only real failure."

Alastor smiled at me.

"Come here," I held a hand out. Alastor laid back down next to me. I laid my head on his chest, and he started playing with my hair. The next thing I knew, I woke up with the sunlight shining through the window.

I felt dizzy, and my head was pounding. I didn't think I had drank enough to cause a hangover, but I felt awful. I quietly got out of bed and into the kitchen to get water. There was a woman bent over, looking through the fridge. Her yellow thong showed a perfectly round butt, and her flawless brown skin immediately made me feel self-conscious.

"Um, hello?" I said quietly.

The woman quickly turned around and stood up. Her big, curly hair bounced around, and I could see her pierced nipples through her white tank top.

"Oh my god," she said. "I am so sorry. I was trying to be quiet so that I wouldn't wake anyone up. I just wanted to surprise Maddi with breakfast."

"Holy shit," I exclaimed. "Colbie? Colbie Adams?"

"Yeah?" she said.

"You were in the grade below us in high school," I said. "You used to date John Harrison, right?"

"Ew, don't remind me," Colbie said, pushing her hair back.

"Are you and Maddi-?"

"Fucking?" She interrupted me. "Yeah. A lot. She's great. Do you want some coffee?"

"Um, sure," I responded.

"Do you need to take care of whatever that is?" she asked, pointing at my stomach. My colostomy bag was full of gas and was blown up like a balloon under my shirt. I awkwardly walked off to the bathroom and changed my bag. It was odd farting out of a hole in my stomach without any control. My doctor gave me stacks of paperwork explaining what foods should be avoided, especially before bed. The spicy food and alcohol from the night before made my colostomy bag so full of gas that the bag was beginning to pull away from my stomach.

I washed my face and brushed my teeth before returning to my room to wake Alastor up. He looked so peaceful in my bed. His cheek pressed into the pillow, and his mouth slightly open made me wonder if that's what he looked like as a child sleeping. I sat down and listened to him breathing before I leaned in to kiss his cheek. Suddenly his eyes opened, and he grabbed my arm, letting out a low guttural growl. The irises of his eyes were completely black. I gasped and tried to pull my arm away. He blinked, and his eyes softened. They didn't look all black anymore. It must have just been the lighting in the room, or maybe his eyes had dilated.

"Oh my god, Emma, I'm so sorry," he said, letting go of my arm. "You scared me."

"No, I'm sorry," I said, still startled. "I didn't mean to scare you like that. Are you okay now?"

Alastor nodded and sat up, hugging me.

"I'm sorry," he repeated. "You know I would never hurt you on purpose."

"I know, it's okay," I assured him, rubbing my arm. "Get some pants and come have some coffee. Maddi's, uh, friend is making some. Also, she was only wearing underwear and a see-through tank top. And she's got a nice body. And perfect hair. You know what? I can just bring you your coffee in bed."

"Don't be ridiculous," Alastor laughed. "I could be in a room full of women and still only see you."

I kissed him, and we went into the living room, where Maddi and a now dressed Colbie were sitting together on the couch.

"I wish you didn't have to go to work," Maddi said, kissing Colbie's cheek.

"I know," Colbie smiled. "I'll see you after I get off, right?"

Maddi nodded, and they kissed for a long time. I gave Alastor an uncomfortable look, and he started making my cup of coffee. Colbie stood up, and Maddi gave her a smack on her butt.

"It was nice meeting you properly," Colbie smiled at me.

"Nice meeting you too," I replied.

"Have a nice day at work," Alastor added.

The door shut behind Colbie, and I looked at Maddi.

"What?" she shrugged.

"Why didn't you tell me you were seeing one of the most popular girls from the grade below us or that she was going to be standing in our kitchen in her underwear?"

"I'm sorry," Maddi replied. "She wasn't going to stay the night, but I had the apartment to myself, and she brought dinner over and just ended up staying. That was the first time we spent all night together. Emma, I *really* like her. She's so beautiful, fun and sexy."

"Does she know about your parents?" I asked. Maddi jumped at the mention of her parents.

"Yeah, I told the hot black girl I'm fucking all about my racist, homophobic, religious parents. *No!* I don't want to scare her off. I'm catching feelings for her; every time I tell girls about my family, it usually ends things."

"Maybe this time will be different," I said.

"I'm not risking it. Luckily, she doesn't ask about my family, so I don't bring them up."

"Parents not approving of their daughter's dating life," Alastor chuckled. "Sounds familiar."

I shot Alastor a dirty look.

"I think your dad will be more understanding than my dad," Maddi sighed.

"He's probably going to call and apologize any minute," Alastor said.

As if right on cue, my phone started ringing. I looked at it.

"Oh!" I exclaimed. "It's my dad."

"Weird," Maddi said.

I watched it ring while Maddi and Alastor stared at me.

"Are you going to answer it?" Alastor asked.

I hesitated before hitting the green button.

"Hello?" I answered.

"Hey," my dad muttered. "What are you up to?"

"Just hanging out with Maddi and Alastor."

"Oh," he said stiffly. "Well, I won't keep you. I just wanted to tell you that I'm sorry for how I reacted. I want to make it up to you by inviting you and Alastor over for dinner. If that's okay."

I thought about it for a moment.

"Sure," I finally answered.

"Okay. How does tonight work for you guys? Around six?"

I held my head away from the phone to ask Alastor.

"If you don't want to," I started.

"It's fine," Alastor said. "He's not going to scare me away that easily."

"Okay," I said into the phone. "Well, then I guess we'll see you tonight."

"All right," my dad replied. "Bye."

He hung up without telling me he loved me. He had never done that before. I looked over at Alastor.

"See?" he smiled. "That wasn't so bad!"

"We'll see how tonight goes," I rolled my eyes.

7

I sighed heavily as we pulled into the driveway at my parents house. Alastor grabbed my hand and squeezed it.

"It'll be okay," he smiled at me. "Are you sure you aren't too hot in that?"

He pointed to the sleeveless turtleneck sweater I was wearing.

"I couldn't get the concealer to cover the huge hickey you gave me!" I said. "My parents would be pissed if I went in there with that thing showing."

"And it's not suspicious that you're wearing a sweater in 80-degree weather."

"It's sleeveless. No one is going to say anything."

Simon ran out the door to the car.

"Emma!" he yelled.

I got out of the car, and he hugged me.

"It's weird not having you here," Simon said.

"You miss me?" I asked.

"A little bit," he smiled.

"I *just* moved out like a day ago," I said.

"Well, after the fight you and Dad had, I wasn't sure when I'd see you again."

"Oh my god," I laughed as Alastor got out of the car. "Come on."

We all walked through the front door, and the house smelled strongly of garlic. My mom was standing in the living room, ready to greet us.

"Hey, guys," she smiled.

"Hi," I replied as she reached in for a hug.

"Honey, why are you wearing a sweater?" she asked. "It's 80 degrees outside, and you're all sweaty."

"Thanks, Mom."

Alastor moved towards my mom.

"Alastor," she sniffed. "How are you?"

But Alastor didn't reply. Instead, he reached around my mom and gave her a big hug. She looked surprised and then laughed before hugging him back.

"Hope you guys are hungry," my mom said before walking toward the dining room.

"Starving," Alastor answered.

We walked into the dining room, and the table was already set. My mom had made spaghetti and meatballs with salad and garlic bread. It all looked so good. I knew that as much as I loved living on my own, my mom's cooking would be one of the few things I would miss.

"Everyone go ahead, sit down," my mom gestured to the table. "Your dad should be finishing up out back."

Simon sat on one side of me while Alastor sat on the other. My mom took the seat on the other side of him. As we sat down, my dad came in through the back door.

"Just in time," my mom scooted her chair closer. "Wash your hands and come sit down."

"Hey, Carl," Alastor stood up to shake my dad's hand. He looked at Alastor and then his hand.

"Got to- uh- wash my hands first," my dad awkwardly muttered.

Alastor sat back down. My mom looked from my dad to Alastor to me. My dad walked to the sink while my mom grabbed the salad bowl. She used the tongs to put some in a small bowl in front of her before passing it to Alastor. As the salad came to me, my dad sat between Simon and my mom. He cleared his throat loudly and took a drink of his water.

"Did you get the lawnmower fixed?" my mom asked him as she grabbed a piece of garlic bread.

"No."

"What's wrong with your lawnmower?" Alastor asked him. My dad didn't say anything. My mom nudged him under the table.

"It's broken," my dad finally said.

"Carl can't get it to start," my mom added.

"If you want to bring it up to the shop, I'll take a look at it for free," Alastor said.

"What shop?" I asked.

"Well, I was going to wait until after dinner to tell you, but I finally got a job at Repair/Restore. I'll learn how to fix things like cars, lawnmowers, boats, or bikes. Pretty much anything that runs on a motor. They're going to start taking computers now because of me and my background of computer knowledge."

"Alastor, that's awesome!" I burst out, hugging him.

"It's not much," he added. "But they said depending on how quickly I learn and how much clientele I bring in, I can move up pretty quickly."

"Well, congratulations, Alastor!" my mom smiled.

"Repair/Restore?" my dad asked. "Mike Kelly's shop?"

"Uh, yeah," Alastor said. "His son just started as assistant manager, and that's who hired me."

"I went to high school with him," my dad smirked. "There was one night all the baseball guys got together and bought a bunch of beer from the gas station down the road from the field. The old guy working there was going blind and selling alcohol to minors."

"Carl," my mom side-eyed my brother.

"Mom," Simon rolled his eyes. "I know high school kids sometimes drink, and yes, I promise I never will."

"Anyways," my dad continued, rubbing his stubble. "We all got rip-roaring drunk out on the field. We decided that if any of us passed out, they had to clean up the field the next morning. Poor Mikey passed out, so we left all the cans and other trash all over the field, not thinking anything of it. We figured the next day was Sunday, and no one would be there. We didn't know our coach was stopping by the field on the way to church to look for the whistle he left in the dugout. He found Mikey snoring on the pitcher's mound surrounded by a bunch of crap."

"What happened?" I asked.

"He woke Mikey up, told him to pick up his mess, and kicked him off the team."

"Oh no!" I gasped. Alastor and Simon started laughing.

"Horrible," my mom shook her head and took a bite of spaghetti. "Poor kid."

My dad chuckled.

"Did he tell on you guys?" Simon asked.

"Nope," my dad replied. "Never said a word."

Cheeseball rubbed against my leg and purred. Alastor looked under the table and held his hand out to pet her. She yowled at him before biting his hand.

"Ow!" he yelled. "God damn cat!"

He stood up quickly and charged at the cat.

"Alastor, are you okay?" I asked.

Cheeseball ran down the hall, and Alastor picked up his empty cup and drew it behind his head like he was going to throw it.

"Oh my goodness!" My mom gasped. Alastor slowly put his cup back down. "Here, let's go clean you. I am so sorry! She's never attacked anyone like that before."

Alastor went into the kitchen with my mom, and Cheeseball was nowhere to be found. My mom bandaged up Alastor's hand, and we finished dinner, no one speaking except for Simon. After dessert and some forced conversation, I told Alastor it was time to leave. My parents insisted we stay longer, but I lied and said I had to get up early the following day for work. It was nice knowing I was returning to my home, away from them. Alastor dropped me off in front of my apartment and kissed me.

"Are you sure you can't come up for a little bit?" I asked before kissing him again and moving his hand around my butt.

"I wish I could, but I have some things to get done before I start work in the morning," he replied. "I hate every second that I have to be away from you. But I'll see you in a couple of days, okay?"

I nodded and kissed him again before getting out of the car. I went inside and got into my pajamas. Maddi was watching a movie, so I made us a bowl of popcorn and joined her on the couch. She looked over at me.

"Thanks for moving in with me," she smiled. "You seriously saved my life."

I smiled back.

"And thanks for always accepting me the way I am."

"Same here," I said. "Thank you for never treating me like the 'weird poop girl with allergy problems.' You're why I was as cool as I was in high school."

"Please!" she laughed. "*You* were the cool one of the group. I was always so jealous of how cool your family was. They go to church but still cuss, drink, and act like normal humans. My house constantly felt like I was in church."

Maddi grew quiet, and I glanced over at her, watching her wipe tears from her cheek.

"What's wrong?" I asked.

"I have to tell you something. But I don't want Whitney to know, okay?"

I nodded.

"You have to swear you won't tell anyone," she said. "Not Whitney or your parents or Alastor or anybody."

I paused a moment before nodding again.

"This summer, when I told you guys my parents sent me to a retreat," she started, "that wasn't true."

"What do you mean?" I asked.

"They sent me away to a conversion therapy camp."

"What?"

"Yeah. They talked me into signing up for this retreat for young adults. I signed up because, in my mind, it was better than spending the summer at my parents' house. Back in March, my cousin's friend told her that she saw me at a club 'hooking up with girls.' I made out with one girl at that club, just one! It's not like I was part of a big lesbian orgy. But that's all it took for everything to start spiraling. She told my cousin, who told my aunt, who then told my mom. I came home one day, and my parents were sitting down on the couch, staring at me. My mom had her Bible in her lap. I wasn't expecting it at all. My dad stood up and just asked if I was sexually attracted to girls. Emma, I didn't even answer him. I looked at them in shock, and before I could speak he backhanded me so hard across the face that I thought my eye had popped out.

"I started crying, begging him not to hurt me. He grabbed me by the wrist and started hitting me. I tried to cover my head so he would hit me in the back or the stomach. I figured any bruises or cuts on my face would raise questions that I didn't want to deal with. I cried for my mom to stop him, and she just turned her head away. She didn't cry, didn't blink, nothing."

"Oh my god," I gasped, covering my mouth with my hands.

"So about a month went by after that happened," Maddi continued, wiping her eyes again. "I barely spoke to my parents, even though they had taken my car keys from me. My dad drove me to work every day and picked me up every evening. I lied to you guys when I said my car was broken down. It was running fine. I was just trapped. When they told me about the retreat, they gave me a brochure. It talked about movie nights and an on-site swimming pool. It was a Christian-ran thing, but I thought I could deal with it. I'd be spending my time there alone, away from everyone. They made it sound tolerable. Again, I'd rather be at a lame Christian resort than with my parents. I looked at the dates and told them it wouldn't be possible to miss out on two months of work. My dad said he'd already talked to my boss about it and got it approved. My dad is how I got that job in the first place since he knew my boss. So I signed off to go. And because they tricked me into signing myself off, there wasn't anything I could do about it once I got there. And obviously, it wasn't anything like the brochure said."

"What was it like?" I asked.

"I showed up and had to turn in everything I brought with me. I thought they were taking everything to my room for me, but they went through all my belongings to ensure I didn't have anything 'indecent.' My phone was confiscated, and they took several pairs of my underwear I had packed and my tampons."

"What!"

"Yeah," Maddi scoffed. "They replaced my tampons with pads and my cute underwear with god-awful granny panties. Also, they took the swimsuit I had packed. There wasn't even a pool there. So, those were the first red flags. My room was horrible. No television, no radio, and no reading material besides a Bible. There was also a notepad and a pen in the room. My bed was uncomfortable and smelled like piss. After checking out my room, I went out to explore. It was this dumpy little motel with a small courtyard and a chapel. That's all there was to this place. And the whole place was gated off with high fences. I stopped some woman and asked her where everything was, and she wouldn't even look at me, just kept walking. After walking around for a while, this man introduces himself to me. Reverend Mullens."

Maddi gulped.

"Emma, he was so horrible to me," she cried. "The two months I spent there almost made me want to kill myself. They had me watch hours of lesbian porn while force-feeding me medication that made me sick. I was puking and shitting so much, and they'd have me just strapped to this chair watching porn. They had me in this

messed-up form of therapy where Reverend
Mullens kept trying to get me to admit that a
woman sexually abused me at some point when I
was younger or that there was some type of trauma
that gave me this 'false sexuality.' They made me
write verses about lust, sin, and Hell. At first, I
refused to write them. I'd get slapped until I
complied. They just kept trying all these different
things, and I told them nothing was wrong with
me, and nothing changed how I felt. I kept trying
to tell them this was how God made me and that I
truly believed that God still loved me. They told
me how broken I was and were willing to do
anything to save my soul because I was still a child
of God underneath all my sin. They kept telling me
how much they cared about me and wanted to help
me."

Maddi started sobbing. I just looked at her,
waiting for her to continue, even though I was
scared of what was coming next.

"He raped me, Emma," she said, not
looking at me. "And not just once. I'd wake up in
the middle of the night with him on top or with his
fingers inside me. He repeatedly told me he was
helping me and doing God's work. I stopped eating
and started wetting the bed, which pissed them off.
Finally, I snapped out of it. I thought, 'just lie to
them. Tell them what they want to hear and get
out of this place and away from your parents as
fast as possible.' So I flipped a switch and started

acting obedient, telling him that he must have cured me. I said some gross shit like how much I enjoyed him, which made me want to throw up. I was only there for 60 days, but it felt much longer. My parents picked me up at the end of my stay there and were so happy to see me. My dad told me how proud he was of me and hugged me. My mom told me that she prayed for me every day that I was gone and how her prayers were answered. They thought I was straight and fixed."

"What happened after you got back home?" I asked.

"I gained their trust enough to get my car back. I found out that my dad had gotten me fired from my job, so I spent the end of summer scrambling to find a new job, got all of my stuff moved in here before you moved, and then I went to a lawyer and got a restraining order against my parents. I'm never seeing them or talking to them again. My grandma isn't talking to them anymore either. She said my dad keeps calling her, leaving hateful messages, and asking where I am, and she won't answer or call him back. He showed up at her house once, and she said he threw a bunch of her stuff around and broke stuff. My parents are completely fucked up."

"Jesus Christ, Maddi," I shook my head. "How did you manage to keep all of this from us?"

"I don't know," Maddi shrugged. "I was feeling sorry for myself over what happened. I was embarrassed. The two people who were supposed to love me more than anyone else caused the most pain I've ever experienced and they did it because they're brain-washed by religion. But my life improved as soon as I got away from my parents. I have a great-paying job and my own place, and I met an amazing woman. It's almost as if I had to go through something horrible like that to get to something great. I almost feel grateful. Almost. I've been seeing a therapist, which my parents would have never allowed. It's helping me get through all the trauma. I'm still working on myself. It's an everyday thing. But I'm working on it. I just don't want anyone to know. I don't want anyone feeling sorry for me."

"I understand that, trust me. I won't tell anyone," I promised. "And I'm here if you ever need to talk about it or need anything."

I held my arms out, and Maddi leaned into me. I wrapped my arms around her and squeezed.

"I don't want it to change how you see me," I heard her say.

"Never," I smiled. "You'll always be the same stunning, smart, classy Maddi to me."

"And you'll always be the weird poop girl with allergy problems."

I playfully pushed her back and scoffed.

"Kidding!" She grinned. "You know you're the hot friend."

"Oh, please!" I exclaimed. "You're so much prettier than me!"

"I'd kill for your long legs!"

"You have a better ass than me," I retorted.

"You have better boobs!"

We both started laughing and went back to watching the movie. I must have fallen asleep at some point because Maddi woke me up to tell me to go to bed. I shuffled to my bedroom and flopped down. I checked my phone to see if Alastor had messaged me. I had a missed call from my parents' house. I called back, and my mom answered.

"Hello?" she said in a sleepy voice.

"I'm sorry for calling so late," I said. "I wanted to make sure everything was okay."

"I was still up, honey," she said softly. "I've been up with Simon."

"Is he okay?" I asked. "Is that him crying?"

"Hold on, let me go to the other room," she replied.

I waited anxiously.

"It's Cheeseball," she finally sighed.

"The cat?"

"Yeah. Simon put out her food bowl, and she didn't come when he called for her. He looked all over the house and couldn't find her. He started getting worried, so Dad and I looked outside for her. Dad found her. In the street."

"Oh my god."

"I don't know what exactly happened," my mom continued. "She rarely gets out, and when she does, she has never gone anywhere close down by the road. She must have been sick or something, with what happened at dinner and then this. Simon hasn't stopped crying. I feel so bad. The poor thing was just ripped to pieces. The only way we knew it was her was from her collar."

"Oh, Mom," I teared up. "I'm so sad for Simon. I know how much he loved that cat. And she loved him too. Does he want to talk?"

"Maybe tomorrow, sweetie. You go ahead and get to bed."

"Okay. Love you."

"Love you too," she said before hanging up.

I laid my head on my pillow and felt terrible for my brother. I laid awake, wondering what had caused Cheeseball to run off like that until I was finally too tired to think anymore. I rolled over and fell asleep.

I'm lying still. I can hear people moving and talking around me. I try wiggling a little bit but am unable to. I hold my hands up in front of me and can feel some type of container surrounding me. It is dark and cramped. I stop moving to hear what is going on.

"The Lord has called Emma home to the kingdom of God. Let us bow our heads in prayer as we lower the casket."

"What!" I yell. "NO! I'M NOT DEAD! LET ME OUT! MOM! DAD! LET ME OUT OF HERE! I'M NOT DEAD!"

"For you shall go out with joy, be led forth with peace."

I listen for anyone else to say anything. I hear nothing. I start shouting again and beating on the lid of the coffin.

"PLEASE, ANYONE! HELP ME! I'M ALIVE! PLEASE DON'T DO THIS! I'M ALIVE! I'M-"

I stop when I hear a soft thud hit the coffin, followed by another one and another one.

"Oh god," I cry. "No, no, no. Don't bury me. I'm alive. I'm alive!"

I start sobbing and crying out again. I then notice that the casket is getting warmer. I start sweating and breathing heavily. It feels like I am in an oven, and I realize I am beginning to burn. Suddenly, the coffin starts falling apart, and I can feel insects crawling on me. Worms try to make their way into my nostrils. I close my mouth as I pull the worms away from my face. I start digging my way out of the dirt and finally make it out of the ground. I look around and am surrounded by fire; everything around me is burning or burnt. The wind is strong and hot on my face. I see a worn-down building in the distance and run to it to get away from the wind and heat. I go inside and shut the door, wiping ash off of my dress and

arms. I turn around and realize I am inside a church. There are pews on either side leading up to an altar and a pile of something on the floor.
I walk up to get a closer look and gasp. There are dead and rotting animal carcasses piled up. There are dogs, cats, rabbits, foxes, deer, raccoons, and rats. Something shiny catches my eye, and I can see a name tag on a collar standing out amongst the fur and guts. It's Cheeseball; her body is mangled and torn. The front door slams shut, and I jump at the sudden noise. I turn around and see people coming in.

"Oh, thank God," I sigh. "I was so scared! I don't know what's happening, but-"

As the group comes closer, I notice that they are all women, or at least what appears to be elderly women. They have ashen skin as if all the blood has been drained from their bodies. They all have thinning gray hair and are wearing long white gowns. They keep their heads slightly lowered and their eyes closed as they move silently toward me.

"Hello?" I say softly.

As the women make their way up to the altar, they suddenly stop and begin sniffing. A few of them get down and crawl through the animal bodies, checking them. One stops in front of me and lifts her head. She opens her eyes, which are empty holes, and blood pours out of them. The rest of the women open their eyes, all with the same bleeding, exposed sockets.

"No!" I cry and try to run. Several of them grab me and pull me down to the ground.

They expose rotting fangs and begin to sink them into my skin, feasting on me while I scream.

I jolted awake to someone knocking loudly on my door. I sat up in bed, panting and sweating. Maddi peaked her head in.

"Come on," she said. "We have to get going. We have to pick up our books today, remember?"

She stopped and looked me over.

"Jesus, are you okay?" she asked.

"I'm fine," I breathed. "I'll be ready in a bit."

"Okay. Are you sure you're good?"

"Yes, I'm fine," I repeated.

Except I wasn't fine. My stomach was hurting badly. After we picked up our textbooks, Maddi wanted to grab lunch. I sipped on my water and didn't touch my food.

"Oh my god," Maddi said, looking at her phone, "Colbie wants me to meet her parents tomorrow night before our date. Do you think that means it's getting serious?"

"Probably," I said quietly.

"Aren't you hungry?" she asked, taking a bite out of her sandwich.

"Not really," I sighed. "I don't know. My stomach is kind of acting up today."

"Probably getting stressed about school starting up," she replied.

"Yeah," I muttered. "That's probably it."

However, my stomach didn't let up the next day when school started. My stomach was twisting in painful knots during every class. I originally planned on wearing a cute outfit but wore a loose shirt and sweatpants. It was hard to concentrate on anything my professors were saying. After classes were over, I met Maddi in the parking lot.

"Well, that wasn't as bad as I thought it'd be," she smiled as we got in the car. "I have a lot of homework but not nearly as much as I expected. How was your first day?"

"It was okay," I muttered. "I had a hard time keeping up with everything."

"Are you feeling okay?" Maddi asked, checking her phone.

"I just feel tired," I replied. "That was a long day."

"I know what you mean. I'm wiped out. Let's get home and try to get through some of this crap. I have to get as much homework as possible before my date!"

When we got home, I went straight to my room and laid down. I slept from four o'clock until the following day. I woke up feeling better but still a little worn down. I checked my phone and had two missed calls from my mom, five missed calls from Alastor, and eight messages from him. I called him and rubbed my eyes.

"Where the hell have you been?" he answered. "I've called you and messaged you a bunch of times!"

"Sorry," I mumbled. "I wasn't feeling good yesterday, so I came home to lay down. I just woke up."

"Well, I was worried about you. I wanted to tell you how my first day at work went."

"Oh yeah," I said, sitting up slowly. "How was it?"

"Awesome," Alastor answered. "It was only one day, but I've already learned so much. I think I'm going to like it. And I gave them my class schedule, so they'll get my work schedule figured out based on that. They were cool about it."

"That's great," I said. "So I guess I'll be seeing you later in Geography."

"Yes, you will," he exhaled. "And then I get to see you again in English a couple of hours after that."

"I'm so excited!"

"For English class or because you get to see me?"

"Both," I chuckled.

"I'll let you get ready. Glad you're feeling okay."

"Thanks," I said. "See you later."

"Bye."

I got up and got dressed before making my way to the kitchen. Maddi was putting a load of dishes in the dishwasher.

"Oh crap," I said. "It was my turn to do the dishes. I'm sorry."

"Hey," she greeted. "Don't even worry about it. How are you feeling?"

"Better," I said. "I feel groggy, but I think I was just really worn out. I'm starving."

"I'm sure you are," she laughed. "We'll drive through somewhere on the way to school."

I was thrilled that it was Tuesday. I had two classes with Alastor on Tuesdays and Thursdays and one with him on Fridays. I couldn't even concentrate in my math class because I was so excited to see Alastor in Geography afterward. When my math professor let us out, I ran to the bathroom and checked on my hair and makeup. My skin color seemed slightly off, but I didn't look too bad. I was the first to arrive in the classroom and picked a random empty seat. Other students started trickling in, and I was beginning to worry that someone might sit next to me before Alastor could get there. Finally, he walked in. My heart immediately started racing, and I waved at him. He smiled and sat down next to me.

"Well, hey there, stranger," he grinned.

"I'm so happy to see you," I breathed. "I never thought my math class would end. And this gives you a good excuse to come to my place and do homework with me."

"Like I need an excuse for that," Alastor winked. "And I plan on doing more than homework."

I blushed as our teacher introduced herself. It was difficult for me to focus with Alastor sitting next to me. He smelled so good and was so cute that I couldn't keep up with what the teacher was talking about. After class, Alastor and I went out for lunch before our next class started. We talked about our courses and professors, laughed, kissed, and enjoyed each other's company.

"You were very distracting in class," Alastor smiled. "I don't think I heard half of what our professor was saying. I couldn't stop thinking about how much I wanted you."

"Same," I said before biting my bottom lip. "I want you right now."

"Right now?" Alastor asked. "We don't have time to go by your place before English class."

"We don't have to go back to my place," I said, turning my head outside to Alastor's car.

"What, the car?" he asked, surprised. I nodded.

Alastor stood up from the table, grabbed my hand, and led me outside to the car. I giggled as I jumped in, and Alastor started the car.

"Where can we go?" he asked, driving.

"I don't know," I said, moving my hand to his lap. "Just find a spot to park where no one else is around."

He drove around until we found a dead-end street. Alastor parked the car and laid his seat as far back as it would go before unbuttoning his jeans. I was so in love with Alastor. As much as I fought it at first, I was completely head over heels. Maybe it was because he was my first boyfriend, but I truly believed it was just meant to be. I was so happy, and everything was going perfectly. Until October.

8

I was beginning to bleed again when I went to the bathroom. I was afraid to tell anyone because I was two weeks from my check-up to see if I could get my colostomy bag removed. I was falling behind in some of my classes because I fell asleep during class, skipped homework assignments, or did not attend the class at all. I was always tired and usually not very hungry or energetic. I started noticing a color change in my eyes and skin. I was developing jaundice. I tried to hide my symptoms, but it gradually became more difficult. I started wearing more makeup than usual and wearing baggy clothes.

All of my relationships were starting to get rocky, except for Alastor. Maddi and I started seeing less and less of Whitney because she had moved in with Sam and was with him all the time. I saw Maddi less often because she and Colbie were getting more serious. Colbie's parents adored Maddi, so they were always either out on dates or with Colbie's family. I was happy for Maddi, but it did bother me how she was more concerned about spending time with Colbie than me. I was irritated with Whitney too, but I expected Whitney to act like a puppy on a leash. Whenever Whitney had a serious boyfriend, she pretty much forgot she had friends. But it's always been Maddi and me. I asked her three times if she wanted to do something with Alastor and me. Every time she would either already have plans with Colbie or ask if Colbie could also come along. It was getting on my nerves.

"Colbie means a lot to Maddi," Alastor would tell me. "Just like you mean a lot to me."

I get it, I guess. It's just hard to share my best friend. I was just so used to being the center of attention with my friends and family. I didn't see much of my family anymore either. Between work, school, and Alastor, I had little time left for my parents and brother. My mom called often, but most of the time, I let it go to voicemail. When I remembered, I'd send her a text message touching base and letting her know I was still alive and well.

We were two weeks away from the fall Homecoming dance, and I still didn't have a dress. My mom asked several times to go with me. I knew she'd spend most of the time telling me how thin and sickly I looked, so I avoided dress shopping with her. Maddi and Colbie had gotten theirs together. Whitney wasn't planning on going because she and Sam thought the dance was stupid. Granted, we had already been through all the dances as teenagers in high school. This was different, though, because I had an actual date. I didn't have to rely on going with a group of friends to have fun. Alastor asked if I wanted him to take me dress shopping, but I didn't want to ruin the surprise of me wearing a killer dress.

"It'll still be just as amazing if I see you in it at the store. Of course, I'll think you'll look amazing in all of them so we might be leaving with twenty dresses," he teased.

"I just don't want you to see me in it before the dance because it won't have the same effect."

"Well, I can drop you off at the dress shop and then come back later to pick you up," he suggested.

"So you want me to be alone?" I asked. "Like *that's* fun."

"What the fuck do you want, Emma?" Alastor snapped at me. "It's not like you're wedding dress shopping. Calm down. I don't care what dress you end up wearing."

I stared at him.

"What?" he said. "You're such a buzzkill. You have to complain about everything. Homecoming, your dress, Maddi and Whitney, school, not feeling good all the time-"

"Oh, I'm sorry that my Crohn's disease is a 'buzzkill' for you," I replied.

"That's not what I mean, and you know it," he scoffed. "God, I am so sick of your little pity parties. If Emma isn't getting her way, all she has to do is bring up her tummy issues, and everyone is suddenly too afraid to hurt Emma's feelings. That's all you care about; yourself. I'm working and going to school full time too. You expect me to spend every second of my free time with you, which is unfair. It's not fair that it has to be about you all the time."

"Then just stop seeing me," I said, fighting back the tears. "You've made it obvious that you're tired of being around me, and I'm such a buzzkill as you say, so just stop hanging out with me."

"Fine," Alastor stood up and put his jacket on.

"You're an asshole; you know that?" I cried.

"At least now you don't have to worry about getting a stupid fucking dress," he said before walking out the door and slamming it shut.

I buried my face into the couch and started sobbing. I cried until Maddi came home.

"What's wrong?" she asked, running over to me.

"I think Alastor and I broke up," I wept and told her what had happened.

"Maybe it was just a bad fight," she said, moving a piece of hair out of my face. "Why don't you go take a hot shower, get in some comfy clothes, and I'll order us a pizza?"

"I'm not hungry," I mumbled.

"Well, I'll order one in case you change your mind after a shower."

I nodded and got up slowly before heading to the bathroom. As I let the shower warm up, I checked my phone—no new messages or calls. I thought about messaging Alastor and then decided to wait until after my shower. Surely he'd call or message me by then. Maddi was probably right. It was just a nasty fight. That's all.

I checked my phone as soon as I got out of the shower—still nothing. I could hear Colbie and Maddi in the living room talking and laughing. I quietly tiptoed from the bathroom to my bedroom and shut the door, smelling pizza along the way. I got into pajamas and stared at my black phone screen. I kept waiting for it to light up and to hear Alastor's voice say how sorry he was and that he was outside my door so he could apologize in person. But the screen stayed black as I crawled into my bed and covered up. Finally, I picked up my phone and messaged him.

So are we broken up?

I waited for him to respond, hoping he would immediately. Tears filled my eyes as I waited, and I buried my face in my pillow, eventually falling asleep.

I opened my eyes and looked around, awoken by a noise. It was dark outside. I looked at my phone and saw that it was a little past midnight. Still no response from Alastor. The noise that woke me up was Maddi and Colbie moaning in Maddi's bedroom. I wanted to storm in there and tell them both to shut up. Instead, I reached over the side of my bed, grabbed a shirt of Alastor's that he had left, and put it up to my face.

123

I started crying again and fell back asleep, smelling his shirt.

I am standing in the woods. It's cold enough that I can see my breath. I look around and see nothing but trees. As I walk, I look down and notice that I am completely naked, my colostomy bag hanging from my bare stomach. I cross my arms over my chest and shiver. Suddenly, I hear a twig snap behind me. I spin around and see something large and black moving through the trees in the distance. I turn back around and start walking a little faster. I hear the thing moving behind me, so I start running.

The thing following me sounds closer, so I push myself to run as hard as possible. I trip and fall to the ground just as I come to the forest's edge. I look down at my foot and see a small branch has gone through it. I slowly pull the stem out of my bleeding foot and try to get back up. I hobble a few times before falling again. I see a cliff ahead and start crawling towards it. Whatever is chasing me will surely get me now. I go to the cliff's edge and look to see the ocean beneath it. I look back at the forest and see Alastor coming out of it.

"Run!" I yell. "Something is chasing us!"

Alastor doesn't change his pace or his expression. As he gets closer, I notice his eyes are entirely black. I hold my hand out so he can help me to my feet, but instead, he grabs me by the throat. He lifts me until my feet are off the ground.

"Don't!" I gasp.

"I almost let you get away," he smiles. "But you're mine."

Before I can say another word, Alastor throws me off the cliff. I fall backward and hit the water. I flail my arms and try to reach the surface. I am pulled back down as a hand grabs my right arm. I look in the water and see a decomposing naked woman looking at me with one eye missing.

"You belong to him now," she says.

A rotting naked man grabs me by the other arm and starts to pull me down.

"We all belong to him," he said.

Suddenly, I'm surrounded by corpses of men, women, and children, their hands grabbing me and pulling me further into the darkness.

I woke up the following day dizzy and nauseous. I ran to the bathroom and threw up in the toilet. My head was pounding. After throwing up a few more times, I brushed my teeth, returned to my room, and sat on the edge of the bed. I looked at my phone. Still no response. I slowly got myself dressed for school, having to take multiple breaks to sit and catch my breath. I went to the kitchen and got myself a glass of water.

"You okay?" Maddi said from the couch. Colbie was sitting with her legs spread over Maddi's lap. I nodded.

"You want to talk about it?" she asked. I shook my head.

"Can you give me a ride to school?" I asked quietly. "I don't feel like riding my bike."

"Sure," Maddi replied.

When we got outside, I thought Maddi would say something to Colbie about letting me sit in the front. But Colbie got in the front seat before I could get to the car. I pushed a bunch of trash, papers, and clothes around in the backseat and buckled. The two of them talked the entire ride to school. At one point, Colbie turned the radio up really loud.

"Can you turn that down, please?" I asked sternly.

"Sorry," Colbie said, turning the volume back down. "I just really like that song."

"Well, you'd be able to hear if you didn't talk nonstop."

"What did you say?" She turned and looked at me.

"Emma, what the fuck?" Maddi looked at me in her rearview mirror.

"Wow, you finally acknowledged me," I said. "I was beginning to think I was invisible."

"What is your problem?" Maddi asked. "You could have chimed in at any time during the conversation."

"How can I when it's all 'remember that guy' or 'did you like that restaurant' or 'we should check out this place?' It's always about just you two."

"Wow," Maddi scoffed. "Kind of exactly like you and Alastor? Or does that not count because it's you and *your* significant other? I'm sorry you two broke up, but you don't need to act like a bitch, especially towards Colbie."

"It's okay," Colbie said. "We should have tried harder to include Emma."

"Oh, shut up with your self-righteous, hippie, 'let's all get along' bullshit," I raised my voice.

Maddi pulled the car over.

"What are you doing?" I asked.

"You can walk from here," she said. "We're not far from the parking lot, and you need the extra space right now anyways."

I unbuckled and got out of the car before slamming the back door hard.

"I'll see you at home," Maddi said, wiping her face. I flipped her off and turned around to head towards the building. Maddi's tires squealed as she drove off.

I was in my math class, not feeling great. My headache was throbbing, and my stomach felt a little more bloated than usual, but I tried to shake it off to get through class. I just needed to get through math, and then I'd see Alastor and confront him before Geography started. We were in the middle of taking a test when suddenly the room started spinning. I felt like I would pass out, so I stood up to let my professor know I didn't feel good. And then I hit the floor.

When my eyes fluttered open, I could hear people talking but couldn't understand what they were saying. I managed to barely get a word out before falling back asleep. I didn't dream at all. It was like I was just stuck in darkness.

"Mom," I murmured.

My eyes opened again, and bright sunlight came through a window on the other side of a hospital room. I looked around the room and saw my mom curled up in a chair at the end of my bed.

"Mom," I whispered.

She lifted her head and ran over to me. I barely recognized her. Her hair was a tangled mess, and she had no makeup on. The dark circles under her bloodshot eyes and her red, chapped nose told me that she had been getting more crying done than sleep.

"What-" I tried to speak. My mom hushed me and ran her hand through my hair.

"I'll let the nurse know you're awake," she said softly. She reached for the remote next to my bed, where I could see IVs and different machines making noises.

"Yes?" a voice from the remote answered.

"She's awake," my mom said.

"Be right there."

I shifted in my bed a little bit, and my mom came back to sit by me.

"How do you feel?" she asked.

"Tired," I whispered.

"You've been in and out of it for two days, sweetie."

I looked at her in disbelief.

"The doctor has been waiting for you to wake up to talk to you, but there are a couple of things he's found out while you've been out."

I listened while my mom began to cry.

"You have jaundice, which is why your skin and eyes have been more yellow-tinted lately. Also, you have liver failure. Emma, I don't know why you didn't say anything-"

She stopped to wipe her nose and sobbed a little before continuing.

"The doctor wants to do more testing to find out what's causing your liver to fail and might end up doing more surgeries."

"No," I said, tears running from my eyes to my ears.

"Emma," my mom started. "Please don't-"

The door opened, and my doctor walked in.

"There's our sleeping beauty," he said through a forced smile. "Are you feeling okay, Emma?"

I wiped my face and nodded.

"So, I guess your mom has already talked to you."

I didn't answer.

"Well, we've got you started on some medications, and hopefully, we can dive in and see the root of the problem."

"Dive in?" I asked. "You mean surgery?"

"Well, yes. To find the issue and treat it properly-"

"Why can't you do an ultrasound or CAT scan or whatever to look?" I asked. "I don't want to be cut open again."

"Unfortunately, your symptoms are pretty severe at this point, Emma. If you had told someone about your jaundice, the bleeding, and extreme bloating, we might not be in this situation right now."

"So, you're saying it's my fault?" I asked.

"No, not necessarily. However, you should know to report any noticeable body changes with your condition."

"How soon can we start the surgery?" my mom asked.

"What!" I yelled as loudly as I could. "I don't want to have any more surgeries!"

"I don't care what you want, Emma," my mom said coldly. "I am your mother, and it is my job to do whatever I can to keep you healthy and safe."

"So I get no say in this?"

"You have the right to refuse medical treatment," my doctor explained. "However, all these years your parents have sacrificed keeping you as healthy and comfortable as possible may be all for nothing. We can do the surgery, find out what is going on, fix it, and send you home to live a hopefully normal life. Or, you can refuse treatment, go home, miss out on school, and probably force one or both of your parents to quit their jobs to stay home and take care of you until you die, which may be very painful. Imagine what that would do to your parents and your little brother."

I immediately started crying again.

"It's just a routine surgery to see what's causing you all these problems," he smiled. "I have another patient to check on quickly, and I'll be back for your answer."

The doctor left, leaving my room silent, besides my mom sobbing. Then, her phone rang. She glanced at it and didn't answer at first. She looked over at me and then back at her phone before answering.

"Hello," she said. "She's been awake for about half an hour now. She, um, is refusing the surgery as of right now."

"Is that Dad?" I asked.

"Yes, she has the right to, and the doctor explained it. I don't know. If you think it would help, sure."

She handed me her phone.

"Hello?" I said.

"Are you out of your goddamn mind?" I heard Alastor's voice say.

I burst into tears again.

"Emma, I'm so sorry for everything I said," he apologized. "I was just angry and hurt, and I was so scared when I showed up to school and saw them putting you in that ambulance. I don't know what I would do if I lost you."

"I'm sorry too," I said.

"I love you," Alastor said.

"I love you too, so much."

"I can't lose you, Emma."

"I'm scared," I said. "What if they find something bad? Something unfixable?"

"You can't think like that, Emma. You need to do whatever the doctor needs you to do to live. It's just surgery."

"What if I need a liver transplant?"

"Then, I come up and cut myself open right there in front of everyone and give you mine."

"That's not funny," I frowned.

"I'm serious. I'll give whatever body parts I can."

I didn't say anything.

"I'll be up there as soon as I get out of school. Now you tell the doctor you'll do the surgery. Okay?"

I paused for a moment.

"Okay?" he repeated.

"Okay," I said.

"I love you.

"I love you too."

I handed the phone back to my mom.

"Thank you so much, Alastor," she said, wiping tears from her face. "All right, I'll see you then. Bye."

I didn't talk to my mom or do anything but look at the wall until the doctor came back in.

"So, have we reached a decision?" he asked.

My mom looked at me. I nodded.

"Are we good to go for surgery?"

I nodded again.

"Good, that's what I like to hear," he smiled. "Let's get started on the paperwork to get the ball rolling pretty quickly."

"Wait," I said. "We're starting it now?"

"Not right this second, but I want to get things started soon. We don't have much time to waste."

"I'm not going into surgery without my dad, Simon, and Alastor here."

The doctor looked at my mom.

"Emma, they'll be here when you get out."

"No!" I said. "I'm not going without seeing them first."

"That will be fine," the doctor explained. "By the time everyone gets here, we should be prepped and have everything ready to go. I'll come back after a while."

After about an hour, my dad, Alastor, and Simon all showed up together. I tried not to show how terrified I was, but it was hard. Judging by everyone's expressions, they were scared too. We all tried joking around and laughing, but everyone could tell it was forced. When my doctor came back to tell us it was time for me to go to surgery, my mom started crying again. Simon gave me such a long hug that I thought my parents would have to pry him off of me. Alastor kissed me and told me he loved me. My mom and dad held my hand down the hall until the doctor told them they couldn't go any further. People were surrounding me, prepping to start. Tears started running, and all I wanted was my mom. A nurse ran her hand through my hair.

"We're going to start the sedation now. It'll be just like falling asleep."

"I'll wake back up, right?" I asked.

"You will. I promise," she smiled. "Now slowly start counting back from ten for me."

I saw the sedative get added to my IV as I started counting.

"Ten...nine..." I started. I felt my body begin to relax.

"Eight...seven..." My eyes fluttered before closing.

"Six..."

Six.

Six.

9

Why is it so dark?

"Scalpel."

What? Who said that?

"And we're in. Let's see what's going on inside this young woman."

Oh shit. Did my sedative not fully work? Why can I hear what's going on in the operating room?

"Oh my god. I wasn't expecting it to look like that."

What's going on? Can anyone hear me? HELLO!

"I was afraid of this. How it got this bad, I don't know. It's always hard telling parents about this sort of thing."

"Poor thing. She's so young."

I don't want to hear anymore. Whatever is wrong, I don't want to find out. I want to just die on this table and not ever wake up.

"They could try chemotherapy, couldn't they?"

"They can, but I think it's too late for that. All they can do now is wait. Unfortunately, they won't have to wait long. She doesn't have much more time. Maybe two months."

"Oh my god."

Oh my god. I'm dying.

"Let's go ahead and finish up. There's not much we can do now."

"Mama," I whispered. "I want...my mama."

"Honey," I heard my mom. "I'm right here."

"I had...the worst..."

My eyes fluttered open.

"Dream" I finished. My throat was dry and my voice was hoarse.

It was dark in my room when I woke up. No one was around. I was by myself.

"Hello?" I asked weakly. No one answered.

"Hello?" I said again.

I reached around for my call button. I found it and pushed the button several times. Soon, a nurse came in and turned my room light on. It momentarily blinded me because it was so bright.

"How are you feeling?" she asked.

"Where's my family?" I asked. "My mom and dad and my brother? Where's my boyfriend, Alastor?"

"You have a few people waiting for you in the waiting room. I'll let them know you're awake in a moment. How are you feeling?"

"Sore," I said, trying to wiggle around a little bit.

"That'll get better with time. I'll page your doctor and let him know you're awake now."

"How did my surgery go?" I asked.

"The doctor will talk with you and your parents shortly," she smiled. "Is there anything I can get you?"

"Water," I answered, scowling. "But everything's fine with me, right? I mean, I'm still here. Nothing is missing; all my parts are still intact?"

"The doctor will be in shortly to discuss your surgery with you and your parents. I'll be right back with your water and your family."

Without letting me get another word in, the nurse walked out of my room. I could feel the bandages on my stomach and a dull throbbing. I must have been given some good painkillers because I didn't feel as sore as I thought I would. The door opened, and my mom, dad, brother, and Alastor walked in. I smiled at them but did not get a single smile in return.

"What's wrong?" I asked.

"How are you feeling?" Alastor asked quietly.

"I feel a little sore, but....what's the matter with all of you?"

The door opened again, and my doctor came in. He looked around at everyone in the room before looking at me.

"How are you feeling, Emma?" he asked.

"Um, a little sore. And nervous. How did my surgery go?"

Dr. Steinbeck began talking, but my mind only picked out certain words. When they opened me up, they found that my gallbladder was filled with cancer. The tumor was so large that they immediately took my gallbladder out. My liver was failing, and Dr. Steinbeck wanted to put me on the transplant list immediately. However, patients with a history of cancer cannot be placed on a transplant list. He also wanted to get every inch of my body scanned for any more cancer. By the time he was done talking, everyone was crying. Simon had his face buried in my dad's chest. I sat there in shock. A piece of my body was no longer there. A whole organ, covered in cancer, was taken away from me. My mom asked how my gallbladder had gotten so bad so quickly, and the doctor explained that it's not uncommon for gallbladder issues to go undetected since other organs hide it.

My dad asked a lot more questions than my mom did. When would I get my tests and screenings done, how long would a new liver take, how long would the healing process be from my surgeries, etc. My head was spinning. I kept looking at Alastor, waiting for him to do something. Say something. React at all. He stood perfectly still the entire time. The only thing about him that moved was the silent tears that ran down his cheeks.

"Emma?" Dr. Steinbeck looked at me. "You haven't said anything about any of this. Are you all right?"

I looked back at him and nodded slowly, lying to everyone in the room. Simon, at this point, was sobbing so hard that my dad asked my mom to take him down to the hospital's cafeteria. My dad went out into the hallway to talk to Dr. Steinbeck more. I was scared to look at Alastor. I knew if I did, I would start crying.

"Emma?" I heard him finally say. Silent tears began rolling down my cheeks.

"Emma, look at me, please."

I wouldn't.

Alastor sat directly in front of me on the bed. He put my face in his hands and lifted it. I started sobbing uncontrollably and buried my head into his chest.

"I'm going to die," I cried. "I haven't done or seen anything, and I'm going to die before I experience anything. I won't get married; I won't have babies; I won't grow old. I will die young, and the world will keep going without me!"

"Emma, stop, please!" Alastor grabbed my arms and gently shook me. "The world won't just go on without you. My life, your mom and dad's lives, your brother's life, your friends' lives; our world will get turned upside down without you. I can't live without you. I don't *want* to live without you. I can't imagine a world without you in it."

By now, Alastor was also crying and hugging me. I realized that I couldn't be afraid. I had to be strong for everyone.

"Hey," I smiled up at him. "I'm not going anywhere. I'm going to fight this with all I have. I'm going to beat this, and who knows? Maybe we can travel somewhere. We can have an adventure together."

Alastor smiled back at me.

"I've never been outside of this state," I added. "Maybe this will be a good excuse to get out of here."

He nodded and wiped his face. My mom, dad, and Dr. Steinbeck came back into the room.

"So what do we need to do to get rid of this shit?" I asked.

"Well, we will have to run extensive tests and scans to see how invasive the cancer is and if it's attacking any other organs. Depending on the outcome, we will begin discussing treatments such as radiation and chemotherapy. It just depends on how much we're up against. Before anything else, however, we will need to perform surgery on your liver. Since we cannot do a transplant, we will have to go in and remove the failing portion of the liver."

"How long do I have?"

The question fell out of my mouth so quickly that I didn't realize I had said it out loud at first. Dr. Steinbeck cleared his throat.

"Based only on the condition of your liver, without taking into account any of your other organs, and assuming everything else comes out clear, we're looking at around six months."

My mom started crying into her hands. Alastor stood up and hugged her. I nodded slowly.

"Wait, you're saying the best case scenario is six months?" my dad asked.

"Yes," Dr. Steinbeck sighed. "Obviously, it's just a guess, depending on how well things go with surgery and treatments. It could be a little more."

"But it could also be less," I mentioned.

"Correct."

"How can you stand there," my dad pointed a finger in Dr. Steinbeck's face, "and tell me that the best guess you can make for my little girl is half a year? That's only one more Thanksgiving! One more Christmas! One more birthday!"

"Dad!" I snapped.

My dad leaned against the wall of my hospital room and slowly slumped to the floor, putting his hands on his head.

"Mom," I said. "Don't tell Simon. Not until we figure all of this out for sure. Why don't you go out there and check on him? He's been sitting out in the waiting room alone for a while. He's probably freaking out."

My mom nodded slowly and left the room. Alastor and I both looked at my dad sitting on the floor. Alastor walked over to my dad and sat down beside him.

"It's going to be okay," Alastor said softly. My dad didn't look at him.

"Hey," Alastor murmured. My dad looked at him. "It's going to be okay."

Alastor slowly put his arms around my dad. At first, my dad pulled away slightly, but then Alastor squeezed harder, and my dad fell into his hug, crying.

"I can't lose her," my dad cried. "I can't lose my baby."

"Everything will be fine," Alastor promised.

Six months, I repeated in my head.

Over the next few days, I had every inch of my body tested, poked, and scanned. I had more blood, urine, and feces tested than I ever imagined. I met with a counselor, an obnoxious bigger woman, who helped with terminally ill patients. I would have rather had more blood drawn and sit through more scans than listen to that woman talk. She was squeezed into a tight, dark-colored dress and sat with her fat ankles crossed. I focused on things like her neck rolls and sweat marks spreading out from her armpits. I don't know if her sole purpose was to get me to cry or scream, but she asked me bullshit questions like, "What about dying makes you sad? What about it makes you angry or scared?" I lied my way through my session and went back to my room.

My mom had ordered my lunch, and it was waiting for me.

"Hey, sweetie," she smiled. "How was it?"

"Are you fucking kidding me?" I said, looking over my plate before putting the cover back over it. "How do you think it was?"

"Aren't you hungry?" she asked, taking the cover back off. "I thought some chicken strips and fries would sound good. You haven't eaten anything since yesterday."

"I'll eat when I feel hungry," I replied, checking my cell phone. "Is Dad or Simon coming up anytime soon?"

"It's hard since Simon has school, and your father has to work."

"Also, hanging out with me sucks because I'm dying. I wouldn't want to be around me if I was Dad either."

"Now, Emma, why would you say something like that?"

"He's barely talked to me since I had my surgery."

"He just doesn't know what to say yet, honey. Just give him some time."

"Yeah, because I have *so much* time."

"Do you want me to turn the tv on? Or maybe I could go pick out a book or magazine from the gift shop?"

"I kind of just want you to leave me alone," I muttered, not looking up from my phone.

"What?"

"I want you to leave me the hell alone."

"Emma..." my mom's voice cracked.

"You haven't left my side since I woke up from surgery. I can't take a shit without you being in my business. But I'm sure you love this. Having to take care of me like when I was a kid. I lived with you and Dad my whole life, and then when I finally got out on my own, I got sick and am now dying. I've lost my apartment, which I guess, thank God Colbie was able to move in with Maddi since I let her down. I lost my job. I had to quit school. So now you get to go right back to hovering over my every move and take care of me. You're dying to have the 'I told you so' speech, and I swear to God if you do, I will throw myself out of my hospital window."

She didn't respond. I looked up from my phone. My mom stood next to me, quietly crying. I looked back at my phone, and my mom grabbed her purse.

"I'm going to run by the house, take a shower, get into some fresh clothes, and maybe make some dinner for your dad and brother since they haven't had a hot meal in a while. I'll be back up later."

She kissed my forehead and left my room. I laid down on my side and tucked my knees up. I covered myself with my blanket and cried myself to sleep.

"Make sure the knots are tight," I hear a voice say.

"She's not going anywhere," a second one replies.

I open my eyes, and two large creatures are looming over me. I am tied to a large wooden table by my wrists and ankles. I try to move, but I seem to be paralyzed. I stare blankly up at the two things moving around me. They are silhouetted, hidden in the shadows, but I can tell they are much bigger than me and are not human.

"Okay, go ahead and start cutting," the first voice says. "I don't want her sitting too long and spoiling."

What does that mean? I wonder. I can see something large and metal out of the corner of my eye. Then, I feel it slide down my torso, from my sternum, and past my belly button. These things are cutting me open! I try to scream or move and can't. I feel like retching, but I can't even do that. I hear my ribs crack and then briefly saw as they were pulled out.

Oh god, I think. *Please, please, let this be a dream. Let me wake up.*

"Ew," the second voice says. "What is that?"

"I'm not sure," the first voice says. "I think that's supposed to be the intestines. Everything looks rotten. This thing must have been sick before it died. Start pulling it all out and see if there's anything that can be saved."

I watched as my insides were torn out, one organ at a time. All the while, the two horrible creatures complain about my body being spoiled and inedible. I feel dizzy and nauseous and want it to end.

"All that's left is the brain," the first voice sighs. "At the very least, we can eat that. Surely that hasn't been contaminated by disease."

I see one of the creatures raise a large mallet above my head. I'm ready for this to be over. When the mallet comes down, I finally wake up.

I opened my eyes and then barfed all over my hospital bed. My mom came over and started rubbing my back.

"I'm sorry," I sobbed. "I'm so sorry."

My mom softly hushed me and moved my hair out of my face. A nurse came in and helped clean me up. After they got me into a new gown and a clean bed, the nurse told us that Dr. Steinbeck was coming in with some results. I looked at my mom, who had somehow aged years in the past few weeks. She looked more like my grandma now, and she seemed very tired. She was worn down. What had I put my poor parents through? All the worry and stress through the years, and I had a feeling that it was about to get even worse. Dr. Steinbeck came in with his fake smile and a stack of papers.

"How are we doing today, ladies?" he asked, pulling a chair up and guiding my mom into it.

"I have more cancer, don't I?" I asked.

Dr. Steinbeck sat on my bed and rubbed his thinning hair.

"We found some tumors," he started. My mom covered her mouth with one hand as she let out a gasp.

"*Tumors*?" I asked. "As in, more than one?"

"We need to start chemotherapy immediately. You have a tumor on your liver and one on your colon. We cannot operate on either tumor until we try to minimize the size through chemotherapy. If we can minimize the size and keep the cancer from spreading, that will make any surgeries we do more successful. There is good news in all of this, however. We may be able to put you on the liver transplant list since there is cancer in your liver. If we can successfully remove the other tumors and get you on the list, we can get you a cancer-free liver."

"How much time do you think I have now that you know I have multiple tumors?" I asked. "Would chemo help add more time, or does it even matter?"

"I would recommend chemotherapy. If it doesn't work, you know how much time you most likely have. However, if the chemotherapy *does* work, it will only add more time."

"How likely is that to happen, though?" I asked.

"We've given patients six months before. I gave one young man a six-month prognosis, and he is still alive. That prognosis was given to him two years ago."

He smiled softly at me and then looked at my mom. She looked scared and pale.

"I promise I will do everything possible to keep Emma with us as long as possible."

But his promise wasn't worth shit.

Come to find out; my tumors were all in inoperable locations. Surgery was no longer an option. They had me start chemo right away. I had to do it every day for a week, get three weeks off, and start a new cycle. I had a nurse with me throughout the session, explaining everything. I guess she could tell I was scared because she held my hand a lot and even put her arm around me. While I had my chemo treatment, my mom went home to nap and shower. But the nurse who was with me made me feel better. Several other people were getting their treatments when I entered the room, but I tried not to look at anyone. The nurse started my IV and gave me a blanket.

"Would you like a snack or something to drink?" she asked. "Sometimes patients complain about having a metallic taste in their mouth while getting treatment."

"Could I have some orange juice?" I asked. She nodded and left.

"How old are you?" I heard a quiet voice ask. I looked around.

An older black woman, maybe in her late sixties, was looking at me. She had a pink knitted cap and matching shawl on.

"You look way too young to be here," she scoffed. "How awful. But that's the thing about cancer. It doesn't give a shit if you're young, old, black, white, ugly, beautiful, rich, or poor. As long as it steals some of your life from you, that's all it wants. Look at this."

She pulled her shirt down and revealed two large scars where her breasts used to be. I felt very uneasy and wondered where my nurse had gone.

"I know. Hideous, right?" She laughed. "My ex-husband hated it so much he left me for a younger, bigger pair. But I'd rather have no tits and be alive still."

I didn't say anything. Her smile faded.

"How long?"

"What?" I asked.

"How long did they give you?"

"Six months."

"You're so young and beautiful. Any babies?"

"No."

"I have three. You at least have a man?"

"I have a boyfriend."

149

"That's good. What kind do you have?"

"Um, I'm not sure. I think they said something like metastasis. I had a gallbladder, but they took the whole gallbladder out. I have tumors in my liver and my colon. They can't operate on them, however. So here I am."

She nodded at me.

"So you have breast cancer?" I asked.

"It started as breast cancer. They removed both breasts. I went into remission for about four years. Then they found a damn spot on my lung. Can't have those removed, though."

"Jesus Christ almighty, you're going to talk the poor girl into a coma," an old man in the corner thundered.

"I'm trying to be comforting, you bitter old bag, and don't take the Lord's name in vain," the lady spat before turning back to me and smiling. "That's Hector. Don't pay any attention to him. He's just a mean old man. I'm Kim. What's your name, baby?"

"Emma," I said as my nurse returned with my juice.

"Everything going okay in here?" she asked.

"Could you turn the heat up, sugar?" Kim asked. "I'm freezing."

"Are you out of your damn mind?" Hector yelled. "It's like an oven in here. How are you still cold with all those layers you have?"

"You got the devil in you; that's why you're so hot all the time!" Kim snapped. "Now mind ya business and take a nap or something."

Hector waved her off and went back to reading his book. Suddenly, I felt sick to my stomach. I started heaving, and the nurse put a bag in front of me. I threw up while she rubbed my back.

"Poor thing," Kim sighed. "I know, it's terrible. Next time you come in, ask for the pre-chemo cocktail. Anti-nausea and a steroid. No puking, and you'll have energy afterward."

"No, you want the anti-nausea and the anti-anxiety," Hector argued. "No puking, and it'll make you relaxed."

"Do you two know each other?" I asked after I was done throwing up. "Like, did you know each other before this?"

"No," Kim replied. "But we spend so much time together here; it feels like we've known each other our whole lives."

"Sometimes I think we know too much about each other," Hector chuckled.

"You love me, and you know it," Kim smiled.

Hector, grinning, closed his eyes and fell asleep instantly. There was a long period of silence. Finally, Kim spoke; her eyes were filled with tears.

"If and when you get done with all this crap, you go and live," she cried. "Before I had breast cancer, I spent my life taking care of my kids. I'm glad I could be there for them, but I never gave myself time. I spent too much of my time working and caring for everyone else; I never did anything for myself. And now, I may not ever get to. I wanted to travel, get a tattoo, and eat ice cream for breakfast. All of these stupid things. You always say, 'someday I'll do it.' Well, today needs to be that day. You never know how many tomorrows you'll get."

I started crying, and my nurse started rubbing my back again. Kim's treatment ended, and she slowly got up. She momentarily took her cap off. She scratched her bald head and put her hat back on. She walked over to me and held my hands in hers.

"You don't let this cancer win. You promise me that."

I nodded and smiled at her. After she left, my nurse unhooked my IV and helped me back to my room. I felt nauseous, weak, and tired. At one point, the doctor came in while I was napping to tell my mom that I could go home. My mom and a nurse took me to the car in a wheelchair. I slept the whole way to my parents' house, and when we pulled into the driveway, Simon came out to help me inside. I sat down on the couch as soon as I entered the room. I was exhausted and still felt nauseous.

"I want to go lay down," I said. "I don't know if I can make it up the stairs."

"Just lay down on the couch," my mom smiled. "I'll get you a blanket."

Without arguing, I lay down and closed my eyes. I must have fallen asleep because the next thing I knew, I woke up to Alastor carrying me upstairs. My parents had put an extra bed in my old room, and Alastor put me down gently on it. Something caught my eye. I looked behind Alastor and saw a person-shaped shadow move across the room. I jumped and gasped. Alastor turned around and then looked back at me.

"What's wrong?"

"I thought I saw…"

"Shhhh," he whispered. "It's okay. Just go back to sleep."

I smiled sleepily at him and then closed my eyes again. When I woke up again, I sat up and looked around my old room—some of the things that used to be stored in the basement were now there. I saw my mom's sewing machine and my dad's exercise bike. I looked at the nightstand beside the bed, and there was a little silver bell. Underneath was a note that said, "Please ring for service." I picked it up and jingled it. A moment later, the door opened, and Alastor walked in.

"Hey there, beautiful," he smiled. "How are you feeling?"

"I'm thirsty," I said. "How long have you been here?"

"About four hours."

"You waited that long?"

"I wanted to see you," he came over and sat next to me on the bed. "I've missed you so much. It's been so hard trying to concentrate on school without you."

"How much of my stuff is left to pack at Maddi and Colbie's?" I asked.

"Just the rest of your clothes," he answered. "Your mom said the bed could stay there, so Whitney didn't have to move hers. And your parents have been trying to get a reclining bed approved by the insurance company."

"Whitney?" I asked. "Why does Whitney need a bed over there?"

"She's, um, moving in with Maddi and Colbie."

"What? Since when?"

"Sam broke up with her, and Maddi thought it would be easier to split the rent three ways, so they didn't have to pay so much."

"Oh," I muttered. "Well, good for them. I hope they have a great time living together."

"Emma, don't be like that."

"Yeah, I guess I shouldn't waste my time that's left being angry," I said coldly.

"Don't stress over anything," Alastor smiled. "We're trying to get your room set back up the way it was and make sure you're as comfortable as possible."

I looked at Alastor, eyes filling with tears.

"I can't do this," I cried. "I don't want to do this. I don't want to be bald and sickly and throw up all the time. I just want to live a little longer. I'm so scared of dying."

"Emma, stop," Alastor started crying too. "Don't talk like that."

"Alastor, you didn't see how all the doctors and nurses have been around me. They know I'm dying. I am going to die. And probably soon. They can't operate on me. I'm not going to get better!"

Alastor wrapped his arms around me, and I buried my face into his chest and sobbed.

"I'm not going to get any better," I repeated softly.

We cried together until we had nothing else left. Eventually, we fell asleep holding each other, just like the first time I stayed the night with him. I didn't dream that night, which was fine because my body felt too exhausted to even dream.

10

I woke up the following day, and we got ready to go to my next chemotherapy treatment. Alastor drove me and was planning to sit with me during my appointment. However, they were busy and running behind when we got to the clinic. I gave the receptionist my name. She told us we might be waiting for a couple of hours to get in. Alastor frowned.

"A couple of hours?" he repeated. "How are you guys a couple of hours behind?"

"It depends on when patients get here, how long their treatments last, or any other unknown factors. Now, please sit and wait, and we will call you back when it's your turn."

"Come on," I said softly. "Let's just go sit."

Alastor glared at the receptionist and followed me to a couple of chairs. I watched Alastor as he looked around the room at the other patients. I also looked around. There were all types of people there. Old people, teenagers, men, women; some looked fine while others looked...bad. There were a few people in the waiting room that scared me. Two women and a man. All three were bald, skinny, pale, and looked like they were barely human still. I grabbed Alastor's hand and squeezed it.

"I know," he whispered and smiled. "It's okay, though."

"I hate this," I whispered.

"I do too," Alastor replied. "Do you want anything from the vending machine? I have to do something to keep busy for a little bit."

"Do you want me to come with you?"

"No, it's okay. You stay here and relax for a while."

"Okay," I leaned back in my seat. "I'm good. I don't feel hungry."

Alastor leaned in and kissed my forehead before walking down the hallway. I watched him the whole way, admiring him from behind. As he turned the corner, a large shadow stood facing me. I sat up and stared at it as it turned the corner too. I got up and slowly walked down the hallway. One of the ceiling lights flickered above me as I turned down the hallway Alastor went down. There was no one around.

"Alastor?" I said quietly.

The lights in the hallway flickered and then went off completely. I tiptoed down a little further to the vending machines. I walked up to one of the lit machines and looked at the rows of snacks. Then, I heard someone coming up behind me, breathing heavily. The light in the vending machine went out, and I saw an unrecognizable, twisted face next to mine in the glass reflection. I screamed and turned around.

157

"I'm sorry!" Alastor said quickly. "I didn't mean to scare you!"

I looked around. All of the hallway lights and vending machine lights were on. People walked up and down the hallway, looking over at us as they passed.

"Are you all right?" Alastor asked.

"Where were you?"

"I had to go to the bathroom quickly and then came to get snacks like I said I would."

I rubbed my forehead and sighed.

"Are you sure you're alright?"

"Yeah, I just need to sit down and rest my eyes for a bit."

"Well, we have about two hours of sitting. Come on, let's get you back to the waiting area."

Luckily, we didn't have to wait two hours. It was closer to an hour and a half, which was still a long time to wait. By the time I was called to go back, I was tired and hungry. They drew my blood, took my urine samples, and then made me wait some more. Finally, we returned to the chemo room, where I got my "pre-chemo cocktail" and then had my IV started. Alastor asked many questions about the chemotherapy, at-home care, my diet, my medication, and anything he could do to help. The nurse politely answered all of his questions and brought us drinks and snacks. Kim walked in and smiled when she saw me.

"Hey, baby," she waved. "How are you feeling today?"

"Tired," I sighed. "I slept almost all afternoon yesterday and all night last night."

"Yeah, that's one good thing about chemo. You finally get caught up on all the sleep you've lost throughout the years."

She looked at Alastor.

"Well, hello there," she smiled. "You must be the boyfriend."

"Hi, I'm Alastor," he shook her hand.

"Alastor? That's an interesting name. I'm Kim."

She turned to me.

"Oh, you'll have to start bringing him every time. He's much easier on the eyes than what I usually have to look at around here."

I chuckled and put my hand in Alastor's. I was so thankful to have him there with me. He'd have to go back to school the next day, but I was enjoying his company while it lasted. After my chemotherapy, we returned to my parents' house and watched movies for a while. Simon came home from school and walked in hurriedly.

"Hey, Simon," I said as he walked by. "How was...."

He went straight up to his room and shut the door. I looked at Alastor.

"Maybe he didn't hear you," he smiled politely.

"Yeah," I sighed.

"I'm sorry you have to move back in with your parents," Alastor said. "I know it doesn't feel like it, but Simon is glad you're back home. He's just scared."

"I wish he didn't have to see me like this, though," I said. "I don't understand why no one isn't willing to let me try to stay with Whitney, Maddi, and Colbie. I know we had that fight, but we've gotten into fights before. We could have found a bigger place. I would have at least tried to work and live there. It sucks so much being back here."

"However, your parents know your medical history. You have a sure ride to and from chemotherapy and doctor's appointments. It just makes sense. They can take care of you."

"I don't need anyone to take care of me," I muttered. "I'm a grown woman."

"A grown woman with very aggressive cancer," he replied. "I know you can take care of yourself. But this is something I think you should swallow your pride with and take the extra support."

"I'm further away from you."

"I'll visit as often as possible," he reassured me. "I hate it too. But I want you to focus on getting better."

"I wish you could stay the night," I sighed.

"I know. But I can stay late."

"How late?" I winked.

I reached my hand over to his lap before heaving. I got up and ran to the bathroom, puking into the toilet and all over the floor. Alastor came in and held my hair back. I started crying and apologizing between throwing up. I was so humiliated. After Alastor helped clean me and the bathroom up, he helped me get into my pajamas and bed. He played with my hair until I fell asleep. I was immediately sad the following day when I woke up in an empty room.

My dad and brother were already at work and school when I went downstairs. I saw my mom through the kitchen window sitting on the back porch. She was holding a cup of coffee and crying. She sat there silently, tears occasionally running down her cheeks. She didn't wipe the tears or her nose. She just sat like a statue. I knew why she was crying. It was the same reason everyone I cared about had been crying lately. It was the same reason I had been crying so much. I was dying. Everyone knew it. I knew it.

I opened the back door, and my mom turned her head away from me.

"You're up," she wiped her face quickly. "How are you feeling?"

"So great," I said sarcastically. "I was thinking we could go for a run."

She didn't respond.

"Mom," I said quietly. She turned and looked at me.

"I don't want to do this."

"What are you talking about?" she asked.

"I don't want to be miserably sick just to die anyway. I want to enjoy what time I have left. I don't want to be in bed all day."

"I don't want to hear it, Emma," she stood up quickly. "I know you don't feel good, but adjusting to the chemo will take time."

"You know I don't feel good?" I repeated. "Are you fucking kidding me? I am dying, Mom!"

"Stop it!" She screamed and threw her coffee mug against the house. The cup exploded, and coffee went everywhere. My mom sank to the floor and buried her face in her hands. I sat down next to her and pulled her up against me. I breathed in the smell of her hair and face cream. She smelled like she always did—one of the many things I had always taken for granted. And one of the things I was going to miss the most.

"I can't lose you," she finally said.

"You won't," I said in a shaky voice. "You know a part of me will always be with you. I'll be watching over you and Dad and Simon. I'll just be in a better place."

She sat up and looked at me with tired eyes.

"I have always believed in God," she cried. "I've always believed in Heaven and Hell. That we go somewhere when we die. For the first time in

162

my life, I am terrified that what I believe is wrong. I can't stand the thought of losing you, and that is it. I can't stand thinking I will never see you again when you go. I don't want to live in a world where you don't exist. My heart can't take it."

I sat there while she cried and wiped her face.

"You want to know something crazy?" I asked. "The closer I get to death, the more I believe in all of it."

She smiled at me and stood up before helping me up. I spent the day at home with my mom. We stayed in our pajamas all day, looking at photo albums and watching old home videos. I saw one labeled "Emma's Arrival" and showed it to my mom.

"Is this from when I was born?" I asked.

"I don't think I can watch that one," she replied.

"Okay," I sighed.

"You want to know why we named you Emma?" she asked. I nodded.

"Your name means 'whole.' Before you were born, your father and I separated. We had problems like any married couple, and your father met someone else. I was devastated, but I knew I hadn't been there for him like a wife is supposed to be for her husband. I treated him more like a friend than a spouse, pushing him away from me. Eventually, he found his way back, and we reconciled. We hadn't been back together for that long when we found out we were pregnant with you. It changed everything. You were the missing piece to our lives. You were what made us whole."

I scooted close to my mom and put my head in her lap. She ran her fingers through my hair before stopping abruptly. I looked up and there were a few strands of my hair between her fingers. Before I could say anything, she shook the hairs loose onto the floor.

"Oh, honey, I'm so sorry. I must have been pulling on your hair too hard. Lay back down. It's okay."

I reluctantly laid back. I figured if it were serious, she would have made a bigger deal of it. She played with my hair until I fell asleep.

I continued to go to chemotherapy treatments, even though it didn't seem to be doing any good. Everyone was hopeful that something would improve, but things just seem to get worse for me. One night after my treatment, Alastor came over to visit me. I had been sleeping since I got home and woke up when I heard a knock on my bedroom door.

"Come in," I said quietly. I smiled as Alastor walked over and kissed my forehead.

"How are you feeling?" he asked.

"I wish people would stop asking me that," I whispered.

"Sorry," he smiled.

I sat up in bed slowly, and Alastor stared behind me. I looked at my pillow and saw thin clumps of hair. I gasped and ran my fingers through my hair, pulling more out.

"Oh my god," I breathed.

"It's okay," Alastor said, placing his hand on my thigh. "The doctor told you that might happen."

I didn't respond.

"It's just hair," he continued. "You don't need it. You're just as beautiful without hair as you are with it."

"Alastor, I'm done."

"What do you mean?" he asked.

"I don't want to do chemo anymore," I answered. "I had a check-up appointment with the oncologist today. It's spreading."

"What?"

"It's not going away," I explained. "It's getting worse. I'm dying."

"No, you're not."

"Alastor," I said, grabbing his hands. "I am. I'm dying, and chemo only makes me weak and tired. It's not going to keep me alive. I don't want to live in this bed for the rest of my life. Do you understand?"

He just stared at me.

"I'd rather enjoy a shorter life. I want to get out and do something. I talked to my parents this evening, and even though they fought the idea at first, they understand why I want to quit chemo."

"Wait, they're supporting you quitting chemo?" he pulled his hands away from mine, sounding hurt.

"It's okay, Alastor," I smiled.

"No, it's not okay!" he snapped. "I don't want to lose you!"

"I know!" I cried. "I know. I don't want to lose you either. I don't want to say goodbye to you. You made me feel more alive than anything else in my short existence. Leaving you behind will be the hardest part of all of this."

"Then take me with you," Alastor cried.

"What?" I asked. "What did you just say?"

"I don't want to live without you," Alastor sobbed. "It's too hard. You're the only thing in my life that has ever made sense. You're the only person I can be myself around. I've been surrounded by people who have never made me feel like I'm worth anything. But I feel like I'm worth something because of you! I can't live without you. I don't want to."

"What are you saying, Alastor?"

"When you die, I'm going to too. I'm going to make sure I do."

"You stop it now," I said, my heart pounding. "You don't ever talk like that to me ever again. You don't get to decide that. You have a chance to live a full life. You can get married and have babies and grow old-"

"I wanted to do all of that with you! It's not fair."

"I know," I sighed. "It's not fair. It's not fair that I found the love of my life at the end of it."

Alastor hung his head and cried. A thought occurred to me. I blurted it out without even hesitating.

"What if I did it too?" I asked.

"What?"

"What if I went on my own terms?" I asked.

"What are you talking about?"

"I don't know," I shook my head. "I don't know. Just forget it."

Alastor looked at me. I thought a moment before speaking again.

"It's just, " I explained. "I'm going to die soon anyway. I don't want to suffer anymore. I don't want cancer to have the power to kill me."

"You mean we'd do it together?" Alastor asked.

"No, no, no," I panicked. "I don't want you doing anything."

"We could, though!" Alastor sniffled. "We could die together so we could be together forever."

"No!" I yelled. "That's crazy. I can't let you-"

"I'm going to do it either way. We may as well do it together. I want to go wherever you go."

"You don't have to do this, Alastor," I said. "I can go on my own."

"I love you too much to let you do that," Alastor said, taking my hand and kissing it. "I don't want you ever to be alone again. It would be sort of poetically romantic. Two lovers who couldn't live without each other died together."

I knew it was insane. It was irresponsible. I hoped, deep inside that Alastor would want to change his mind. But we sat there, making plans. We would go out of town, rent a lake house over the weekend, and not return. We were going to take a handful of my pain pills, get as drunk as we could, go out on a boat, and jump into the water together. But, as much of my life goes, nothing goes according to plan.

I woke up the following day in so much pain that I couldn't stop crying. My parents rushed me to the emergency room, where the doctors informed them that the chemo had caused severe nerve damage. I was admitted and put on morphine to help with the pain. People were in and out of my room a lot, meanwhile I was in and out of consciousness. I was mumbling to everyone around me, but no one was able to understand me.

I saw shadows that no one else noticed. People would walk right through the shadows, unable to feel or see them. I could hear my parents telling me to let go and that it was okay to stop fighting. I just wanted to sleep. I felt so tired. I tried to close my eyes and sleep off the worry and the pain, even though I knew my eyes were already closed. I was warm and comfortable but unable to sleep heavily. It felt like when you fall asleep too fast and your whole body twitches, so you wake back up just a little bit. Someone once told me that our bodies do that because we fall asleep too quickly, and our brain thinks we're dying, so it signals our nervous system to jumpstart and wake up. I don't know if any of that is true, but my body knew not to jumpstart itself this time. My brain knew it was time to sleep. And I did. I slept so well.

Death: Part One

11

"Do you want to come inside where it's warm?"

I opened my eyes and saw my breath. I was wearing a coat, gloves, and a scarf, and snow was on the ground. I didn't feel cold at all, however. I watched as my hot breath appeared each time I exhaled.

"Hey, you."

I looked over to my right. A man was standing by me and smiling.

"Do you want to come inside where it's warm?"

I looked at the building behind him and realized where I was. I was sitting on a bench outside the Downtown Theatre, my favorite venue to see shows. The marquee above the door said, "The Broken Chandeliers and The Conservation: Tonight Only." They were my two favorite bands. Maddi, Whitney, and I had seen them once at the Downtown Theatre. It was the best concert I had ever been to. The three of us had so much fun dancing and singing together. I'll never forget how excited I was when my dad dropped us in front of the door.

"Have fun," he said. "But-"

"But not too much fun?" I finished.

"Actually, I was going to say, 'but no hanging with the band backstage.' I don't want my daughter to be a groupie."

"Bye, Dad," I laughed.

"Have too much fun!" he yelled as I walked away from the car.

"Hey," the man said to me. "You comin' or what? The show's about to start."

"I know you," I said, standing up and walking towards him. "You're Matt Kinsley, the lead singer of the Broken Chandeliers!"

"Guilty," he smiled and shook my hand.

"You guys have been my favorite band forever," I beamed. "I own every single album you've ever put out."

"Oh lord, I hope not every album," he chuckled as he opened the door for me. "Even the awful Christmas one?"

"Even the Christmas one," I laughed. "Although, to be honest, I only bring it out once a year."

"Well, that's good," he smiled. We walked into the building, and I stopped. I suddenly realized something wasn't right. Matt turned around and looked at me.

"What's wrong?" he asked. I looked around us. No one else seemed to be in the building.

"You're dead," I breathed. "The whole band died in a bad wreck a few summers ago. I remember you were on tour at the time because you were coming back here. I wanted to see you guys again, but I couldn't afford tickets. Your tour bus was driving through Colorado, and there was a snowstorm. The bus rolled multiple times and killed everyone, including the driver. I remember that happening. I was so sad that I cried, even though none of my friends did."

Matt smiled at me.

"What is this?" I asked. "Am I dreaming?"

"No," Matt smirked. "But you already know that by now, don't you, Emma?"

I looked around and noticed that everything seemed different. There was no one else around, and there was no noise except our voices.

"You closed your eyes and thought about that concert you and your friends went to," Matt said. "How come?"

"It was one of my favorite memories," I explained. "We had so much fun that night. We pushed our way down to the stage, and when our favorite song came on, the three of us started dancing and singing. You pointed us out and asked if we wanted to come up on stage with you guys. We were freaking out and got up there and started singing along with you. You put your arm around my shoulder, rocking back and forth. It was like time had stopped. It was a great memory."

Matt smiled at me and hugged me.

"I'm dead, aren't I?" I asked. Matt looked at me and nodded, still smiling.

"I don't feel anything," I said. "No pain or cold or anything. I feel excellent."

"Take my hand," Matt reached out for me. "I want to show you something."

Matt led me to a door to our right. When he opened it, it led to a bright glowing scene. I walked into a classroom with children running around and a teacher trying to get everyone to line up to go outside. I saw a six-year-old me getting in line before being shoved by a little boy. He stuck his tongue out at me, and I put my head down until we got outside. I watched myself as a little girl sitting on the side of the playground. Another little girl with long, curly, red hair came over and asked if I wanted to play.

"That was my first best friend," I smiled. "Her name was Samantha, but she went by Sam. I always loved her red hair and freckles, and she always said how much she loved my olive skin and how tall I was."

I watched as Sam walked over to the boy who had shoved me in line. He was picking on another kid, and Sam went up behind him and shoved him down, making him skin his knee and cry. She got in trouble for doing it, but from that moment on, she and I were inseparable.

"Her family moved a couple of years later, and I stopped talking to her," I said to Matt. He gave me a sympathetic smile. "But I never forgot how she stood up for me."

"That's really nice," Matt sighed. "We have to move on."

Matt led me to another door. I stopped before we went in.

"So is this like, a job you have now or something?" I asked. Matt laughed.

"Sort of, yeah," he answered. "I was naturally good with people when I was alive and I needed something to keep me busy so here I am. Living out eternity as a greeter. I honestly never thought anything would make me as happy as playing music with my band but getting to do this is pretty awesome."

"Where did the rest of the band end up?" I asked.

"Oh, um, here and there," he smiled weakly. "Come on. This next memory is a good one."

This one led us into a hospital. I walked up to my mom, lying in a bed holding a baby. I watched as a ten-year-old me stepped in with my dad, and I was hesitant to go up to my baby brother. I remember being so angry that my parents were having another baby. I had been an only child for so long that it was a drastic change. I felt like they were replacing me with a kid who didn't have so many medical issues.

"It's okay," my mom smiled. "Come here and meet your brother."

I shuffled over and peeked at Simon. I remember seeing his little face and instantly loving him.

"Oh, I love him just like I love you and Dad," I cried. "I'll always love him."

"Do you want to hold him?" my dad asked.

I sat on the bed next to my mom, and she gently handed Simon to me, showing me how to support his head.

"Hi, Simon," I smiled at him. "I'm your big sister, Emma. I promise I'll always take care of you and never be mean to you."

Simon looked up and gave me a newborn smile. Both of my parents cried and hugged us. I smiled as I watched this scene from my life.

"Let's move on to the next one, shall we?" Matt asked.

I followed him through a door that led me to my high school. I watched a teenage me walking with Whitney and Maddi as we talked.

"I know it would be cheaper to go to a state university," I stated. "But come on! Living in another state throughout college would be so cool! And our state doesn't have any good journalism schools."

"I thought you wanted to be a photographer," Maddi inquired.

"I do!" I answered. "I want to write and take photos that go along with my stories. I want to take pictures of wild African animals. I want to take pictures of the wonders of the world. I want to take pictures at music festivals and movie premieres. I want to take pictures of political rallies, protests, marches, and sports events. And I also want to write about those things. I want to be as involved as I can in the world. I don't want to miss anything! I want to do it all!"

"A little ambitious this morning, aren't we?" Whitney laughed. "I'd be happy with just passing my history test."

"Emma," I heard a voice call from behind me. It was Mr. Way, my newspaper and yearbook teacher.

"We got the results from the journalism conference," he smiled. "They reviewed everyone's entries."

"Did I place in any of them?" I asked.

"You placed first in the Entertainment and Environmental categories and third in the Social News category."

"What!" I beamed. "That's unbelievable!"

"I am so proud of you," Mr. Way smiled. "You did a great job. Also, placing in three categories at that conference will help when applying for journalism scholarships. Especially since you have a teacher who has high hopes for you."

"Thank you so much, Mr. Way," I said. "This is so awesome!"

I looked at Matt.

"What's wrong?" he asked.

"I wish I would have been able to go to college sooner. And I wish I could see more," I replied. "I was so excited about winning awards at that conference. And I didn't even do anything with it."

"Let's go on to the next one," Matt said, putting his hand gently on my shoulder.

We went through another door, and I was in my bedroom. My dad sat down on my bed and woke me up. I was in sixth grade, and it was winter. I woke up and looked up at him.

"Hey, sweetie," he said. "How about you play hooky from school today, and we go ice skating, just you and me?"

We flash-forwarded to see my dad and me at the ice skating rink. It was my favorite memory with my dad. I watched us ice skate for a while until Matt made me move on to the next memory. The next one was when my mom and I spent all day together watching old home movies and talking. I watched how my mom looked at me while I watched the videos. The love in her eyes filled the room.

"Another happy memory," I whispered. "Which one next?"

"The next one isn't a memory," Matt said softly. "But it's something you need to see."

Matt walked up to another door and opened it. We went through to a softly-lit room. There were people I knew crowding the place. Everyone was either murmuring or crying. I walked past co-workers from the daycare, parents of the children I cared for, friends of mine from high school, classmates and teachers from high school and college, and family members. I saw Whitney and Maddi hugging each other and crying while Colbie had her hand on Maddi's shoulder. My grandma was sitting with Simon and holding his hand. Then, I saw my parents standing by a casket.

"I don't know if I can," I said to Matt.

"It's okay, I promise."

I stood by them, looking at myself lying there, dead. I was shocked by how pretty I looked. I had a head full of hair, which was probably a wig. The makeup the funeral home had applied took away any dark circles or lack of color. I looked glowing and healthy. I was happy that this was how everyone would see me for the last time. I was wearing a beautiful dark blue dress and a pearl necklace that had been my grandma's. I recalled her telling me that I could have it when she died. I thought it was a stunning necklace, but it made me feel sad that I would get it when she died. My family must have remembered how much I loved that necklace. I watched my parents holding each other and crying silently. There was a long table filled with flowers, cards, and pictures of me growing up. I walked along the table until I reached the end. There was a mirror on the wall, and my reflection caught my attention. I looked the same as I had in the casket. I was wearing the same blue dress with the pearl necklace. My skin looked flawless, and my hair was full and beautiful. I ran my fingers through it.

"It's not a wig," I wept. "Look at how beautiful I am."

"You've always been beautiful," Matt replied. "That's the crazy thing about dying. You finally see yourself the way everyone always did."

"I hate how sad everyone is though," I looked around.

"They'll be okay," Matt assured me. "Listen to them."

I listened to conversations happening in the room. People said, "she's not suffering anymore," and "she fought so hard." I smiled at Matt, and then my smile faded.

"What's wrong?" Matt asked.

"My boyfriend isn't here," I frowned. "Why isn't-?"

And then it hit me.

"Oh no," I gasped.

"What?" Matt asked.

"My boyfriend would have been here," I said frantically. "But he's not here! We talked about something before I died, and I think he might have done it!"

"What are you talking about?"

"Where do people go when they die?" I asked.

"Well, someone usually greets the person who has just died to ease them into the realization that they've just died. Then, they're led up to the Processing area. After that, it's kind of just up to you."

"Is there a way I could find out if someone I know has died?"

"I'm not sure," Matt answered. "I'm part of the greeting team. When we get up to Processing, they might be able to help you."

"When do we get up to Processing?" I asked.

"Well, as long as you're okay with everything so far, I suppose we could make our way up there now."

"Is there anything else I need to do?" I asked.

"As long as you're okay with not seeing anyone on Earth that you care about for a while, we can go now."

I looked around at my friends and family. My parents were walking around talking to people, making polite small talk. I noticed Simon up by my casket.

"Wait a minute," I said before going over to my brother. He was standing by my casket, looking at my body and crying.

"I miss you so much already," he said quietly. "I know you're not in any pain anymore, and I'm glad, but I'm also not. How am I going to keep going without you? Who will talk to me about high school and girls and stupid stuff like that? I need you back. I'm sorry about all the times I yelled at you and all the times we fought. I'm sorry for every time I called you stupid or didn't want to spend time with you. I just wish I had my big sister back. I didn't tell you how much I love you that often. But I know how much you loved me. I couldn't even talk to you the last time you saw me. I wish I would have. I'm just so sorry for everything. I love you so much, Emma."

I reached out and put my hand on Simon's shoulder. His body jumped slightly, and he started sniveling. I looked at Matt.

"Did he feel that?" I asked.

"They feel us, but it's usually not significant enough for them to notice. It usually feels like a cold chill or static. They don't even suspect it's us."

I looked at Simon again. He was getting so big. I couldn't believe I would miss watching my baby brother grow up. I was going to miss seeing my parents get old. I would miss seeing people I cared about get married and have kids and age. But my death wouldn't stop any of it from happening. Everyone would be sad and miss me, but life would go on. And then I thought of Alastor.

"How long do people usually stick around?" I asked.

"Just depends on the person," Matt said. "Some people have a tough time coping with dying. They try to find ways to stay as long as possible. They try to communicate with loved ones or give them clues as to where their bodies are or who killed them. Stuff like that."

"Like ghosts?"

Matt laughed.

"Not exactly," he chuckled. "We can't really communicate with the living. We're supposed to move on after we die. Some people have a harder time with that than others, which is understandable. It's not easy to leave the ones you love behind. But that's just the way things are. You live, you die, you move on."

I looked around at everyone.

"And I'll see them again, eventually?"

"Absolutely. As long as they live good lives."

"I'm ready to go," I said.

"Let's go then," he nodded.

I followed Matt out of the funeral home and out into the street. In the middle of the road was a giant escalator. I laughed at Matt.

"Are you kidding me?" I chuckled. "Is this real?"

"It is for you," he explained. "They're very accommodating for everyone's interpretations of what exactly happens when we die. You know, to make the transition easier. Some people get stairs, some take an elevator, and some get a tunnel into white light. It isn't about *how* you get there, but *where* you end up."

"Wait, you mean we're not going to Heaven?" I asked.

"No, not quite. We have to get you up to Processing. They'll be able to tell you where you're going. Sometimes Processing takes longer for some people. It just depends on how long you lived and the amount of good and bad things a person did while alive."

"Oh," I said quietly. "Who are *they*?"

"What?" Matt asked.

"You said *they're* very accommodating, and *they'll* be able to tell me where I'm going. Are you talking about angels or something?"

"Yes."

"Really?"

"You sound surprised."

"I don't know," I shrugged. "There's so many religions and beliefs and theories. It's weird when you realize yours is right and everyone else's is wrong. It makes me feel a little sad for everyone else."

"Again, everyone gets their little version of everything," Matt grinned. "God is very patient and understanding. Some people strictly follow Christianity and put God before everything throughout their lives. At the same time, they can treat others horribly, hating gay people, poor people, or foreigners. To be a Christian is to be Christ-like and love unconditionally, even if it's someone who doesn't deserve it. On the other hand, some people are non-Christians but believe in forgiveness, kindness, and love. When they die, they sort of get a crash course in the truth. Whether or not they want to change their way of thinking is up to them."

I stood on the escalator, a million thoughts running through my mind.

"So if there are angels, does that mean Heaven and Hell exist?" I asked.

"Yup," Matt answered. "Although we kind of refer to it as Paradise. And yes, Hell very much exists. As do demons and Satan."

"Wow," I muttered. "What's Heaven- I mean, Paradise like? Is it just hanging in clouds all day praising God with non-stop rainbows and sunshine?"

Matt laughed.

"Not exactly," Matt answered. "Unless that's what you want your Paradise to be like. Paradise is much like Earth, but all the best parts about it. Ice cream and hugs and-"

"What if someone doesn't like ice cream?" I asked.

"You don't have to eat it," Matt said. "But if you like it, you have easy access to it. That's why everyone's personal Paradise is a little different."

"What if my Paradise is so different from, let's say, my brother's that he doesn't want to visit me, and then I get sad because I never see my brother again."

"Everyone visits everyone in Paradise, especially family members."

"What if they don't want anyone to visit them?" I asked.

"Then they don't," Matt said. I noticed a subtle change in his voice.

"How strict are rules on who goes to Hell?"

"Depends on what you consider strict," he said shortly.

"So since I grew up Catholic, I don't need this so-called crash course and can just go right in, right?"

Matt looked at me but didn't answer.

"I'm going to Heaven, right?"

Still nothing.

"Matt?" I said, concerned.

"I have no idea," Matt replied. "I'm not in Processing, so I couldn't possibly tell you where you're going. And everyone has a different waiting time."

"Waiting time?" I repeated. "You mean Purgatory?"

He didn't say anything as we got closer to the top. I could hear the sound of people talking. Neither of us spoke as we stepped off, and I saw hundreds of people walking around what looked like a vast lobby. There were high walls that were painted white with arched doorways on either side. There were men, women, and children of all ages and ethnicities, and most of them had someone with them like Matt (*a greeter, I think he said*). I noticed there were various artworks on the walls and even some statues and sculptures scattered about. Some greeters seemed to be walking around the art with people, maybe to help them calm down. Some people looked worried or confused, but most of the people looked elated to be there. I thought it was strange to see so many people who were happy to be dead.

"Many people died either from disease, starvation, torture, abuse, or some other kind of suffering," Matt said, almost to answer my thoughts.

"This is the first time in a long time that many people are no longer experiencing hunger or pain. Or maybe they could not walk, see, or hear. Now they get to. Dementia, cancer, third world countries, war, poverty. So many awful things can happen to people while they're living. For some people, dying is the best thing to happen."

I put my hand on my stomach, where I no longer had a colostomy bag, and tears ran silently down my cheeks. Matt put his hand on my shoulder.

"I'll take you into Processing, and then I'll have to be on my way," he stated.

"What?" I gulped. "You're not staying with me?"

"I wish I could, but I have a lot of other people to help get here. Not everyone is as easy to convince as you."

"How will I know what to do?"

"You'll be fine," Matt reassured me. "You ready?"

I nodded slowly before following Matt through the crowd. Many people were forming lines, although I couldn't tell where they ended up. Matt directed me to one of the lines, and I got behind a tall black man in beautifully colored clothes.

"You've got this," Matt said before hugging me tightly.

"If this hug had happened when I was alive, it would have been added to my favorite memories," I tearfully admitted. "Thank you so much for helping me through all of this."

"Thank you for being such a big fan of mine in life," Matt said. "Our fans were what kept us going and made life worth living. It's the least I can do for you."

I looked around nervously.

"You're going to be fine," Matt repeated. "It was great meeting you, Emma."

"You too, Matt. Maybe I'll see you again?"

Matt smiled and walked off.

I watched the different people around me. It seemed like the only time the guides stayed with newcomers was if the newcomers were children. Some of the guides were carrying babies in their arms. I watched them take the babies to a different building than where I was going. Every couple of minutes, the line would move forward. I either watched the people around me or looked down at my shoes. The man in front of me turned around and smiled at me. I politely smiled back but didn't say anything.

"How are you?" the man asked me.

"Fine," I replied. "How are you?"

"Oh, I am just fantastic!" he grinned widely. "This is so wonderful. I am so happy to be here."

"Where are you from?" I asked.

"Togo. I lived there with my wife and son."

"Togo?"

"In Western Africa," he smiled.

"You're from Africa?" I asked. "You don't have an African accent."

"We speak primarily French where I am from," he laughed. "Have you noticed that no one has an accent?"

I listened to people around me talking. They all seemed to be speaking clear English.

"Right now, everyone here is speaking French," he said. "To me, at least. We don't hear other languages. We can understand everyone."

"Wow, I didn't even realize that," I exclaimed. "I guess that makes sense."

I looked at his clothes. He was wearing a bright blue shirt with matching pants. His shirt had flowing sleeves and gold trimming on it.

"My name is Philippe," he said, putting his hand on his chest.

"My name is Emma," I stuck my hand out to shake his.

"It's very nice to meet you, Emma," he replied, shaking my hand.

"So, what do you think about all of this?" I asked.

"It's a lot to take in," he replied. "But I am ready to get through the processing and find my family."

"Your family?"

"My wife and son that I mentioned earlier," he smiled softly. "They both died from malaria. My precious son was only three years old when he died. My wife had already been sick for some time, but she stopped fighting when we lost our son."

"Is that how..." I started.

"No, I did not have malaria," Philippe answered. "No, I was working outside one day and had a heart attack."

"I'm sorry," I apologized.

"Don't be," he said. "After I lost my family, I had nothing left on Earth. I welcomed death with open arms. I practically ran here."

I smiled.

"If you don't mind me asking, how did you get here?" Philippe asked.

"Cancer," I shrugged.

"For you, I am truly sorry," Philippe shook his head. "You are so young and beautiful. You should have lived a lot longer."

"Yeah," I sighed. "I thought I was going to. I had just started school and had an amazing boyfriend who loved me more than anything."

I looked around before looking back at Philippe.

"And I'm worried he might be here just between you and me."

"What do you mean?" he asked.

"Right before I died, we made a pact to kill ourselves together."

Philippe looked at me uneasily.

"I know," I sighed. "I'm worried he went through with it and now is going to Hell because of it."

"But you didn't go through with it?" Philippe asked.

"No," I answered. "I died from cancer before I could do it."

"How would you know if he did it?"

"I don't know," I replied. "I'm hoping someone up there can help me."

As we made our way up to the front of the line, we could see that there were little booths with doors every person went into when it was their turn. They reminded me of the old, wooden confessional booths at church.

"Any idea what that's about?" I asked, pointing to the doors.

"No idea," Philippe answered. "I wish you the best, Emma. I hope you get your answers."

"Thanks, Philippe," I smiled. "I hope you see your wife and son soon."

A door in front of us opened, and Philippe stepped forward. I watched as he walked into the booth and closed the door. I was feeling extremely nervous. I knew I hadn't been a bad person while alive, but I didn't necessarily do anything that good. I started thinking about everything I could have done to improve my chances. I could have gone to church more often, given more to the needy, or spent time with the homeless. The booth in front of me opened, and I hesitated.

"You're next," I heard from behind me.

I walked forward and shut the door behind me. A short, plump lady was sitting at a desk, smiling at me. On the other side of the room was another door identical to the one I had just come through. The room looked like a stereotypical office, except very small. There were a few potted plants on shelves, soothing music playing in the background, and a miniature sand garden on the corner of the desk.

"Go ahead and have a seat, Emma," the woman said as she pointed to the chair in front of her desk. I sat. A nameplate at the front of the desk said, "Hannah B., Processing Assistant."

"You know my name?" I asked.

"Oh, it's my job to know everything about you and your life," she grinned. I could see that she had some pink lipstick on one of her front teeth. "How has your experience been so far?

"Oh," I paused. "It's been okay, I guess. Matt was nice."

"That's good to hear," Hannah said. "Well, my job is to review everything in your life, take notes on both the good and the bad, and then figure out when we'll move you along."

"Wait," I scowled. "Doesn't God decide where we go? Why are you the one who decides?"

"God *does* decide where you go. In fact, I already know where you're going. It's all right here in your file. However, everyone has a waiting period, depending on the circumstances of their lives and choices. We try to move people along as quickly as possible, but you can imagine how busy we get here."

"Can you tell me where I'm going?" I asked nervously.

"I think you already know the answer to that," Hannah smiled.

"I'm going to Heaven?" I asked. She nodded.

The feeling of relief that came over me was overwhelming. I started crying, and Hannah came around and hugged me.

"Okay, now that you know, the wait may be a little more bearable," Hannah chuckled. I nodded. Hannah sat back down and handed me a tissue.

"So, looking through your file, I'd say it will take about 35 days to get you fully processed and moved along. In the meantime, we'll get a room here set up. You're welcome to go wherever you'd like. Just make sure you're back before this runs out."

She handed me what looked like a digital watch. I looked at the screen, and it had a countdown from 840 hours.

"It is essential to get back here before that runs out," Hannah repeated.

"What happens if I'm not?" I asked.

"You'll be stuck wherever you are," she said solemnly. "You know about ghosts, right?"

"Seriously?" I scoffed.

"Sort of," Hannah answered. "They're stuck souls. Sometimes when people wait, they want to visit loved ones who are still living or try to understand why they died the way they did. They become almost obsessive over it and become trapped."

"But Matt said once you come back here from visiting, you don't get to go back."

"Our greeting committee encourages new arrivals to get here for processing as quickly as possible. Also, they don't know who gets a waiting period and who doesn't. So they're not in the position to tell people they can go back and visit."

"Could I visit anywhere on Earth?" I asked. "Like if I wanted to visit places I've never seen before."

"Anywhere you want," she reiterated. "But keep in mind, what you do while you wait also goes into your file. I want you to understand that."

"Okay," I said. "So, where will I be staying?"

"Come with me," Hannah stood back up. "I'll show you."

I followed Hannah out of the back door of her office and into a crazier world than I could ever imagine. It looked like a cleaner, brighter, happier version of Earth. Everyone walking around looked healthy and friendly and had a slight glow to their skin. Then, someone-*something*, caught my eye. A tiny woman with butterfly wings flew by me. I noticed her fly over to a small man with moth-like wings.

"Whoa," I gasped.

"I know, right," Hannah beamed. "I love seeing people react to them."

Another couple of the small, winged people flew past us. They were about as big as my hands but looked like fully grown adults.

"What are they?" I asked. "Are they fairies?"

"They're angels," Hannah explained.

"What!" I exclaimed. "But they're so tiny. And they don't look like what we've always been told angels look like."

"Well, there are different types of angels," Hannah explained. "There are angels who watch over humans, guide their spirits through birth and death, give inspiration, try to sway humans away from war and destruction, and so much more. There are archangels who are warriors. They're the ones who fight demons and guard Heaven. Then, there are the seraphim. They are the highest ranked angels who stand guard at the throne."

"Like, *the* throne?" I asked. She nodded.

"Wow," I gasped. "This is crazy! Wait a second. We just walked out of your office. Did you just leave the other people in line?"

Hannah laughed.

"I'm not the only one who works in Processing. We walked out; someone else walked in."

"It's like magic."

"Except way cooler," she winked and then laughed.

A couple more angels flew past us and waved. I smiled and waved back. As we walked down the pathway, I looked up to see what looked like a big hotel. A big lit sign on the front of the building said, "Nuakh" on it.

"That's where you'll stay until your waiting period is over," Hannah explained. "You'll meet with me a few more times to go over a couple of things, but it shouldn't take too long since your time on Earth was pretty short."

Ouch.

Hannah stopped and looked at me.

"Oh, I'm sorry. I didn't mean anything by it," she smiled weakly.

"It's okay," I sighed.

The inside of the building also looked like a hotel—one of the fanciest hotels I had ever seen. The lobby was buzzing with people laughing and talking. People were sitting in chairs drinking coffee. There was even a family of a dad, a mom, and a little boy in one corner who played "I Spy" together.

"Is that a family that died together?" I asked.

"It's not super uncommon," Hannah looked at them. "Car accidents, floods, tornadoes, house fires, armed robberies that end tragically. There are several reasons a whole family can come in at once."

We approached an elevator, and Hannah handed me a card.

"Here's your keycard. This gets you into your room and your room only. If you lose it, just ask for a new one. But try not to lose it, okay?"

I nodded.

We rode the elevator to the 387th floor before getting off and heading down the hallway on the right.

"The building doesn't seem that tall."

"Magic," Hannah winked.

"Are there that many people in the building?" I asked.

"Let me put it this way; roughly 150,000 people per day die globally."

"That's a lot of people!" I exclaimed. "You get that many people here every day?"

"Pretty close. The only ones who don't go through processing are the babies."

I got quiet.

"I know," Hannah sighed. "I don't like it either. But it happens."

After walking for a few more minutes, we reached room 387E4624. *I'll have to write that down,* I thought. We walked through the door, and I couldn't believe what I saw. My room had photos of my mom and dad, Simon, my grandma, Whitney and Maddi, and some of my favorite kids from the daycare. On the walls were posters of bands I loved, wild animals, and different landscapes. There were shelves filled with all of my favorite movies and books. There was a king-size bed facing a huge tv. And on a table in the corner was the most wonderful surprise. There were all kinds of photography equipment, including a very expensive-looking camera.

"Is this all mine?" I asked.

"We try to make everyone's rooms as cozy as possible while they wait."

"Does everyone get the same type of room?"

"More or less," Hannah bobbed her head from side to side. "We wouldn't give a television to someone who has never seen one, if that's what you mean. When Abraham Lincoln came through here, all he had was some books, a journal, and a chess board. He was inviting everyone to his room to play chess while he waited to move on. We do tend to do a little more for those who die younger. Some of the little kids get full arcades in their rooms. Yours was a pretty easy one. It's cute, right?"

"I love it," I beamed. "Thank you so much."

"Just think, it only gets better from here," she said. "While you wait, you're free to spend your time however you want. I know 35 days seems like a long wait, but I promise you it will go by quickly."

I frowned as I noticed something missing.

"What's wrong?" Hannah asked.

"Nothing," I replied. "I think I just feel a little worn out. Is that even possible? Do I still need sleep here?"

"You don't necessarily need it anymore, but it's something that is missed and appreciated more here. Many people say their favorite thing was either sleeping or napping."

"A nap does sound pretty nice, actually," I smiled.

"I'll let you get settled, and if you have any questions, just dial 0 on the phone."

I looked at the nightstand next to the bed. There was a standard telephone perched on top.

"I'll be back around 5:00 to conduct your first Processing review. We'll cover about five years, depending on how long we take."

"Okay, thank you," I smiled again. "See you later."

"See you later, Emma," Hannah beamed. "And welcome."

Hannah shut the door, and I double-checked every inch of my room. There was no sign of Alastor's existence anywhere.

12

I waited about fifteen minutes before heading out of the building, just in case Hannah lingered around. With my keycard in my pocket, I made my way down the elevator, through the lobby, and out into the sunshine. The weather here was gorgeous. It wasn't too hot or too cold. It made me wonder if it ever rained or snowed. I liked both things on Earth, so it'd be a little disappointing if I never got to experience either again. I looked at my stopwatch and noticed it was already down to 838 hours. If I were to figure out what happened to Alastor, I would need to start back on Earth. I hurriedly walked past crowds of people, avoiding the tiny angels flying around. I could see the escalator straight ahead of me when I felt someone tap on the back of my arm. I turned around to see a little blonde girl smiling up at me.

"Do you know how to get to the hotel-looking place?" she asked. "I can't remember which way it is."

I pointed to the sidewalk that led to the building.

"Just follow this path for a few minutes, and once you get past these trees, you should be able to see it."

"Can you please walk with me?" she asked, raising her tiny hand out for me to take. I looked around.

"Are you here alone?"

"No," she shrugged. "My mommy said I could play for a little bit while she talked to the other grown ups, but I kind of got too far from the building."

I slowly took her warm hand in mine and she smiled at me before we started walking.

"I think my mommy's afraid my daddy followed us here," the little girl said quietly.

"What?" I asked.

"He came home and was mad at Mommy and started hitting her. Mommy was going to take me away from Daddy so he wouldn't be mean to us anymore but he found out. I tried to make him stop hurting her but then he hurt me too. Real bad. I was lying on the floor by Mommy and then all of a sudden we were at a carnival! I wasn't hurt anymore and Mommy was smiling for the first time in a really long time. And then we came to this big hotel and Mommy said I could go play with other kids. I never got to play outside with other kids. Daddy wouldn't let me."

"Annie?" a mousy, blonde woman called to us.

"Hi, Mommy!" the little girl waved.

"Where have you been? I was worried!"

"She got a little too far from the hotel so I was helping her get back," I said shyly.

"Thank you so much," she smiled.

"You're welcome," I responded as Annie let go of my hand.

"Thank you!" Annie exclaimed before skipping to her mom. I watched Annie's mom run her hand through the little girl's hair and kiss her on the forehead. As they headed back inside the hotel, I turned to continue on my way.

I got on the escalator, thinking about which place I wanted to start with first. I would check at Alastor's job, then check the school, swing by Maddi's apartment, and end at my parent's house. It would have been nice to know where Alastor's house was because that would be the obvious choice. But on the off chance he had decided to go through with what we talked about, *someone* would be able to give me some clue. I stepped off the escalator and stood in front of Repair/Restore, the store where Alastor had been working. The sign said, "OPEN," so I went through the door. Literally.

"Holy shit!" I said out loud. I could phase through doors. I really was like a ghost!

I looked around and watched a couple of customers in the store talking to Mike, the owner. I didn't see anyone else in the back room, so I headed out. Outside the shop, I closed my eyes, thought about the college building, and then opened my eyes. I was standing right in front of it, miles away from Repair/Restore.

I checked the digital calendar in the main hallway just to be sure Alastor might be there. It was a Thursday afternoon. *Alastor will be in our English class.* I ran down the English hall and peeked inside. My professor stood at the front of the room, reviewing the book assigned for reading. I could see my old seat, empty still. Next to it was where Alastor sat. It was empty too. Panic started flooding over me. The young woman in the chair closest to me yawned. I looked down at the quiz on her desk, sitting next to her book and a water bottle. I noticed that three of her answers were wrong.

"Are you kidding me?" I slapped my finger on one of the answers. The water bottle tipped over, spilling water on the woman's paper and book. She stood up quickly, and everyone in the room stopped to look at her.

"I'm sorry," she said. "I don't know what happened! I'll go get some paper towels."

"Oops," I said, "I know you can't hear me, but I'm sorry. I didn't mean to do that."

I left the school feeling defeated. *Why wasn't Alastor in class?* I thought. Next was the apartment, which didn't take long because no one was home. I peeked into my old room, which was Whitney's now. I looked around at the piles of clothes and the unmade bed. I walked past the trash can, and something in it caught my eye. It was a pregnancy test with a plus sign on it. Whitney was pregnant! I wondered if Maddi and Colbie knew yet. Was it Sam's? Was it a boy or a girl? Probably too early to know. I looked inside Maddi and Colbie's room. It looked the same as when I last saw it, except there were two nightstands now instead of one. There was a paper on one of the nightstands, and I leaned in to read it:

Emma,

I can't believe you're gone. The last time we talked was the worst fight we had ever been in. I regret that day so much and wish I could take it back every day. I also wish I had visited you after you got sick. I was just being stubborn and stupid. But when I came to see you the night you died, I realized I was too late. I'm glad I got to say goodbye to you, but I don't even know if you knew I was there. And I guess I'll never know. I'm not sure why I decided to write this letter. Do they get mail in wherever you are now? Anyways, I hope you're okay, having fun, and surrounded by a bunch of cool dead people wherever you are. Tell Matt Kinsley hi for me, will you? You're my very best friend forever and always. I love you so much and miss you more than words can say. I hope I see you again someday. If I had to pick anyone to be my guardian angel, it would be you.

Love,

Maddi

"I wish I could tell her I read her note," I whispered before leaving. All that was left was my parents' house.

I slowly walked through the house. It was oddly quiet. There was a kitten I didn't recognize sleeping on our couch. The dining room light was on. I entered and saw my dad sitting at the table, drinking a glass of whiskey. My mom was standing at the sink, rubbing her forehead.

"Did he say when he would be back?" she asked.

"No," my dad answered. "He just said he was going to visit Emma and that he'd be back. And he turned off his fucking phone!"

I wondered if they were talking about Alastor until I heard the front door shut.

"Simon?" my mom called. My brother walked in.

"You're grounded," my dad said immediately.

"I know," Simon sighed. "I'm sorry. My phone died, and I just realized it about ten minutes ago. I came home as fast as I could pedal."

"I don't care," my dad snapped. "You're still grounded."

"Okay," Simon replied.

"And I don't want you taking Emma's bike anymore."

"Okay, Dad."

Simon turned to walk away.

"YOU TURN AROUND AND LOOK AT ME; GOD DAMNIT. WE'RE NOT DONE HERE!"

His sudden yelling made both my mom and me jump. What was wrong with him? He never yelled at us like that. My little brother slowly turned around and waited for my dad to say something. He buried his face in his hands and started crying. Simon went over and hugged him from behind.

"I miss her so much," Simon whispered. "And the flowers on her grave are already starting to die."

"We'll go up this weekend with new ones," my mom smiled, hugging Simon.

"I love you, buddy," my dad said, kissing the side of Simon's head.

"I love you guys so much," Simon said as my family hugged each other.

"I love you guys too," I quietly said.

The light flickered slightly. Simon looked up. I immediately turned to walk out of the house. I made my way to the living room, and the kitten walking toward the dining room stopped in front of me. It looked right at me and started meowing. I turned around and saw Simon watching the kitten. I ran through the front door onto the porch, and the door opened behind me.

"Emma?" Simon called. I stopped on the bottom stair and peered back at him, seeing his eyes fill with tears.

"If you're there, I want you to know I love you."

I smiled at him and watched as he stood there, waiting for something else to happen. I fought the urge to try and make contact, but I didn't want it to cause problems between Simon and my parents. He waited a moment longer before going back inside. I knew it was getting close to my appointment with Hannah, so I returned to the escalator as it reappeared and headed back. As I walked through the lobby, I glanced at the front desk and noticed a man, or what almost looked like a man, staring at me. He had blonde, almost white hair and aquamarine eyes that I could see clearly across the lobby. He watched me as I made my way to the elevator. Hannah was standing outside as I approached my room door, waiting for me.

"Am I late?" I asked.

"No, I'm always early," Hannah smiled. "I'm glad you made it back on time for our appointment."

I let us in with my keycard, and Hannah immediately sat at the corner table and started getting papers out. I moved the camera equipment out of the way.

"Been doing anything interesting since the last time I've seen you?" she asked. "Visit the pyramids or the Eiffel Tower?"

"Just checked in on friends and family," I shrugged.

"Ah, well, that's nice of you," Hannah gestured to the chair on the other side of the table. I sat down.

"I thought you knew where I went."

"I do. Just making small talk."

"I think I accidentally interacted with a couple of people."

"It happens. Most people make things happen when they visit Earth, whether accidentally or intentionally. Doing stuff on purpose is what's going to get you in trouble."

I nodded slowly and scooted my seat forward.

"This will go pretty quickly," she explained. "The first decade of life generally doesn't have much to it unless you're in a gang or something wild like that."

I sat with my hands between my knees and started slightly rocking back and forth.

"Emma Rose Hawthorne. Age 21. Born in Oak Woods, Missouri, on April 24, 1989. The parents are Carl and Sue Hawthorne. You've lived in Oak Woods your whole life. Healthy birth, healthy upbringing. Several moderate allergies, a couple of severe allergies, and Crohn's disease. You bit a couple of kids at daycare as a toddler."

Hannah paused.

"Do I get a point taken away or something?" I asked. Hannah laughed.

"No, dear," she said. "As I said, there's usually not much to go through during the first couple of sessions. It looks like you had a great upbringing. You had a very loving family."

"They're the best," I beamed. Hannah flipped through a couple more pages without looking at me.

"All right, well, I think that's about it. You told some minor white lies, stole a sucker from a gas station, and threw up on a little boy's shoes. As of age five, pretty great record. So far."

Hannah winked at me. I laughed nervously.

"Okay, if you will just sign on this line," she pointed to the last paper in the stack. "That'll be that until next time. I'll be back in a few days, but I'll call you ahead of time in case you're off wandering around somewhere."

I watched Hannah get all her stuff together and leave. I rummaged through the dresser and found all of my favorite clothes in them, mostly jeans, t-shirts, and sweatpants.

"Gotta love the basics," I said to myself. I changed into a t-shirt and sweatpants and picked a movie to put on until I got too bored with it. I then realized I hadn't eaten since I arrived. I didn't feel hungry. Would it be weird to eat even though I didn't feel hungry? I looked over at the phone on the nightstand. I picked it up and dialed 0.

"Yes?" I heard a voice say.

"Yeah, um, dumb question," I started. "I don't feel hungry."

"You won't while you're here," the person on the other line said. "You won't feel hungry, tired, cold, hot, sick, or any pain."

"Would it be okay if I still wanted to eat?" I asked.

"Sure," the voice said. "You'll still enjoy all the foods from life."

"And what happens to the food?" I asked.

"What do you mean?"

"Like, do I need to take care of it later?"

Silence.

"My bathroom only has a tub."

"No, you don't need to pee or poop here," the voice sighed. I fought back a chuckle. "What would you like to eat, Emma?"

"Is there a menu?" I asked.

"No menu, just whatever you want."

"Can I have ice cream?"

"What flavor?"

"Chocolate please."

"Is that it? Any toppings?"

"Really?"

"You can have whatever you want."

"Actually, can I have a banana split?" I asked.

"Sure. Anything else?"

"That's all. Thank you."

"No problem. It'll be up in a bit."

I hung up the phone and sat on the edge of my bed. I was going to have ice cream for the first time in years with no worries of an upset stomach. Nothing would ever hurt ever again.

There was a knock on the door. I opened it, and there was a large platter on the ground. I picked it up and brought it inside. I took the lid off and saw a giant banana split. There were two whole bananas, a big scoop of vanilla ice cream, a big scoop of chocolate ice cream, a big scoop of strawberry ice cream, chocolate sauce, pineapple chunks, strawberry chunks, whipped cream, and a cherry on top. It was picturesque. I almost didn't want to eat it because it looked so perfect. But I did. I ate every single bite of it, and it was delicious. After eating, I laid back on the bed and watched my movie. I looked around at all of the photos on the walls. I was surrounded by everyone who cared about me, except for one person. I immediately sat back up.

"What am I doing?" I asked out loud. I was wasting time. I needed to figure out what happened to Alastor.

I slid a pair of sandals on and went down to the lobby. Mr. Super-Blonde-Hair was still sitting behind the desk. He was reading a massive book in another language with a scowl on his face. I slowly approached the desk, and he looked up. His frown turned into a smile.

"How was your banana split?" he asked.

"Excellent," I said. "Were you the person I talked to on the phone earlier?"

"Guilty," he said, going back to the book. "How can I help you, Emma?"

I didn't say anything at first. I watched him flip through pages of his book quickly, making marks next to different words in the book.

"What language is that in?" I asked. "I thought everyone could understand everyone and everything here."

"It's the Holy language. Humans, dead or alive, can't understand it. This book contains everyone staying in this building and about to come in. Once someone's processing is complete, their name vanishes from the book."

I nodded as I listened and looked at the book.

"It just helps us keep track of everyone," he smiled and stuck his hand out. "I'm Elijah, by the way."

"You're not human?" I asked, shaking his hand, which was incredibly soft.

"Nope," he said. "Never have been. I'm an angel. A virtue, more specifically."

"A virtue?" I asked. Elijah sighed.

"We encourage humans to strengthen their faith. We also assist in miracles and are authorities over nature."

"Could have used a miracle when I got sick," I rolled my eyes.

"We can't be everywhere," Elijah replied. "Plus, we've been short-staffed up here, so we have to take shifts between up here and down on Earth."

Suddenly, a thought occurred to me.

"Did you say that book has everyone staying here or about to come in?" I asked.

"Yes," he said. "Why?"

"Could you, by chance, look up a name for me?"

"Um, I suppose I could do that for you. What's the name?"

"Alastor King," I breathed.

Elijah paused for a moment before flipping through the pages of the book. He moved so quickly through the names that his hands looked like a blur to me. He reached the back of the book and closed it.

"There is no Alastor King here or on the way here."

I sighed and put my head down.

"Someone you were expecting?" Elijah asked.

"No," I answered. "Not really. I thought he might be here, but I'm glad he's not."

"Is he still alive?"

"I guess so if he's not in your book."

"The name was Alastor King, correct?"

I nodded.

Elijah got onto the computer in front of him and started typing. He looked at me, then back at the computer, typing more.

"Oh," he said to himself.

"What?" I asked.

"Does he live somewhere far away from you?" Elijah asked. "I'm not getting anything in that area."

"He lives pretty close to me," I said, confused.

"Nothing is coming up on him."

"What does that mean?" I asked. "If you can't find him here or on Earth, does that mean he's already in Heaven?"

"No," Elijah said quietly. "No, I remember every person's name who has moved on from here."

I stood there, holding my breath.

"He went...somewhere else," Elijah finally said.

My eyes widened, and I gasped.

"I'm sorry," Elijah murmured.

"Are you saying Alastor went to Hell?" I asked. "Is that what you're telling me?"

"I said I'm sorry," Elijah repeated. "It's not up to me to decide where people go."

"But he was a good person!" I yelled, leaning on the desk towards Elijah.

"Please keep your voice down," Elijah looked around. "Look, there must have been something he did that got him sent there. I really am sorry."

"He didn't do-!" I stopped. I stepped back and put my hand over my mouth.

"Are you all right?"

"D-d-do people w-w-who-" I stuttered, tearing up, "who commit suicide...."

Elijah slowly nodded.

I started sobbing, slumping down onto the floor. A few people nearby watched as Elijah walked around the desk and knelt next to me.

"Oh no," I cried. "Oh no, oh no, oh no."

"Do you want me to help you to a chair?" he asked.

"No," I shook my head. "I just want to go back to my room."

Elijah helped me up to stand and walked me to the elevator.

"If there's anything you need, just let me know, okay?"

I nodded as the elevator door shut. I went on autopilot, finding my way back to my room in a haze. Eventually, I flopped down on the bed, covered myself up, and cried until I fell asleep, thinking about Alastor.

I woke up the following day to my room flooded with sunlight. I covered my head with the blanket. Maybe I could just spend the next 815 hours in bed, waiting for whatever happened next. I knew visiting my family and friends would just drive me insane. I could always take my camera equipment and go sightseeing, but I didn't feel like it. Alastor was in Hell because of me. A person I loved was sent to Hell, possibly forever, because I convinced him that dying with me would be better than living without me. My phone rang, and I leaned over to pick it up.

"Hello?" I answered.

"Good morning, sleepyhead!" I heard Hannah's voice on the other end. "Were you still in bed?"

"Yeah, I'm still in bed," I answered.

"I told you some people love to sleep!" she chuckled. "Well, I just wanted to let you know that something happened with a newcomer that pushed your next appointment up. I'll be by tomorrow evening to go over years five through ten with you. Sound good?"

"Sure," I mumbled.

"All right, awesome. Just be sure to be in your room around 5. See you then!"

I hung up without saying goodbye. I rolled back over in bed and stared at the wall. I closed my eyes and thought about laying in bed with Alastor, feeling his chest rise and fall as he breathed. I remembered burying my face into his chest and him wrapping his arms around me, smelling the top of my head. I remembered him kissing my forehead and my nose and cheeks and lips. I remembered listening to his heart beating, feeling his fingers lightly trace my spine. A lump formed in my throat, and I started to cry again. Even though I was dead, I felt heartache.

Knock. Knock. Knock.

I jumped at the sound. *Who could that be?* I wondered. Hannah wouldn't be over until the following evening, and I didn't order anything. Maybe if I just lay quietly, they would go away and think I wasn't there.

Knock. Knock. Knock.

I waited.

Knock. Knock. Knock. Knock. Knock.

I got up angrily and opened the door.

"What!" I snapped.

Standing before me was a little girl with long, curly, red hair and freckles. Her smile faded, and she crossed her arms.

"Sam?" I gasped.

"Desperate times call for desperate measures," she pushed past me into the room. I gaped at her as she hopped up on the bed, her feet dangling back and forth.

"What are you doing here?" I asked.

"You seemed like you could use a friend," she smiled. "And who better than your guardian angel?"

13

"Guardian angel?" I asked.

"Yup!" Sam grinned. "I got promoted pretty quickly after I got here. You know I've always been a bit of a suck-up."

"Wh-what are you talking about? Are you dead?"

"Duh. How else do you think I became a guardian angel?"

"But how? When?"

"Shortly after we moved, I got pneumonia," Sam shrugged. "Couldn't shake it."

"Seriously?" I asked. "Why didn't we ever hear about it?"

"We moved halfway across the country. After we moved, my parents tried to start all over and forget about everything from before the move. My dad had been cheating on my mom, and they wanted to try and make things work for me. But after the move I got sick. My mom hadn't forgiven my dad, so she left him. I was the only thing keeping them together."

"Sam, if I had known...." I started. "I thought you moved and just forgot all about me."

"Are you kidding me?" she asserted. "You were my very best friend. You were my only friend. I always thought we would grow up and go shopping for prom dresses, talk about boys, and get our driver's licenses together."

"You died so young," I said.

"So did you!" Sam remarked. "You barely beat me in years. It's not fair. I can't believe cancer got you. You were so beautiful and just had so much life left."

I gazed at Sam, looking the same as I had always remembered her.

"Sam?" I asked, tearing up.

"Yeah?"

"Can I have a hug?"

She leaped off the bed and ran to me with her arms outreached. I got down on one knee and hugged my childhood best friend, frozen in time as an eight-year-old little girl.

"Okay," Sam said, finally letting go. "We need to get you out and about. I didn't have them fill your room with this awesome camera stuff for you just to lay around and mope."

"You did this?" I asked, looking around my room. Sam nodded.

"How come there aren't any photos of Alastor anywhere?"

"What?"

"My boyfriend, Alastor. I figured there would be a picture of him."

"Oh, it, uh, wasn't allowed."

"Why?"

I watched Sam turn and look out the window.

"Oh," I realized.

"Why don't we leave this room for a bit?" Sam asked, smiling. "Come on, pack up some of that fancy equipment, and we can go anywhere on Earth you want to."

I thought about it for a moment before agreeing.

"Change out your sweatpants and do something with your hair," Sam laughed. "You can't smell bad anymore, but you look like you do. I'll wait for you out in the hall."

I changed into jeans and a blue shirt and put a button-up flannel over the shirt. I pulled on a pair of sneakers and brushed through my hair before deciding to put it in a ponytail. I met Sam out in the hallway with my camera.

"Ready?" I asked.

"When you are, Lady Lumberjack," she said, pulling on my flannel shirt.

"Your shoe is untied," I smirked. "Do you know how to tie your shoes, or do you need help?"

We both laughed as we started walking.

"So, where do you want to go?" Sam asked.

"Where *can* we go?"

"I can go literally anywhere. You have a few limitations that I don't have, but we can go anywhere on Earth you want to."

I thought about it as we approached the escalator.

"Africa?" I asked. "I've always wanted to see African animals up close."

"Oh my gosh, it's so amazing!" Sam squealed. "Are zebras still your favorite animals?"

"Yes! I can't believe you remembered that. I don't even remember the last time someone asked me what my favorite animal is."

"Adults kind of stop caring about that stuff. When I wasn't watching over you, I'd sometimes follow some kids from your daycare home and watch them. Kids are so much more fun than adults. Adults constantly think about bills and sex and money and how tired they are. Kids think up so many amazing things, most of the time made-up nonsense."

Sam let out a big sigh.

"I miss being a kid."

"Aren't you technically still a kid?" I asked as we got off the escalator and into the African savannah.

"Physically, yeah, I'm stuck looking like this forever," Sam pulled on her cheeks. "But I feel much, much older. I mean, I know the secrets of the universe now! I know what happens to everyone when they die. I have VIP access to Heaven, Earth, space, and even some parts of Hell."

"Wait, you can go to Hell?" I asked as we made our way through tall, yellow grass.

"Yeah, angels can enter all realms," Sam shrugged. "One of the perks of the job. It's mostly to retrieve some people in the higher levels of Hell. The ones who can still redeem themselves."

I gaped at Sam. She sighed.

"Depending on what the person did and why they go to Hell, they only spend a certain amount of time there. Sort of like a prison sentence. I know most of them who wait are people who don't believe in God. Even the people who believe in other religions don't have to spend time in Hell. But the ones who flat out disregard any religion or God, because let's be honest, it's all the same thing, they have to spend time down there. I honestly don't know much about it because I haven't had to go down there to get anyone yet. Honestly, I'm not looking forward to the day I have to."

"What's Hell like?" I asked. "It's not all fire and brimstone, is it?"

"Not exactly," Sam laughed. "Different levels have different....scenery. Oh, Emma, look!"

Sam pointed to my left, and I saw five zebras grazing. I gasped before grinning at Sam. She smiled at me and then started moving towards them. I almost told Sam to be quiet before realizing it didn't matter. We were standing right next to all of them, and none reacted to us. I got my camera out and started taking pictures of the zebra.

"Will I be able to save these when I go to Heaven?" I asked.

"Yeah, we'll figure out a way to let you take them with you somehow," she nodded.

I continued to take photos and watch. Suddenly, a couple of the zebras perked their heads up and stopped eating. They looked around, startled by something we couldn't see. A fourth one stopped eating and looked up too. One of them made a high-pitched noise, and suddenly a group of lionesses appeared out of nowhere, pouncing at the herd. I watched the zebras run away until one of the lionesses finally lunged and grabbed one of them by the throat, flipping it over. I started moving closer, looking at the enormous cat, her teeth puncturing deep into the zebra's throat. Then, the other members of her pride came over to help her. Two more lionesses grabbed the zebra from behind and brought it down. They started tearing into the body as three more joined them.

"You want to take some pictures?" Sam muttered. I shook my head, unable to take my eyes off what was happening.

"That poor zebra," I finally said.

"Lions have to eat too," Sam said. "Besides, there are many mouths to feed."

I looked where she was pointing, and two lion cubs joined the group.

"It's weird feeling sad for the zebra but gratifying for the lions," I remarked.

"Yeah, life is like that. Can I share something with you? If you don't mind being done here."

"Sure."

Sam grabbed my hand and closed her eyes. I closed mine as well. Suddenly, the bright sunshine disappeared. I opened my eyes. It was nighttime, and we were surrounded by snow.

"Where are we?" I asked.

"The Arctic," Sam smiled. "Isn't it so cool?"

I looked around. It was the quietest place I had ever been.

"Come here," Sam grabbed my hand again.

We lay down in the snow, the tops of our heads touching.

"What are-"

"Shh!" Sam hushed me.

I lay still, looking up at the night sky. I could see thousands of stars, more than I ever saw when I was alive. It was so beautiful and peaceful. Suddenly, something large blocked the moonlight on my right side. I looked over, and a massive polar bear walked by us. Its giant paws crunched into the untouched snow, leaving tracks behind it. I got my camera out and took pictures of it while it stopped and sniffed the air. After getting a couple of good shots, I put the camera away and watched the polar bear until it was out of sight. I laid back down and continued looking up at the stars.

"Emma?" Sam said quietly.

"Yeah?" I answered.

"What's it like?"

"What?"

"Kissing a boy."

I looked at her, her tiny body next to mine.

"Eh," I scoffed. "It's not that big of a deal."

"Emma, don't bullshit me," she laughed. "I'm not a baby. I can handle it."

I felt uneasy. I didn't want to explain how wonderful things were that I knew she had missed out on.

"Hey," I rolled over and faced her. She turned to me. "Boys suck for the most part. For every one that's great, there are five who are assholes. They play a lot of mind games, like suddenly changing their minds about you after telling you for a whole summer how much they like you. I had a huge thing for a boy going into my freshman year of high school. For a whole summer, we would talk for hours on the phone. He kept telling me how much he wanted me to be his girlfriend once school started. And then school did start, he ignored me for the first week before finally admitting that he was just too cool for me."

"Wow. What a dick."

I laughed out loud.

"A lot of them just want in your pants, whether they like you or not."

"Gross," she groaned.

"I'm telling you, Sam, you're not missing out on anything," I continued. "I had the biggest crush on this other boy. He had shaggy hair and was an artist and was just the coolest guy I had ever seen."

"What happened?" Sam asked.

"I, uh, finally got the courage to ask him out. And he shot me down immediately. Because I was taller than him. I mean, forget anything to do with me as a person, right? Because I was taller, that was it. As if I wasn't already self-conscious about being a taller girl. As if I didn't think I was a freak because of my medical issues. I just wanted to be normal. Whatever the fuck that means."

"I would have rather been an abnormal teenager than a dead kid."

There was a long pause.

"Sam?" I finally said.

"Yeah?"

"Did you say you've been to space?"

"Yeah."

"Do I get to go to space?"

"Maybe, at some point," Sam smiled. "Depends on what you want Paradise to be."

"What do you mean?"

"It's more than I can explain to you right now. You'll learn more once you're done with Processing."

"What's that supposed to mean?" I sat up and looked at Sam. She looked back at me. "It's more than you can explain? Like, because I'm a dumb human I can't understand stuff an eight year old angel can?"

"You're still attached to your human life. That's why Hannah's going over everything with you. Once you finish your appointments with Hannah and get through processing, you'll be ready. You're lucky, however. Your waiting period is pretty short compared to a lot of people. Not people like me, of course, who die as kids, but still not too bad. And technically, I'm the same age as you."

"Can I be honest with you about something?" I asked.

"Anything," Sam said, laying back down.

"Knowing that Hell really exists scares me. I'm not sure why, because I already know I'm going to Heaven. But still. Knowing it's there, full of demons and torture is brutal."

"Honestly, it's not that bad," Sam explained. "Some people go to Hell and have no chance of leaving. And those levels of Hell are much, much worse. The temporary parts of Hell are just bad enough to make people realize they were wrong. Everything sucks. Food tastes terrible. You can't sleep even though you're tired. It's constantly cloudy and windy. It's not torture; but it's just miserable enough to drive people to be better."

"What about people who kill themselves?"

"What about them?"

"Do they get the temporary part or the....permanent part?"

"I'm not sure. Again, I haven't had to go down there yet. I just know what I know from....training, for lack of a better word."

I sighed.

"What's going on, Emma?" Sam asked.

"Well, you know my boyfriend, Alastor?"

"I know of him, yeah."

"Wait, haven't you seen him?"

"Actually, no," Sam replied. "Every time he was around you, I had another assignment."

"I thought you were *my* guardian angel?"

"You don't think you're the only one I guard, do you?"

Sam started laughing. I frowned.

"Sorry," Sam said. "I'm super busy. I'm constantly taking jobs and had to make a special request to spend the day with you. We're short-staffed right now."

"That's what Elijah said, too," I rolled my eyes. "How is that even a thing? For angels to be short-staffed? What, you guys don't host a yearly Heaven job fair?"

"You must think, Emma, how much there is to all of this. People have been around for thousands of years. Thousands are born every day. Thousands die every day. Angels have to keep up with guarding Heaven, trying to protect people, trying to sway people to do the right thing without screwing with free will, and then we lose some to the other side."

"What does that mean?"

"Some angels turn. I don't fully understand what happens. Maybe they get bored or fed up with taking orders. Maybe they think going bad will make them more powerful."

Sam shook her head slowly. I could tell this was a sensitive subject to her.

"I am so grateful to be where I am," she said. "I died at such a young age. I missed out on so much of life. But I also never faced a lot of life's pain and suffering. I died young to fulfill my true destiny of becoming an angel. I've been able to watch over you and my parents. I get assigned to other kids who are dying at young ages. Once they get to Paradise and see me, they recognize me! Sometimes when kids say they have imaginary friends, it's us angels they can see and communicate with. Children are so much more in tune with us than adults. They don't have a billion things distracting them from us. So it's nice when some kids die and see me because they're delighted to see a familiar face. We talk about our favorite things about Earth and enjoy them in Paradise together. Kids who couldn't walk could beat me in races—kids who couldn't see play hide-and-go-seek with me. Kids who spend their short time on Earth starving daily can enjoy chicken nuggets and ice cream. It's the best part of my job. It's hard watching kids die but watching them enjoy Paradise is what it's all about. It's why I love my job. And granted, you're not a kid, but it's going to fill my angel heart with so much joy to see your face when you enter."

I wiped tears from my cheek, and Sam hugged me.

"I have to go check in on someone," Sam said, breaking our hug. "I'll stop by in a couple of days, and we can hang out again. You pick the next place."

I nodded, and we stood up. The escalator appeared, and we made our way back up. As we made our way down the pavement towards the building I was staying in, I abruptly stopped Sam as a thought occurred to me.

"Sam!" I exclaimed. "Angels can visit Hell!"

"Yeah, and?"

"Alastor is there."

"What?"

"Alastor is in Hell, and it's because of me," I started crying. "Right before I died, we made this stupid pact to commit suicide together because we couldn't stand the thought of being anywhere without each other. I think he went through with it, and I have to do something about it."

"Emma-"

"No!" I interrupted. "You can help me. I know you can. You just said that angels can go pretty much anywhere. You have to do me a favor and try to find him! Find him and see if you can get him out of there."

"Listen," Sam said in a low voice as we entered the building lobby. "I've told you before. I've never even been to Hell. I don't know my way around, and even if I did, I have no business down there. I can't just go anywhere anytime; I must have a reason."

"Try!" I pleaded. Sam grabbed me by the shoulders.

"Emma, stop! I don't even know if people who kill themselves *stay* in Hell! Just wait a while and see if he shows up."

"You want me just to wait and what, *hope* Alastor shows up? Do you know how unfair that is?"

"I do know, and I'm sorry, but I don't know what to tell you. Something like this could get me in a lot of trouble. I know it's tough for you to see past yourself and think of others-"

"I *am* thinking of others!" I snapped. "I love Alastor. I know he was my only boyfriend in my short, shitty life, but he was always there for me. He loved me for who I was and would have done anything for me. If the roles were reversed, he'd be fighting to do the same for me right now. So please, Sam. Try to think of something. *Anything.* Please."

"I'll see you in a couple of days," Sam said. "In the meantime, I'll see what I can find out."

I wrapped my arms around Sam and hugged her tight.

"Thank you," I sighed.

"I can't guarantee anything," she pulled away from me. "But I'll try, okay?"

"Thank you, Sam," I repeated.

"Go get some rest. See you in a couple of days."

"See ya."

I watched Sam walk out the front door before turning towards the elevator. Elijah was standing right behind me, making me jump.

"You know, if I weren't already dead, you would've just given me a heart attack!"

"I couldn't help but overhear your conversation," Elijah said.

"Or you were eavesdropping," I rolled my eyes. "Yeah, not to be rude, but it's none of your business."

"Sam has never been to Hell," Elijah continued. "If you're going to have any chance of finding this boyfriend of yours, you need someone who's been down there."

"Have you been?" I asked.

"No, but I know someone who has. He's been quite a few times and knows his way around pretty well."

"Do you think he would help me out?"

"Let me contact him, and I will let you know. Don't tell anyone we had this conversation. Not even your guardian angel."

I nodded.

"Go to your room, and I'll be in touch."

Once I reached my room, I didn't feel tired anymore. A laptop was sitting on my table with a written note beside it.

Keep yourself busy and edit some photos.

See you soon.

Stay out of trouble.

-Sam

I got my camera out and uploaded the pictures I had taken with Sam onto the computer. I carefully looked through each photo, admiring the zebras with their black and white stripes and golden brown eyes. Something in the background of one image caught my eye. I zoomed into the tall, yellow grass behind one of the zebras and saw one of the lionesses. She watched while crouched down with her shoulders hunched, ready to ambush the zebras with her fellow pride members. I went through the pictures of the lion cubs, their faces bloody with zebra entrails hanging out of their tiny mouths.

How could something so young and cute also be so terrifying? I thought. Finally, I edited photos of the polar bear that I took. Those were a bit more tricky since they were taken at night, but I still had fun looking through them and editing them. I stayed awake for hours working on the pictures until I finally decided to get some sleep.

I woke up the next day to a knock at my door.

Surely I didn't sleep until my appointment with Hannah.

I opened the door, and there was no one there. I looked down and noticed an envelope on a silver plate. I took the envelope inside and sat down on the bed. I opened the envelope and pulled the note out before reading it out loud.

"Found your guy," I muttered. "Five days."

It was from Elijah.

14

I went to the lobby as fast as possible and ran to Elijah's desk. He was flipping through his giant book, occasionally marking pages.

"I assume you received my note?" he said without looking up.

"Who did you find to take me?" I asked.

"Take you where?"

"To Hell," I muttered.

Elijah looked up at me.

"I beg your pardon?" he smirked. "I never said anything about anyone taking you. You're not going."

"How else is your guy going to find Alastor?" I asked. "He's going to need me to help find him."

"No," Elijah shook his head. "Absolutely not."

"Why not?" I asked.

"Because it's too dangerous."

"I'm *dead*. It's not like I can get hurt."

"Your body is dead," Elijah leaned closer to me and lowered his voice. "Trust me, your soul may be immortal, but there are things much more powerful than you that are still dangerous."

"What, like demons?" I asked.

"Among other things, yes. Besides, how much time do you have left on that thing?"

He pointed to my stopwatch.

"789 hours," I replied. "Why?"

"Because if it runs out while you're down there, you'll be stuck in Hell forever."

"Have any humans gone from here to Hell and come back?"

"No."

"Oh," I gulped.

"That's why it would be better to stay here and wait."

"Why does everyone expect me to wait all the time? Is that what you angels think humans want to do when they die? I don't want to wait around and take pictures! I want to help!"

"Okay, shh!"

"If there is anything I can do to help get Alastor here- or at the very least have the chance to apologize to him, I want to."

"Let me talk to Dumah," Elijah said. "I can almost guarantee he'll say no, so just don't get your hopes up."

"Dumah?" I asked. "Is that your guy?"

"Dumah is known as the angel of the stillness of death and the authority over wicked deaths. He's not exactly a 'people person.' He's an angel who is armed with a flaming sword. If anyone can get you through Hell untouched, it would be Dumah. Just know that he's probably not going to want you to go with him."

"I'll convince him to take me," I grinned.

"Yeah, you're pretty convincing," Elijah smiled back. "You would have made a decent politician when you were alive."

"My dad used to tell me that too."

"Great minds think alike," Elijah beamed as he went back to flipping through his book.

"Elijah," I whispered. He looked up at me. "I can do this. I don't care how scary or dangerous it is. I can do it. Tell this Dumah that I can do it."

Elijah sighed, rubbed his eyes, gave one slight nod, and returned to his book.

"Thank you," I muttered before walking away.

When I got to my room, I took a long bath before deciding to order some food. I picked up the phone, and I recognized Elijah's voice immediately.

"What can I do for you, Emma?" he answered.

"I want to order some stuff," I laughed. "Can I get some scrambled eggs with shredded cheese on top, some crab legs, a lobster tail, a banana, and a bowl of strawberries?"

"Anything else?" Elijah asked.

"Hm, what's good that's made with soy?"

"I don't know. I don't eat. Tofu? It's made from soy."

"I'm good," I said. "Just the other stuff is fine. Oh! And chocolate milk to drink!"

"It'll be up in a bit."

"Thanks, Elijah."

"Yep."

I hung up the phone and went to my dresser to look for something to wear. After sifting through all my options, I decided to try the closet. The clothes in the closet were fancier than the ones in the dresser. I looked through the dresses, skirts, and jumpsuits before settling on an emerald green evening gown towards the back of the closet. I threw on a pair of black and white checkered sneakers and put my hair in a high ponytail on top of my head. I went to the bathroom and put on red lipstick, bright pink blush, and blue eyeshadow.

"Why is this makeup even here?" I giggled to myself.

There was a knock on my door, and I laughed in the mirror one more time before opening it. Hannah's smile immediately went to a more startling reaction.

"Playing dress-up, are we?" she smiled.

"I thought I'd get super fancy for you this time," I answered, trying to keep a straight face. "Don't I look pretty?"

I gave Hannah a huge, cheesy fake grin. Hannah cleared her throat and let herself in. I stood by the door and watched her sit down at the table. I plopped down on the bed and waited for Hannah to get her paperwork.

"All right," she sighed. "We'll pick up where we left off and try to get through age 13 or 14.

Then, we'll try and cover the rest during your next visit. Get you moving right along!"

"I thought we would go over ages five through ten today?" I asked.

"Yes, well, I've been reviewing your life, and most of this involves a year of homeschooling, some doctor visits, family dynamics, and a couple of family vacations. There's not a whole lot to go over until-"

There was a knock on the door.

"-Until middle school," Hannah finished. "Are you expecting company?"

"Oh, my room service!" I exclaimed, jumping off the mattress towards the door. I brought in a cart full of food and pulled it up by the bed. I uncovered the three plates and started scooping eggs into my mouth. Hannah gaped at me.

"Do you mind if I eat while we do this?" I asked with a mouth full of eggs.

"Not at all," Hannah cleared her throat again. "You spent a lot of time in these years resenting your parents for coddling you. You wanted to be a normal kid and hated how protective your mom was over you. Your life continued like this for several years until your brother, Simon, was born. Your parents had to be more attentive with him, so you weren't getting as much attention anymore, which made you unhappy."

"Isn't that just a normal kid reaction, though?" I asked. I picked up a crab leg, staring at it in confusion.

"You use those plier-looking things to crack them open," Hannah pointed to a silver tool next to the plate. "And yes, it is. However, you and I know it was a prominent thought in your everyday life. Would you agree that you were unhappy during that time?"

I cracked open a crab leg.

"I did it!" I exclaimed. "Look, Hannah!"

I pulled the meat out of the shell and took a bite.

"Oh, that's gross," I said, politely spitting the crab into a napkin. "Oh man, how do people enjoy that?"

"Emma," Hannah said. I looked at her.

"Were you unhappy?" she asked again.

"Yes."

"Did you ever think about hurting yourself?"

I looked down and slowly nodded.

"Did you ever think about hurting your brother?"

"No! I would never hurt him!"

"Did you hate him?"

"No!"

"Emma-"

"Maybe there were moments when I thought I did, but no. I never hated my brother. And I never told him I did either."

"You told your parents that you hated them quite a few times."

"Every kid says it. I didn't mean it!"

"At the moment, you did," Hannah said. "It's okay. Your feelings were validated. Truth be told, your parents had moments of resenting you too."

"What?" I asked.

"They spent a lot of their time taking you to doctor's appointments or hovering over you because they were afraid of you dying."

"That's a little harsh."

"It's human nature," Hannah shrugged. "No one is perfect, Emma. But this is why everyone gets different waiting periods while they're here. We have to go over terrible thoughts, lies, theft, and any type of pain you may have inflicted on yourself or others. I know bringing up anything negative in your life is hard. But it's all part of the process."

I nodded and tried a bite of lobster tail. I grimaced, and Hannah laughed.

"Not a fan of that either?" she asked. I shook my head.

"Hopefully, I like the strawberries!" I giggled.

I took one of the strawberries and smelled it. The smell kind of reminded me of my mom. She was always baking with fresh fruit and had a sweet smell to her. I took a bite and immediately was overwhelmed with the flavor. It was lovely and tart and slightly juicy but also had a bit of a meaty texture like peaches. I sat and ate every strawberry in the bowl and even started crying at one point. I finished the last one and glanced over at Hannah. She sat, smiling at me, waiting patiently as I enjoyed a new food for the first time.

"I really missed out on these," I pointed to the bowl. "Thank you for letting me indulge for a little bit."

"You're welcome," Hannah cleared her throat.

My appointment with Hannah went on for another hour before she stood up and started putting her papers back in order.

"Well then, that should do it," she smiled. "We got through a big chunk of it today, so I think one more session ought to do it."

"Once that's over, I'll still have whatever time is left on this thing, right?" I held my watch up.

"If I can get things moving along quickly enough, we should be able to get your last appointment done in about a week. After your last appointment with me is finished, we'll try and get you moved along immediately. We're swiftly getting through the years of your life, so I need to see your watch for a moment."

I took it off reluctantly and handed it to Hannah. She pushed some buttons on her watch before handing mine back over.

"166 hours?" I asked frantically.

"Yes," Hannah said, making her way to the door. "That's exactly one full week from today's appointment."

"You've cut my time in half!" I snapped. Hannah looked at me.

"Believe me, it's for the best," she smiled. "The sooner we can get you moved along, the happier you will be."

I watched Hannah open the door before glancing back at me.

"Emma," Hannah sighed. "Remember what I told you about the watch. You have to be back here when the time runs out. It's imperative. Understand?"

I nodded, and she smiled again before shutting the door. I started breathing heavily and looking around my room. My time was running out. I needed to figure out a way to reach Alastor and do it sooner than later. I ran over to the phone and dialed 0.

"Don't tell me you're still hungry," Elijah answered. "No one likes a glutton."

"Elijah, listen to me," I breathed.

"What's wrong?" he asked.

"There's been a change of plan. You need to get a hold of your guy as soon as possible."

"How soon do you need him?"

I looked down at my watch. Almost five minutes had passed since Hannah left.

"Now."

"Not possible."

"I'm coming down there."

"You don't need to do that," Elijah said sternly. "Dumah is already not thrilled about this little mission. Also, I haven't even had a chance to discuss the possibility of you going. If I tell him you want to move it up to 'as soon as possible,' he'll probably call the whole thing off."

"Then let me talk to him," I gritted my teeth. "Please, Elijah. Hannah just moved my transfer time up."

"By how much?"

"One week is all I have left."

"She must be desperate to get rid of you," Elijah chuckled.

"What's that supposed to mean?"

"Hannah likes- and don't take this the wrong way- interesting lives."

"What?"

"She tries to push along people she doesn't find fascinating. Her throat clearing is a giveaway that she's bored and not interested. I think it's a little rude, but it's not my place to say anything."

I felt tears run down my cheeks.

"Please don't cry," Elijah sighed.

"I'm not."

"Yes, you are. It'll be alright. I'll talk to Dumah as soon as possible and see what I can do. For now, get some rest."

"I don't want to rest!" I yelled. "I'm tired of fake sleeping and fake eating and pretending I'm happy. I have no friends or family here. I didn't get to live long enough to have any passions I want to spend my days doing while I wait."

"Then what do you want to do, Emma?"

I sat there and thought about it.

"I want to train."

"What do you mean?" Elijah asked.

"When I meet this Dumah, I want to prove to him that I can handle myself. Is there anywhere I can train with, like a former knight, Spartan, or something?"

"You're not going to find any of those around here," Elijah laughed.

"Then I guess I'll look elsewhere," I said before hanging up the phone.

I changed out of the dress and into a pair of leggings, a tank top, and a jacket. After taking the makeup off my face and redoing my ponytail, I looked around my room one last time. I ran over to the wall, took a picture of my parents and Simon out of the frame, and put the image in my jacket pocket. I left knowing there was a good chance I wouldn't see my room again, at least not without Alastor.

I stepped off the elevator and made a beeline for the door.

"Emma!"

"Go away, Elijah," I panted, not looking at him.

"Emma, stop!"

I sighed and turned to him.

"What?"

"Where are you going?"

"Earth."

"Why?"

"I was thinking about checking out an army base or maybe a boxing gym. Are ninjas still a thing? I could see if there's like a secret dojo somewhere."

"I think a military base is a good place to start," Elijah smiled. "Not the army, however. There's a Marine base in California. I'll write it down for you. You'll see some of the best hand-to-hand combat there."

"Hand-to-hand combat?" I asked. "What about guns?"

Elijah started laughing as he pulled a small piece of paper and a pen from his pocket.

"Guns won't do you any good in Hell."

"So I'll just make my way through Hell, punching demons in the face then?"

"Go," Elijah laughed. "Good luck."

"Yeah, thanks," I replied, taking the note. "See you around, Elijah."

I walked down the escalator and read the address on the note. I closed my eyes for a moment and then opened them again. I was surrounded by men shouting and rows of people jogging in formation. I walked around and watched people doing push-ups and pull-ups, crawling in mud under barbed wires, and climbing up walls. I went into a building and found a large room where groups practiced fighting with each other. I tried mimicking some of the moves, but it felt silly. I was punching and kicking the air when a large dark shape caught my eye. I saw a glimpse of the figure walking through the open door of the building. I quickly followed it outside.

I glanced around the complex but only saw humans. I ran around searching for what looked like a giant crow. Finally, I saw something massive move along the tree line. I sprinted as fast as I could to catch it, but when I reached the trees, I couldn't see it anymore. Panting, I leaned over and put my hands on my knees.

"What do you want?" a deep voice said behind me. I turned around slowly and gasped.

A very tall figure stood before me, dressed in all black. Most of his face was covered by a masked hood, but I saw that the skin on his forehead was as black as his clothes. I also noticed two entirely white eyes staring out at me from under the hood. He wore black leather armor with matching elbow-length gloves and boots almost up to his knees.

"You can see me?" I asked. "How?"

"Same way you can see me," he said. "We're not...from here."

"What are you?" I asked.

"An angel," he answered. Giant, black, raven-like wings stretched out from his shoulder blades.

"I've never seen an angel like you before."

"Sorry I'm not pretty enough for you. Now, my turn to ask some questions. Are you following me?"

"No," I lied.

"Did Elijah tell you I was here?"

"You know Elijah?"

"Are you playing stupid, or are you just stupid?"

"I beg your pardon!" I scoffed. "I don't even know who you are! Elijah didn't tell me anything about you. He suggested I come here."

"*Elijah* suggested you come here?" he sighed.

I nodded

"And why's that?"

"I'm not answering any more of your questions until you tell me who you are."

"You really haven't figured it out yet?"

I looked at the hooded angel standing in front of me.

"Dumah?" I said hesitantly.

"Good job," he sighed again. "I guess you're not as stupid as I thought you were. Now, you can go back to Processing and wait in your room until I've decided if I will follow through in five days."

"You are unpleasant; you know that!" I snapped. "I was just asking Elijah if he could get in touch with you. I need to go sooner."

"Excuse me?"

"Hannah moved my date up to next week. If we have any chance of finding out what happened to my boyfriend, we need to get going as soon as possible."

"We?" Dumah crossed his arms.

"Oh, right, Elijah didn't tell you," I exclaimed. "I'm going with you to Hell."

"The hell you are!" Dumah said without missing a beat.

"Yes, I am," I argued. "You're not going to be able to find my boyfriend. You don't even know what he looks like."

"I'm good at finding people. You'll only slow me down and get in my way."

"Could you be any more of a stereotype?" I laughed. "Seriously, this whole 'I work alone,' brooding thing is so lame. I can help you."

"The answer is no. Now, I have something I need to take care of. I'll report to you in five days.

I'll take notes about your boyfriend and be on my way."

"I'm going with you," I said firmly.

"Goodbye, Emma."

I grabbed Dumah's arm and was instantly transported with him. The air was thick with smoke. We were surrounded by destroyed buildings and cars, charred and on fire still. I put my hand to my mouth as I started noticing the bodies around us. Occasionally, I could hear rapid gunfire or an explosion in the far distance. Somewhere, someone was screaming.

"Are you serious?" Dumah growled at me. "Go home, Emma."

"I don't have a home," I whispered. "Don't you get that? I'm not going to pretend that I'm staying at some sort of resort with unlimited room service and fun activities. I'm miserable not knowing where my boyfriend is."

"Shh," Dumah put his finger up to his mouth. "Be quiet."

I watched him silently move around one of the cars. A woman holding a child was lying on the ground breathing quickly. Blood was coming from her mouth, and I could see a puddle of blood spreading out from her. The child wasn't moving, and there were several bullet holes in the child's back. Dumah leaned down and put his face close to hers. She seemed to look right at him as her eyes widened, and her breathing slowed and then stopped. Everything around us went silent. I couldn't hear guns, explosions, fire crackling, or even the wind.

As Dumah stood up, the chaotic noises around us returned, and I jumped at the sound of a man screaming.

"What-" I started. Dumah put his finger to his lips again.

He started moving, and I followed closely behind. The wailing grew louder as we approached a car that had been partially crushed by a fallen light pole. A man was sticking out of the driver window screaming in pain. His lower torso seemed to be pinned down by the overbearing weight of the light pole. As I went around the car, I could see that the whole interior was covered in blood and other human remains. I noticed a torso and legs of another person under the wooden pole in the passenger seat. The man cried out in desperation as Dumah leaned over him. The man looked directly into his eyes, stopped crying, and began to whisper to him. After a moment, the man's speech slowed and then stopped. Everything around us went silent as the man's eyes closed. I looked at Dumah.

"He was praying and asking for his wife," Dumah explained. "Fortunately for him, he couldn't see what was left of her sitting right next to him in the car."

"Can they see you?" I asked.

"As they're about to pass, yes."

"Why did the noise around us stop when they died?"

Dumah looked at me.

"You noticed that?" he asked before he started walking. I followed.

"Yeah, why?"

"I don't usually meet humans who are so....in tune with death. Were you sick a long time before you died?"

"Cancer," I answered.

"Ah," Dumah hissed. "Yes, cancer takes many. I'm sorry for your passing. You seem young. I've seen many much younger people, however. Death takes all."

"Were you there when I died?"

"No, I cannot be present at every passing. But I am not the only death angel."

"Death angel?" I asked. "I've never heard of such a thing. I thought angels were supposed to be beautiful and help people."

"Angels of death do help people, just not in any circumstances people like," Dumah sighed. "Not all angels are the same, however. And most do not wish to converse with the likes of us."

"Too much 'doom and gloom' and not enough 'sunshine and rainbows?'"

"Something like that."

"I can handle myself, you know?"

"It's too dangerous."

"It's too dangerous," I mimicked his deep voice. "But I'm the reason he's there. How can I possibly ever be okay with that? How can I move on without knowing what happened to him?"

"I'm sorry, but my answer is still no. You'll be fine once you get to Paradise. And before long, your family will be joining you so you won't be lonely."

"Ugh, what a horrible thing to say!" I scoffed. "I hope I don't see my family for a long, long time. I hope they all live long, happy lives. In the meantime, if I can help someone else, I'm going to."

"How do you think you can help him?"

"I don't know, but I'm going to try to do *something*! Trying is better than sitting around and doing nothing!"

Rage built up inside me, and I screamed before running to a car nearby. I punched the window, glass shattering all over the backseat. I was shocked that I could break the window, and judging by how Dumah was looking at me, he was too.

"How the hell did that happen?" I asked.

Dumah slowly walked up and placed a heavy hand on my shoulder.

"All right," he said, his white eyes staring into mine. "I've changed my mind."

"Are you serious?" I exclaimed. "Thank you so much! You won't regret it, I promise."

"We need to get started right away."

"Yes, I agree!"

"Are you ready?" Dumah asked, putting his hand out. "No going back now."

"I'm ready," I answered, putting my hand on his.

"Close your eyes," he said.

I closed them and felt a strong *whoosh!* My hair blew around my face, and my body went weightless. I grabbed Dumah with both hands, afraid I'd fall if I let go. My teeth chattered from the cold wind (although I technically couldn't *feel* cold), and I'm almost sure that if my stomach were still fully functional, I would have thrown up. Suddenly, my feet hit the ground, and the rest of my body followed. I looked up at Dumah from all fours and frowned.

"You could have held onto me, so I didn't fall," I gritted my teeth and stood up.

"Sorry, I don't usually have passengers," Dumah said. "Are you all right?"

"I'm fine," I looked around. "Where are we?"

"The In Between," Dumah started walking. "It's where everything in Processing takes place. Many angels reside here."

"Not in Heaven?" I asked.

"No."

"So *this* isn't Processing?"

"No."

I waited for him to elaborate on his answer, but he didn't. I decided not to ask about it. The ground beneath us grew less firm, and I realized we had started walking on white sand. After a while, I was able to hear waves.

"Is this Limbo?" I asked.

"Mmhmm," Dumah mumbled. "Most people get stuck here for quite some time, either right after passing or from Hell. They use this as a 'transitional' place. In my opinion, it's one last way to make people feel guilty about what they did in life. People spend their own lives experiencing pain, sickness, hunger, abuse, and trauma. They don't need to suffer after they die unless they go to Hell."

I scowled at him and felt myself rubbing my arms with my hands.

"The further away from Processing, the further away from Heaven you are. This also means that the further away from Processing you are, the more you start to feel again. In the In-Between, you can still feel cold, hunger, and tiredness. The further into Hell you get, the more intense those sensations get."

"So both Heaven and Hell make you less human," I said. "Only one is more pleasant than the other."

Dumah nodded.

We finally arrived at what looked like a giant hut. It was a round building made primarily of wood and straw on the outside.

"Is this where you live?" I asked. Dumah nodded.

"Considering I don't eat or sleep, I don't need much. Just a place for some solitude."

We walked inside, where there was no floor, only more sand. Candles lit up the hut, showing many different weapons and relics. I walked along the wall, admiring the swords, daggers, shields, books, crosses, jewelry, and vials.

"What is all of this stuff?" I asked.

"Miscellaneous things I've picked up throughout the years. This," he said, picking up a small piece of wood, "is from the cross."

"As in, *the* cross?" I asked. Dumah nodded.

"These," he pointed to the vials, "contain either holy water, blood, or tears."

"Why do you have bottles of blood and tears?" I asked.

"Some are from saints. I have a few from Christ himself."

"So Jesus existed?"

"Of course he did."

"And he's the son of God?"

"That's open to interpretation. There are many religions in the world, and most of them get it wrong. Honestly, God doesn't look at specifics of what a person believes in life. He knows there's no way for one person to get it completely right. But how you treated others in life, how much happiness you spread, how much of your life was spent doing good...those things matter. What you do for a job, your house, your status, or your religion doesn't matter nearly as much as what's in your heart."

"'It is easier for a camel to pass through the eye of a needle than for a rich man to enter the kingdom of heaven,'" I recited.

"Precisely."

"Do I get a weapon?" I asked quickly. Dumah grunted.

"What?" I said. "I don't get any form of protection?"

"*I* am your protection."

"Please," I rolled my eyes. "A little self-defense wouldn't hurt. Imagine you're fighting off five demons alone-"

"Easy," he interrupted.

"Okay then," I sighed. "Imagine you're fighting off twenty demons alone. One of them knocks your sword out of your hand. They're swarming you. You look over at me, just standing there with nothing, and think, 'man, I should have given Emma a sword and some vials of holy water. That would come in handy right about now.'"

"All right!" Dumah growled. "You never let up, do you?"

"Nope," I smiled. "Now, which one is mine?"

I reached for a long sword, but Dumah smacked my hand away.

"No," he said sternly. "Not that one."

He looked at the wall for a moment before pulling down a long, slender dagger.

"This is an Italian stiletto," Dumah handed it to me carefully. "Pope Julius II blessed it. It's lightweight and extremely sharp."

I examined the silver handle And noticed the horses carved into it. It also said "Dominus vobiscum" on the blade.

"What does this mean?" I asked, pointing to the inscription.

"The Lord be with you," Dumah answered. "It's Latin. Do you not know Latin?"

"No. Most people don't."

"That's a shame. Beautiful language."

I looked around for something to put the dagger in.

"There's a scabbard that should fit that on the bottom shelf."

"A scabbard?"

"A long purse to put your dagger in," he muttered.

"Oh, found it!"

"Congratulations."

"You know, if we're going to be spending time together, you could lighten up a little."

"Quiet," Dumah became still.

"Yeah, I talk a lot. But you don't talk hardly at all, so I have to fill the silence-"

"I'm serious," he put a hand out to me. "Be quiet."

"You are so rude and grumpy!"

Dumah grabbed one of the larger swords on the wall and slowly walked toward the door.

"What-!" I started. Dumah put a finger up to his mouth to hush me.

He swung the door open and raised his sword, ready to strike.

15

"Don't!" I heard a small voice say. "I'm just looking for Emma!"

I looked around Dumah and saw Sam standing in the doorway. Her eyes caught mine, and she frowned at me.

"What do you think you're doing?" Sam asked me. "I've been looking everywhere for you!"

"I've been keeping myself busy," I said. "Like you told me to."

"I also said to stay out of trouble," Sam crossed her arms.

"I'm not in any trouble."

"Not yet, at least," Sam eyed Dumah. "Are we going to continue the conversation like this, or can I come in?"

"You can stay right there," Dumah grunted. "This is my home."

"Last I checked, death angels don't have homes."

"And what of you, little girl?" Dumah growled. "Where do you call home? What things have you seen?"

"I'll talk to you outside," I said to Sam. I pushed past Dumah and walked with Sam. We made our way down to the shore before she started talking.

"What were you thinking?" Sam scolded me. "Running away with a death angel! What do you think you're doing?"

"I'm going with him," I breathed.

"To where?" she asked.

"To find Alastor."

Sam stopped and looked at me.

"*What?*"

"Look," I sighed. "Dumah has agreed to take me with him to search for Alastor-"

"In Hell?"

"Yes," I continued. "He will make sure I get back before my time runs out. But Hannah has shortened my time, so we'll have to go immediately."

"No," Sam shook her head. "I asked Hannah to shorten your time."

"What, why?"

"Because, Emma, you have been restless since you arrived. I already know your life didn't have much for Hannah to go over anyways. I asked her to speed up the process to get you to Paradise sooner. You'll be happier there. Until you are in Paradise, you can't fully let go of your Earthly self. You still have wants. You still have guilt. Your heart isn't beating anymore, and yet it still breaks. Please let me help with the pain your soul still feels. Let me free your soul."

"And what about Alastor's soul?" I cried. Thunder boomed in the distance, and I could see clouds forming over the sea. "I know you were my first best friend in life and my guardian angel in death, but I'm dead now. You don't have to worry about me anymore. Guard someone else. Let me make my own decision about something. I never did anything great when I was alive. There won't be statues of me or buildings named after me. I'll never be mentioned in books or movies. So I will try and do one great thing while I still can. I want to find out what happened to Alastor and save him if I can."

Sam gazed out at the water for a long time. She seemed to be thinking long and hard about what she would say next.

"I can't have more time added," Sam finally said. "If your time runs out before you get out of Hell, you'll be stuck there."

"I know."

"And I don't think I'll have any say in getting you out."

"I know."

Sam sighed.

"Is he really worth it?"

"Yes," I whispered.

"I'm coming too, then."

I looked at Sam, astonished. She let out a laugh.

"I'm still technically your guardian angel."

"All right," I chuckled. "Well, good luck."

"What, you don't think I can handle myself down there?"

"No, I mean good luck convincing Dumah to let you come with us."

"*You* convinced him."

"He likes *me*," I smiled.

"Dumah doesn't like anyone," Sam laughed. "He's the angel of the silence of death. He only wants quiet and the stillness of the dead."

"I don't know," I shrugged. "I think he's warming up to me."

We walked back to Dumah's hut. I stopped Sam at the door.

"Let me talk to him," I said. "You'll end up just pissing him off."

Sam rolled her eyes, then nodded. I knocked on the door, and we went inside.

"Ah," Dumah muttered. "Are you on your way? I'm sure it's past your bedtime."

"Actually," I said. "I was wondering if I could ask you something. A favor."

"Another one?" Dumah asked.

"Just one more," I looked at Sam. Dumah also glanced at her and then back at me.

"No," Dumah bellowed. "No, no, no. Haven't you ever heard the term, 'three's a crowd?'"

"I'm familiar with it," Sam said.

"Two angels are better than one, though, right?" I asked. "Dumah won't feel the need to babysit me. That way he can focus more on the mission."

"Oh, so *I* have to be the babysitter?" Sam asked.

"That's your job, isn't it?" Dumah chuckled. "After all, guardian angels are just babysitters. Only reason you get to go is to keep Emma out of harm's way. And to keep her out of my way."

"Fine," Sam crossed her arms. "But I still get to bring a weapon."

"Of course," Dumah pointed to the wall. "I assume you need a blankie and a lunch box also?"

"I'm bringing my own," Sam scoffed. "I can be back before morning. We'll leave then."

"Sounds like a plan!" I smiled, trying to break the tension. "We'll see you first thing in the morning then!"

"Make sure you get some rest," Sam said to me. "You might not have a body that needs rest anymore, but your soul will need some rest before the journey."

I nodded and showed her to the door. After Sam left, Dumah gathered a bunch of blankets and robes to build a makeshift bed for me.

"Apologies," Dumah said. "This is the best I can do."

"It's fine," I replied, laying down. Dumah made his way towards the door.

"You're leaving?" I asked.

"I must get a few things before we leave tomorrow. You'll be asleep anyway."

"You're going to leave me here alone?"

"You're safe here," Dumah sighed. "You won't even know I'm gone."

"Can you stay until I fall asleep?"

Dumah sighed again and then sat down on the opposite side of the room from me.

"Can you at least tell me a story or something instead of just sitting there sighing?" I asked.

"A bedtime story? What next? Tuck you in?"

"Just tell me about somewhere you've been. In another time and place."

Dumah sat in silence. I turned and lay facing away from him.

"Very well," he said. "I was at the Battle of Gergovia."

"The what?" I turned around.

"The Battle of Gergovia," he repeated. "It took place in 52 B.C. and was fought between Gallic tribes and a Roman army."

"Never heard of it."

"It's a historic French battle. Ever heard of Julius Caesar?"

"Yeah, that sounds familiar."

"He was leading the Roman Republic against Vercingetorix. Although Caesar and his men lost that battle, Vercingetorix surrendered to

Caesar and was executed. Anyways, the Battle of Gergovia was great."

Dumah began to tell me about the battle, the people and groups involved, and all of it was so boring that I fell asleep quickly.

I woke up the next day with the sun shining into the hut. I heard footsteps outside and watched a figure make its way towards the door.

"Dumah?" I whispered.

I slowly grabbed my dagger from the floor and got up, tiptoeing along the wall. The door swung open, and I raised the blade above my head.

"Cute," Dumah scoffed. I let out a sigh of relief.

"You scared me," I exhaled. "Are you just now getting back?"

"I've been preparing the boat while you get your rest. You plan on staying in bed all day, or are we going to Hell?"

I got my shoes on and belted my scabbard to my waist. Dumah kneeled in the back of the hut and lowered his head, murmuring to himself. After saying a prayer, he stood up, grabbed the long sword from the wall, and sheathed it. I followed Dumah out the door and down to the shore. Sam was standing next to a sailboat with her arms crossed like they usually were. She was wearing a pink backpack and started tapping one foot on the sand.

"Are we leaving sometime today?" Sam put her hands up in the air.

"Talk to the princess," Dumah nodded towards me.

"Sorry," I apologized. "I think my soul was trying to figure out how to die from boredom from the story Dumah told me last night."

Sam giggled and turned towards the boat.

"Aw, what a cute little backpack," Dumah said. "Are those puppies on it?"

"And kittens," Sam took the backpack off and tossed it at him. "As a matter of fact, I brought this as a gift for you. My bags are already onboard."

"Now, now, children," I groaned, taking the backpack from Dumah. "Enough of the bickering. How are we going to get the boat from the shore?"

"You and Sam get in, and I'll push us out."

I looked out at the clear blue water and then to the boat. The one, large sail in the middle was gray and tattered. There was enough room on the deck for about eight people to move around comfortably. Dumah clearly didn't have a crew to sail with him though. There was one long oar on the back of the boat and Dumah was putting most of his belongings back there by it. The wood of the boat had many deep scratches and dents in it, like it had taken a few beatings before.

"This is....nice," Sam said sarcastically.

Dumah frowned at her.

"What are those symbols?" I asked, pointing to the painted side of the boat.

"It's the name of the boat," Dumah answered. "It's in Greek."

"What does it say?"

There was a pause before Dumah answered.

"It says, 'boat.'"

"You named your boat, 'Boat?'" Sam chortled.

"I didn't name it," he sighed.

"I've never been on a boat," I said.

"Good thing you don't have to worry about getting seasick," Sam chuckled. "Come on."

Sam climbed up into the boat, then helped me up. I sat down as Sam started moving bags and equipment around. I noticed a small, wooden bow and a quiver full of arrows.

"Are those yours?" I asked, pointing to them.

"Oh yeah," Sam smiled. "I took up archery after I died and fell in love with it. I've only ever shot at targets, but I'm pretty good. Hold on tight. Dumah's about to push us."

I turned and saw Dumah at the end of the boat. He leaned up against it and spread his wings out a little as he started pushing the boat through the wet sand and into the water with ease. Soon, we were floating in the water, and Dumah pulled himself aboard. He steered and commanded Sam to occasionally do something with the boat.

"Ease the sail," Dumah instructed.

Once the sail was out, we started to pick up speed, moving along with the current. I looked out into the water and back at the shore. Everything around us was beautiful. No one talked for a long time until I finally broke the silence.

"So where are we going exactly?"

"Straight to Hell," Sam answered.

"Wait," I said. "We're just taking a boat to Hell? How?"

"The sea will lead us to the shore on the other side," Dumah explained. "This is the only way in or out of Hell."

"So what do we do in the meantime?" I asked.

"Just enjoy the silence," Dumah answered. "There won't be any once we get there."

Sam shifted in her seat uncomfortably. I looked back over the water. Quite some time passed as the sun moved from one side of the boat to the other. I hadn't seen the land in hours and was getting bored. There was nothing to do, and no one was talking. Dumah and Sam seemed okay with it, though, so I decided to endure it. I looked down at my watch and sighed. 119 hours. Sam looked at me.

"What's wrong?" she asked.

"Just getting nervous."

"Don't be," she smiled. "We'll be there soon."

"All the more reason *to* be nervous," Dumah sighed.

"I can't believe the sun is already setting," I shivered, wrapping my hands around my arms. Sam grabbed a blanket and handed it to me.

"Why don't we take turns singing songs we know," she suggested. "Just to help pass the time. Dumah, why don't you go first?"

"I don't know any songs," Dumah muttered.

"That's a lie," Sam laughed. "Someone who's existed for centuries and doesn't know a single song? Give me a break. Probably just too chicken to sing in front of us."

"If I sing one song, will you promise to be quiet the rest of the ride there?" Dumah growled.

"Yes!" we both exclaimed.

"All right," he sighed. "This is an old Viking song they would sing while traveling."

Sam and I huddled in close as Dumah started bellowing the song. His loud, deep voice almost seemed to vibrate the boat.

My mother told me
Someday I would buy
Galleys with good oars and
Sails to distant shores.
My mother told me
Someday I would buy
Galleys with good oars and
Sails to distant shores.
Stand up on the prow

272

Noble barque I steer
Steady course to the haven
Hew many foe-men
Hew many foe-men."

Dumah finished singing and we sat in awe. The sun was hugging the horizon now.

"Wow, Dumah!" I said. "That was really good!"

"It was a lot better than I was expecting," Sam added.

"All right, you promised no more talking."

"You picked the wrong profession," I laughed.

"Shh!" Dumah said instantly.

"You could have a Vegas residency with that dreamy voice," Sam cackled. I giggled along with her.

"I mean it!" Dumah snapped. "Quiet!"

Sam and I grew silent. The ocean had swallowed the last bit of sunlight, and as the light around us began to fade, I started feeling afraid. Sam grabbed a lantern, and light filled the boat. I heard a slight splash from behind me and peeked over the boat's edge. Something was moving around us in the water. I braced myself, holding on to the side of the boat. I leaned closer to the water to get a better look. Suddenly, a cold, slimy hand reached out and grabbed my hair. The skin hanging off the bone was pale, and I could see tendons and muscles like torn rags. Before I could see what the arm was attached to, I started to shriek. A hand from behind me covered my mouth. Dumah muffled my screaming as he reached for my dagger and cut my hair, freeing me from the hand. Dumah and I fell backward, still keeping his hand over my mouth. He looked at me and put a finger up to his lips. I nodded, and he removed his hand from my mouth.

Sam shined the lantern over the boat, and I could see what surrounded us in the water. Hundreds of corpses floated around the boat, all in various stages of decomposition. The closer the light got to them, the deeper they would sink beneath the surface. Sam leaned in to whisper.

"Don't make any loud noises," she breathed. "These are lost souls, wandering in the sea for eternity. The light drives them away, so stay close to the lantern."

I nodded and backed away from the side of the boat. Dumah pointed forward, and I could faintly make out land ahead of us. Something hit the boat and made a loud *thud*. I jumped backward and knocked the lantern out of Sam's hand. It fell and smashed against the deck, snuffing the light. The boat rolled side to side, and I could see hands reach up on the boat's sides.

"Dumah," I gasped.

Sam and I huddled closer to Dumah as the corpses started pulling themselves onto our boat. Some were missing eyes, leaving empty black sockets staring back at us. They made no sound besides the shuffling of their feet. One pulled itself onto the boat, and I noticed everything from the hip down was missing. It slowly dragged its body by the arms across the deck. There were several closing in on us.

"Dumah!" I yelled.

Dumah drew his sword, and it was glowing with red flames. The corpses started backing off, covering their eyes with their hands. Dumah swung his sword around furiously and kicked some of the corpses back into the water. As he stabbed one corpse with his sword, it caught on fire. Dazed, it flailed its arms around while the other corpses backed away from it, making them fall off the boat's sides. Sam rushed to get another lantern lit and handed it to me. She was looking frantically behind me, and I turned to see the land approaching very quickly. We were going to crash right into the dock.

"Dumah!" Sam cried. "The pier!"

Dumah looked at the land, getting closer, and ran back to the steering oar.

"Emma!" he called. "Lower the sail!"

"What!" I yelled. "I don't know what that means!"

He plunged the sword into the deck, still blazing, and tried to gain control of the boat. Sam grabbed her quiver and bow and spun around, ready to aim at anything that would be trying to crawl back onto the boat. The corpse that was still on fire collapsed next to Dumah, who seemed to be focusing on only one thing now.

"Everyone, hold on!" Dumah called out. "We're going to crash!"

I braced myself as our boat hit the dock. I lunged forward, hitting my head hard on the side of the deck. My ears started ringing, and I cradled my head in my hands.

"Emma, are you okay?" Sam rushed to me.

"Ouch, shit!" I groaned.

"Are you okay?" she repeated, looking at my head. "You're bleeding."

"What?" I touched my forehead gingerly and glanced at my hand. I winced as I wiped the blood on my shirt.

"How is that even possible?" I asked, feeling dizzy. "I'm already dead, but I'm bleeding and can feel pain?"

"Rules are different here," Dumah sighed, helping me to my feet. He carefully got himself off the boat and onto the broken pier before helping Sam and me down. I looked down at the ground. The sand, unlike where Dumah lived, was black.

"Black sand," I murmured out loud.

I looked back at the water. There were many pairs of eyes looking back up at us. I gasped as I grabbed Dumah's arm.

"They can't get to us," Dumah explained. "They're not welcomed here."

A sound drew my attention away from the water. I watched the corpse on the boat, still on fire, started slowly crawling towards the edge before falling off, onto the shore. As the body hit the ground, it turned into black sand.

"Come on," Sam helped me off the dock and onto the beach. "You sit here while I help Dumah unload some stuff from the boat. I'll see if I can find something for your head."

"Don't bother," Dumah said from the boat. "It's already starting to heal."

I touched where the wound was, and it felt smooth other than some dried blood.

"I told you," Dumah muttered as he brought some bags. "The rules are different here. You can get hurt and feel pain, but it heals quickly, so you can keep getting hurt and feeling pain."

"So people can suffer for eternity," I added. He nodded. A shiver ran down my spine.

Death: Part Two

16

"Hey!" a voice from behind us shouted. A shirtless man waved at us. He looked to be about in his forties. Dumah sighed heavily. I watched the man come closer, with something large following him. At first, I thought it was a tiger, but as it got closer, it went from walking on all fours to two legs. It was a woman with the head of a lioness. She had bluish-green-tinted fur, human hands, and human feet. It wore a usekh, a large, multicolored beaded collar; but was bare otherwise. The man, if he was a man, had marks on his pale-white skin that looked like blue tree branches spreading all over.

"What the fuck!" the man shouted as he came closer. "You broke my boat!"

"Baraqiel," Dumah growled. "We were attacked. About a dozen or so Restless attacked the boat. You're lucky they didn't take the whole thing down."

"I told you to leave at first light," the man spat. "Why ask for help and advice if you're not going to follow it?"

The man stopped and looked at Sam and me. I gulped.

"What the fuck is this?" he asked Dumah. "Who are you?"

279

"This is Sam and Emma," Dumah answered for us. "Emma and Sam, this is Baraqiel. A coworker, for lack of a better term."

"*Coworker?*" Baraqiel laughed. "We're a little closer than that, aren't we? What, are you making new friends now?"

He held his hand out at me. I slowly put mine out, and he shook it. The hair on my arms stood up.

"You can call me Barry," he smiled at me. "You, my dear, are not an angel."

"No," I replied softly. "I'm not. I'm Emma."

Barry glanced back at Dumah.

"You got some balls bringing a guardian angel and a human soul here. What are you up to?"

"We're looking for my boyfriend," I answered. Dumah cleared his throat. "We're going to see if we can get him out of here."

"A rescue mission?" Barry rubbed his bald head and chuckled. "So not only did you grow a pair of balls but a heart as well?"

"Dumah has always had a big heart," the creature said.

"I would have acknowledged you sooner," Dumah said to it, "but Baraqiel has been talking nonstop. How are you, Sekhmet?"

The cat woman hugged Dumah.

"Sekhmet?" Sam asked. "The Egyptian goddess?"

"I'm not a goddess, but yes," she replied, letting go of Dumah.

I gave Sam a confused look.

"I got into Egyptian mythology for a bit," she shrugged. "She's the goddess of war and plague."

"Not a goddess," Sekhmet pointed out again. "But yes, I was a little...bloodthirsty when I was mortal."

"Are you feeling charitable?" Dumah asked.

"If *you're* asking," Sekhmet brushed Dumah's face with her hand. "You know I can't say no to you."

"Where do you plan on staying?" Barry asked.

"I was hoping you could help us with that," Dumah answered.

"First, you ask to borrow my boat, which you wreck," Barry complained. "Now, you need a place to stay."

He looked at each of us, one by one. Sekhmet nudged him in the side. Barry sighed.

"Fine," he finally said. "Come on."

I had one hand on my dagger the whole time we followed behind Baraqiel.

"So..." Sam said, reluctantly to Sekhmet. "You said you're not a goddess?"

"That's correct," she answered.

"Why are you known in mythology as a goddess then?"

Dumah and Baraqiel gave each other a look.

"I had nothing to do with that," Sekhmet explained. "I was human before I died; a slave in Egypt."

Sekhmet showed us her palms, which had scarred markings on them. She returned to walking on all fours while she talked.

"Branded, to show that I was property of the pharaoh," she continued. "I was his personal healer. Usually women slaves were used only as concubines, but when the pharaoh saw how gifted I was in the art of healing, he kept me close and told me how special I was. No one knew he was fighting disease except me. One night I insisted that I needed to go out and find a special flower that only bloomed at night time. There was no flower really; I used it as an excuse to run away. I escaped and eventually started a new life in the desert. I met my husband and we had two young daughters. I continued to use my gift of being able to heal those who were sick. People traveled to visit me when no one else was able to help them. The pharaoh's men sought to imprison me once they discovered my hiding place. I had run away from slavery, which made me a criminal in their eyes, even though I was using my freedom to heal others.

One day, a man came to my home, asking for a cure to his ailment. I offered him some fresh fruit and water while he waited. My daughters played outside with my husband's mother while I worked so they wouldn't be around the sick. As I was putting together some medicine, I was suddenly struck over the head, leaving me unconscious. When I woke up, I had been tied up and bound with rope by the man who had come to my house. The man was taking me back to the pharaoh for his reward. For miles, I screamed and cried and fought as hard as I could. Eventually, I stopped fighting, my body dragging and scraping along the ground behind his camel. When we finally stopped for a drink along the way, I didn't move. I think the man thought I was dead. He got very close to my face to check my breath. I grabbed his dagger and stabbed him in the neck. Then, I proceeded to stab him in the chest, face, and stomach, screaming with rage. I just kept doing it over and over, long after he had died. I stabbed him until I almost passed out from exhaustion. Two men who were nearby heard the commotion and ran at me. One managed to hit me in the mouth, shattering my teeth. I don't know how I found the strength to fight them both. I sort of blacked out. But next thing I knew, they were both lying on the ground too. I had almost completely decapitated one of them with the dagger.

I covered my face with one of the dead men's cloaks and took off on the camel, going back to warn my husband. When I arrived, my home had burned down and my husband and his mother were impaled, propped up by long stakes. They had also placed my daughters' bodies on stakes. They were only one and two years old. So small."

Sekhmet stopped a moment before continuing with her story.

"I walked through the desert that night. The moon and stars were the only light I had. I wandered, praying to the gods to show me any sign of what I should do. I was hungry, covered in blood, and smelled horribly. I stumbled across a group of men, sitting around a fire. When they saw me, they knew immediately who I was. Word spread quickly of the slave witch who had been slaughtering men. I walked slowly towards them, the dagger in my hand. Out of nowhere, a lioness attacked the men. I stood there in horror as she clawed and bit into the flesh of the men who were sent to kill me. One of the men got away, fleeing on horseback and screaming as he disappeared into the night. Never once did the lioness turn to me. She feasted on the others as I followed the one man who got away. I knew he would return, warning others about me.

As the sun started to rise, I entered the city of Heliopolis. I had broken, jagged teeth that resembled almost fangs. My whole body was painted with blood. I'm sure it was a frightening sight. The people around me whispered. An old priest came out onto the street in front of me.

'Woman,' he called. 'We have heard of you slaughtering men in the desert with a great cat by your side. What is your name?'

'Sekhmet,' I answered. 'My family was murdered so I am seeking revenge!'

A great, hot wind blew in from the desert behind me. Everyone in the streets cowered from me.

'Great Sekhmet!' the priest called. 'These innocent people do not mean to harm you! Please, if you come with me, I'm sure there is something we can do to help you.'

I hesitantly followed him to the temple. He led me to a great room where we were greeted by more priests.

'Is this the woman?' one asked. The old priest nodded.

'What's going on?' I asked.

Suddenly, they were all closing in on me. I raised my dagger and felt a sharp blow to the back of my head.

'How dare you come into our temple threatening our lives!' the old priest yelled at me.

I was hit repeatedly until I was knocked out. When I regained consciousness, I was tied to a large log that was sticking out of water. Fur and blood surrounded me, and I felt something heavy and warm draped over my head; I was otherwise completely naked. I glanced around through blurred vision and noticed I was in a lake, a large crowd of people surrounding me.

'Sekhmet, goddess of destruction!' I heard a man's voice from behind me. 'You have come to quench your bloodlust and we must do so to send you back to Ra!'

I felt a sudden jolt of pain as I was stabbed in the back several times. The water around me quickly turned red as my blood mixed with it. The crowd gasped.

'See, we have turned this water into blood, so that you may drink and be satisfied!' the priest behind me yelled.

I tried to speak, but only gasped in pain. The log lowered towards the blood-stained lake and I could see my reflection. My right eye was black and blue, almost swollen shut. However, I could still see what was on my head. They had captured and skinned the lioness and placed her head on top of mine. Organs and bones removed, her skin dangled over my body. They dunked me under water for what seemed like an eternity. They raised me up, stabbed me again, and lowered me into the water. They repeated this until I finally died."

Sam and I waited for her to go on, but she stopped talking.

"That's so terrible," Sam finally said. "So you were killed and turned into legend by the very people who killed you?"

Sekhmet nodded.

"When I died, I was given the choice to become an angel; a dark angel specifically. No paradise for me, even though it meant seeing my husband and daughters again. I think I was always meant to be a fighter *and* a healer. So here I am, an eternity of fighting those who try to tip the balance of good and evil. I used to hate how I look, but I came to embrace it. I look like the monster they thought I was. I remember when the people who killed me died. They thought they would be ushered into the afterlife by Anubis. None of the gods they worshiped existed. But when they saw me and realized what they had done to me and so many other innocent people, they were terrified. They spent their lives making sure Osiris would give them a peaceful afterlife, only to spend eternity in Hell for being the real monsters."

"I'm so sorry," I said. "For everything that happened to you."

"Thank you," she smiled. "I appreciate that."

"You could imagine how shocked I was when I first met her," Dumah chuckled. "And then when I found out what had happened to her..."

"Dumah and I were pretty fast friends," Sekhmet gently rubbed her head against Dumah's thigh. He patted between her ears.

"Why do you choose to walk like that, Sekhmet?" Sam asked.

"I'm faster on all fours," she explained. "Also, I can pounce from down here if we're attacked. I feel more powerful in this position."

Sam and I looked around.

"Don't worry," Dumah said. "Two dark angels and a death angel? You're as safe as you can get."

"Until you get to Hell," Barry laughed.

"Aren't we in Hell already?" I asked.

Barry and Sekhmet chuckled.

"This isn't Hell, love," Sekhmet replied. "This is The Space Between Spaces."

"Huh?" I prodded.

"There are five realms," she explained. "There's Earth, which is where you are when you're alive. When you die, you are sent to Processing or The Space Between Spaces until you are sent to either Paradise/Heaven or Hell."

"So, are we still in Limbo?" I asked.

"Yes, that is an alternative name," she purred.

"And Processing is Purgatory because it prepares you for Heaven or Paradise?"

"Yes," Sekhmet nodded. "Processing is only for those who are about to go to Paradise. Sentencing is Hell's version of it."

"Sentencing?"

"When a person dies, they go to either Processing or Sentencing. If you go to Processing, you're welcomed by a greeter. If you go to

Sentencing, you kind of just 'wake up,' not really understanding what happened. If it's a bad enough sentence, you go straight to Hell. Otherwise, you wait around in the Space Between Spaces. This gives people the chance to realize the situation and become a better person-"

"Or continue being sinful pricks who could care less where they end up," Barry interrupted.

"What about the souls in the water that attacked the boat?" I asked.

"The Restless? They're souls who don't move onto either Heaven or Hell. Sometimes when people die, they get stuck somewhere outside of Processing. The problem with that is there's nowhere for them to go, and they have to go *somewhere*. They refuse to go to Hell to wait out their sentence, and Heaven won't take them, so they wander until they end up at the shore. The Sea of Anathema draws them in like moths to a flame. There's something almost hypnotic about the water."

"So they all get dumped in the sea to float around forever?" I insisted. "That seems almost crueler than Hell."

"Trust me," Barry cleared his throat loudly. "It's not."

"Wait, what's the difference between dark angels and death angels?" I asked. "Also, what makes you all different from other angels?"

The three of them glanced at each other before Baraqiel spoke.

"Death angels are pretty much what humans refer to as grim reapers. Their sole purpose is to be present at death to usher them into the afterlife. God doesn't like the idea of anyone being completely alone when they die."

"That's probably why you didn't have a death angel with you when you died," Dumah looked at me. "You were surrounded by family. A lot of people don't get that."

"Dark angels," Baraqiel continued, "are soldiers for God. We do the dangerous, dirty work."

"Like the archangels?" I asked.

"Not at all like the archangels," Sam laughed. "Those guys are God-made. Dark angels and death angels, like guardian angels, used to be human."

"Archangels are the elite of Heaven," Barry continued. "They're there to guard Heaven in case it ever is attacked."

"Which it won't ever be," Dumah grumbled. "Satan isn't *that* stupid."

"They also supervise over all other angels," Sam added.

"They *do* respect us dark angels though," Sekhmet pointed out. Dumah scoffed.

"They do!" she repeated. "We're the ones out in the field working to keep demons at bay. If it weren't for us, things would be out of control. And you know that."

"Things already are out of control," Sam murmured.

"We're more or less border patrol," Baraqiel laughed. "Which is why a lot of us stick to the shorelines. We're the first line of defense in case any demons try anything nutty."

"Nutty," Dumah mimicked. "Interesting choice of words for demons trying to take over Heaven."

"Could demons ever do that?" I asked.

"No," Sam, Sekhmet, and Baraqiel said at the same time. I looked at Dumah, who just slowly shook his head.

I saw a small house about a hundred yards from us in a clearing up ahead. I stopped for a moment. I could still hear the water, but we were far away from the shore. I could also hear things moving around us in the trees, but no one else seemed bothered by it. The chittering and low growling of unseen creatures made my hair stand on end. I picked up the pace to get closer to the group, feeling like we could get ambushed any second. Barry and the others reached the house and began to walk inside. It felt like something was right on my tail, so in a panic I sprinted towards the house. I jumped through the front door and landed hard on the floor. Everyone turned to me. I looked back at the front door and saw shadows quickly approaching, just outside.

"What the fuck are those?" I cried. Barry slammed the door closed.

"Exactly what you think they are," Barry sighed.

"Demons?" I whispered. He nodded.

"The edge of Hell isn't a safe neighborhood during the daytime," Baraqiel chuckled. "But at night? Forget about it."

"We have to stay inside at night time," Dumah said.

"But that cuts our time in half!" I snapped. "We can't stay cooped up every single night!"

"We can," Dumah growled. "And we will."

"None of us need sleep!" I yelled. "This is a waste of time! You can just use your sword to get past them. We're not even in actual Hell yet! We should get going if-"

"WE WILL LEAVE WHEN I SAY SO," Dumah's voice boomed. The space around grew silent as he continued. "YOU HAVE NO IDEA WHAT YOU ARE GETTING YOURSELF INTO HERE, SO YOU WILL DO AS I SAY."

I glared at him until he stormed off. Sam came over and put her hands on my shoulders.

"It'll be fine," she assured me. "We'll crash here until morning and then be on our way. We're right outside Hell, so we'll get in and start finding your boyfriend. Emma, I promise I will ensure you're back before your time runs out."

"That's not what I'm worried about," I started to cry. "I'm worried I'll have to leave before my time runs out, and I won't be able to get to Alastor quickly enough."

"Trust me," she smiled. "We'll find him. Come sit down and relax."

"Would anyone like some tea?" Sekhmet asked.

"I would love some," Sam replied. "And one for Emma as well."

"No tea," Dumah mumbled.

"It's been blessed," Sekhmet assured him. "And it's chamomile. It'll help relax you."

He shook his head.

"I'm fine," I muttered, sitting down on some pillows on the floor.

"Sam?" I whispered. She leaned in. "Is this crazy? Seriously. It wasn't like we were married or even together that long."

"Are you regretting your decision?" Sam snorted.

"No, I'm genuinely concerned for his soul. I don't know how I can spend the rest of eternity knowing I was the reason someone killed themselves."

"You didn't make anyone do anything, Emma."

"I know. God, if he would have just waited...maybe-" I started crying. "Maybe he wouldn't have done it. Maybe he would have just mourned for me and healed from it over time."

"What if..." Sam trailed off.

"What?" I asked.

"Um," Sam hesitated. "What if we do find Alastor? What will you say to him?"

"I'm sorry, I love him more than anything, and I wish he hadn't done it, and I'll do whatever I can to fix it."

"And what if he doesn't take your apology well?"

"I wouldn't blame him," I exhaled. "I keep playing different scenarios in my mind. But I know I won't know what to do when the time comes. I have this weird feeling in my gut that no matter how much I prepare for this, it will not go as planned. So I might as well not stress over what could happen."

"I think that's a smart idea," Sam smiled. "Just focus on the now. One step at a time."

I nodded and watched Sekhmet and Baraqiel talking on the other side of the room while Dumah sat silently.

"What do you think about Dumah?" Sam asked. "Do you think we can trust him?"

"I hope so," I answered. "At this point, we don't have a choice."

"We can tell him we'll take it from here and trek on, just the two of us."

"Two gals who have never been to Hell, walking around alone?" I laughed. "Not the smartest idea."

"Yeah," Sam chuckled. "You're right."

"Do you remember when we went on the field trip to the zoo?" I asked.

"Yeah."

"Everyone was too scared to pet that baby alligator even though the zookeeper told us repeatedly that nothing bad would happen. You were the only one brave enough to go up and touch it. They even let you hold it, all by yourself!"

"Emma," Sam rolled her eyes. "Its mouth was tied shut. It wasn't going to hurt anyone."

"We were all still too afraid to go near it, though," I explained. "You've never been scared of anything."

"I was scared when I was dying," she tucked her knees up to her chest and hugged them. "All I could think about was how much I would miss. I was so sad and angry, and confused. I almost didn't leave Earth when my time ran out. I wanted to stay behind, watch over my friends and family, and see where their lives ended. I guess I was so good at it that they offered me a job. When they asked who I wanted to guard, you were the first person who came to mind."

A tear rolled down Sam's cheek, and she wiped it away.

"It's funny that all you remember about the zoo field trip was the alligator thing," Sam snorted. "My mom didn't send me lunch money for the field trip. I begged her not to pack my lunch so I could eat at the zoo's restaurant like everyone else."

I felt myself start to blush. I knew what she was going to say next.

"You told me my ham sandwich and chips looked better than anything on the menu at the restaurant and asked if you could buy my sandwich. I was the dirty, poor kid who was made fun of for it. I acted tough and acted like it never bothered me when kids would say mean shit about my family. But it bothered me a lot. And you never cared about my clothes always being too small or that I never wore name-brand shoes. You liked me the way I was."

I started crying too.

"I didn't fully realize what you were doing at the time with the whole sandwich thing," Sam wept. "But thank you. That was the nicest thing anyone had ever done for me. Ever."

I leaned over and hugged Sam.

"All right," Sekhmet sighed. "I'm getting restless. I need some entertainment."

She stood up, stretched, and grabbed a curved blade from the table.

"Where are you going with that khopesh?" Dumah asked.

"I'm just going out to stretch my legs," Sekhmet winked.

"The cat in her can't resist a good hunt," Baraqiel laughed.

"I'll be back at sunrise," Sekhmet reassured. "Lock the door behind me."

Baraqiel unlocked the door, let Sekhmet out, and quickly locked it behind her.

"She wouldn't be able to sit still, even if her afterlife depended on it," he chuckled.

Sam and I spent the rest of the night mainly talking about what I had done during my life. Occasionally we would hear noises outside like growls, screaming, or scratching. Every time, all of us in the house would pause, wait for it to stop, and then go back to what we were doing. Finally, Sam nudged my arm and pointed to Dumah. He stiffly stood up, stretched, and started going through his stuff.

"Is it time?" I asked him.

"I'm going to keep some things here. I don't want to carry a bunch of stuff, especially if we're going to try and get as much distance covered as possible before the next nightfall. I want you to take some of this, though, okay?"

I nodded. Dumah grabbed my belt that held my dagger's scabbard. He started sliding some small bottles and pouches onto the belt. He handed it to me and motioned for me to put it on.

"I'm going to go through everything, and I want you to listen very carefully," Dumah growled. "These bottles here are holy water. You have four, but don't go through them too quickly. Holy water will burn anyone who resides in Hell. If we run into some of the stronger demons, it'll just piss them off more than hurt them. But-"

There was a knock on the door. Baraqiel opened the door and let Sekhmet inside. She was covered in blood and seemed slightly out of breath.

"Have fun?" Baraqiel asked.

"Had a blast," Sekhmet sighed happily before taking a seat in the corner to clean herself off.

"Anyways," Dumah pointed to five dark vials on my belt. "Be very, very careful with those. Those have the blood of the Son in them. You throw them at a demon, and they explode like a grenade."

Next, Dumah described the pouches hanging from my belt.

"The first pouch has crushed cabbage palm in it. It's deadly to demons if they ingest it in any way or get it on their skin. It puts them in anaphylactic shock. The second pouch is wine. Seven popes have blessed it, and it has extraordinary healing properties. You'll feel fatigued easily and this will give you energy to keep going. Not to mention if you get hurt, this is like a liquid elixir. This is the only thing I want you to consume while we're here. There will be many offers to eat and drink while we travel, and you absolutely cannot eat or drink anything from Hell. Do you understand me?"

I nodded slowly.

"I will also carry a pouch of wine, and Sam will have one as well. If you run out, let us know. A lot of things here will tempt you. But you have to stay strong and refuse."

Sekhmet came up behind me with a bowl of white liquid and started painting something on the back of my jacket.

"It is called the 'Eye of Ra,'" she said softly. "The paint I am using is coated with white salt. This will protect you from your enemies. Even those who pretend they are not your enemies."

While Sekhmet painted on my back, Baraqiel came up to me and smiled. He held out a gold necklace.

"Do you know what this is?" he asked as I took it. I looked at it and smiled.

"It's a Star of David," I answered and put it around my neck.

"Yes," he grinned. "Another form of protection. We're not sure what to expect once you get in. Hopefully, no one will notice that you're not supposed to be here. Sekhmet and I have agreed to meet Dumah and you at a secret meeting point.

We'll ensure it's safe for you and set up a hideout for nighttime."

"Thank you," I said. "I appreciate everything you all are doing for me."

"You're a good soul, Emma," Baraqiel said. "We can all see it. Those are worth protecting."

"Thanks, Barry."

"Okay, okay," Dumah grumbled. "We need to get going soon. It's almost daylight. One more thing, though."

Dumah was holding a small silver container in his hand. He opened it and dipped his thumb in what looked like the black sand from the beach. He started muttering in another language and drew on my forehead.

"A cross?" I asked.

"How'd you guess?" Sam asked.

"I grew up going to Ash Wednesday every year," I laughed.

"You're getting the VIP treatment with those saint's ashes," Barry said.

"Saint's ashes?" I asked.

"Saint John," he answered.

I stared at him.

"The prophet, John?" he continued. "John the Baptist?"

"His ashes are on my forehead?" I gasped and lifted my hand to my face. Dumah grabbed my hand.

"Do not touch the ashes," Dumah said, closely leaning in. "I don't give those ashes out to just anyone. They're extremely special. And I've already blessed you, so don't mess up the cross, or I'll have to waste more ashes to draw another one."

"Done!" Sekhmet exclaimed. "Normally, there's a bit of a protection ceremony I like to perform to strengthen the symbol, but it'll still work."

"All right," Sam sighed. "If everyone is finally done with their rituals and talismans, can we please get going now? We're wasting daylight."

Sekhmet hugged me.

"Good luck. We'll meet up this evening, but until then, safe travels."

"Thank you," I replied.

"Are you ready?" Barry asked.

"Yes," Dumah answered. "Let's go."

We walked for almost thirty minutes, none of us talking, so we could keep an ear out for anything dangerous. We came out of the trees and stood in front of a large stone wall. It went on either side of us as far as the eye could see. A large archway was in the middle with a sign carved into the stone.

"Flectere si nequeo superos, Acheronta movebo," Barry said.

"If I can not bend the will of Heaven, I shall move Hell," Dumah translated as if he knew I was wondering what it meant.

I looked through the archway. There was nothing but desert ahead of us.

"This is it?" I asked. "This is the gateway to Hell? But there's nothing here."

Sam looked around, frightened.

"This is it," Baraqiel said. "We'll meet up later."

Dumah and Baraqiel shook hands before he walked back into the trees. Dumah looked at Sam and me.

"All right," he sighed. "Let's get this over with."

17

The three of us slowly walked through the archway. As soon as we were on the other side, the wind whipped at my face, and sand stung my skin. The temperature was scorching, although the sun was overcast with clouds. There was nothing but desert around us.

"Where is everyone?" I asked, looking around.

"There's not much around the entrance," Dumah explained. "We'll be reaching the more populated area soon; Luckily, we don't have to go too far into Hell since we're looking for a recent suicide."

"A *possible* suicide," Sam corrected him. I smiled at her. "We're still not sure what exactly happened."

"Can't you guys just fly there?" I asked. "And one of you carried me? This is taking forever."

"We need to keep a low profile," Dumah said. "Just because angels *can* enter Hell doesn't mean they're welcome. We don't need to draw any unwanted attention to ourselves. This would all be a lot easier if it was just me."

"Well, that didn't happen," I sneered. "You don't have to keep saying that you wanted to come alone. Sam and I know how much you don't want us here. The sooner we find Alastor, the sooner you'll be rid of me."

Dumah stopped as if he were going to respond but continued walking again.

"Why is it so hot?" I asked a few minutes later.

"Emma," Sam smiled. "We're in Hell. Duh?"

I weakly smiled at her before the wind picked up even harder. I put one palm out in front of my face to try and block the sand from kicking up. Dumah reached into the inner pocket of his jacket and pulled out a piece of cloth. He wrapped it around my face, covering my mouth and nose, and then draped it around my head.

"Better?" he asked. I nodded.

"But do I look like you now?" I joked.

"Fortunately for you, no," he softly replied.

We trekked through the sand for a little over two hours before something in the distance caught my eye. At first, all I could see was a stack of smoke, but as we got closer, I could tell that the smoke was coming from a blue car on fire. The sight of it out in the middle of nowhere made me uneasy.

"Someone probably stole it and drove it out here just to set it on fire," Dumah sighed. "Vehicles are constantly being stolen, taken apart, or trashed here. Zero respect for other people's property. Just wait until we get into the city."

"What city?" I asked. Dumah pointed ahead towards the hill we were reaching.

I walked ahead of Dumah and Sam, eager to see what he was talking about. Over the hill was a city skyline filled with dilapidated buildings and rubble. It reminded me of images I had seen of a city after a hurricane or tornado had gone through. Some of the buildings had graffiti written on them or broken windows. The closer we got to the town, the more stranded and destroyed cars we saw. Soon, we also started seeing people as well. Most of them looked unhappy, and they had dirty or torn clothing. I also noticed that everyone wore the same thing: a white or gray shirt and jeans. Some women were wearing oversized shirts with no pants, almost like dresses. The further into the city we got, the worse things looked. I saw people sitting on the sidewalks using drugs. There were people in alleyways having sex. We walked past several fights. This is what I had always imagined Detroit was like at nighttime.

"Everyone kind of just does whatever they want here," I said.

"Yeah," Dumah muttered. "This is the only place in all planes where God doesn't exist. Anyone is free to do whatever they want, except be happy."

"But it's like a prison," Sam said. "They can get out early on good behavior."

"And then they can go to Heaven?" I asked.

"It's a little more complicated than that," Dumah replied. "But essentially, yes. Every soul has a chance for redemption. It's ultimately their choice, however. Many people come here, like their freedom, and spend eternity the same miserable way they did on Earth. I don't understand it."

"You, of all people, should understand," Sam scoffed. "This was how it all started for you."

"What!" I said, shocked.

"How do you know that?" Dumah looked at Sam.

"It's true, isn't it?" she shrugged.

"It....is," he hesitated. "I was originally sent to Hell when I died thousands of years ago. But that's not what's important. What's important is I learned from my mistakes and fully leaned into the healing and rebirth."

"Why-" I started.

"Don't," he snapped at me.

"Don't ask people what they got sent here for," Sam leaned in and whispered. "It's not kosher."

I stared at the back of Dumah while we walked, wondering about him. I was putting my trust in someone who started off in Hell and was now a Death Angel. What if he was dangerous? What if he was planning to betray me? I suddenly felt very unsure of Dumah. Sam could tell how worried I was.

"Hey," she smiled. "Don't look so frazzled. I won't let anything happen to you here, okay? I may be small, but I'm tough."

We exchanged smiles and kept following Dumah through the city. We arrived at a black building with half the letters on its sign missing. I could tell at one time that it said SENTENCING on it. We went inside, and there were very few people in the lobby. It didn't seem as bright and happy as the Processing I was used to. We approached the elevator, and I watched Dumah read the directory. There was a list with floor numbers next to them. I didn't have a chance to read the whole list but noticed the words, Suicides, Greed, Pride, and Wrath.

"We want the third floor," Dumah muttered.

We all got on the elevator, as well as two other men. Dumah pushed the button with a three on it.

"Which floor?" I asked the two men.

"Three for me as well," one of them said softly. He was a kid, no more than sixteen years old. His face was covered in acne, and his hair was greasy.

"Five," said the other man. He was very handsome and tan. I couldn't remember what the fifth floor was, but by judging the look on Sam's face, it wasn't good.

We rode the elevator in silence until we reached the third floor. Dumah, Sam, the teenage boy, and I all stepped off. There was a desk right in front of the elevator with no one sitting at it. I looked back at the handsome man who needed the fifth floor. He was licking his lips towards us, which made me feel uneasy until I realized he was doing it towards Sam and Sam only; then, I felt sick to my stomach. The elevator door closed, and I stood closer to Sam than usual.

"I can fend for myself," Sam whispered. "I could have taken that pervert on easily."

"I know," I replied. "I'd still try and protect you, though."

"Does anyone work here?" the teenage boy asked loudly.

"Yes, yes," said a tiny voice from the other room. "Just one moment."

A short woman with big permed hair came out from one of the back rooms. Under her teased blonde hair, she wore blue eyeshadow behind reading glasses. She wore a purple dress with white polka dots and matching purple heels. She had a name tag on her dress that said, "HELLo, my name is Debbie." I smirked at the pun on her name tag and thought she looked rather friendly for working in Hell.

"What can I do for ya'll?" she asked sweetly in a thick Southern accent. "Starting with who was here first."

"The three of us are together," Dumah pointed to us. "We're wondering if you have records of someone who may have arrived here recently."

"What is the date of the person's death?" Debbie asked.

"We don't know," Dumah replied. "We do know his name, though."

"That won't be much help," Debbie snorted. "But if you don't mind looking through some paperwork, you can help yourself to the new arrival records. We're short-staffed, so it's just me up here. I'm about three weeks behind in filing, so everything is in stacks like this."

She pointed to a large stack of papers on her desk. My jaw dropped.

"We have to go through all of that?" I asked.

"Oh, no," she laughed. "This is what the mailroom just brought up about an hour ago. I'll take you to the sorting room."

Debbie looked at the teenage boy and pointed to the chairs by the wall.

"You just sit yourself down, and I'll be right with you, sugar."

We followed Debbie to one of the back rooms. She turned the light on, and my heart sank. The entire room was full of boxes, which were all filled with papers. Each paper was a person who hadn't been filed into the system yet.

"Most folks who get jobs here don't want the boring desk jobs. Can't say I blame them."

"Where do we even start?" I asked.

"Nothing is in any particular order, but the older files are on the left side of the room and get newer to the right. You're more than welcome to take however long you need."

I looked at Dumah and Sam.

"Let me know if ya'll need anything else!" Debbie smiled before closing the door.

"Where the fuck do we even begin?" I threw my hands up in the air. "This is going to take forever!"

"Not if all three of us are doing it," Dumah said.

"But then we're all stuck in a room when we could be out there looking for him!" Sam argued.

"More hands in here means we'll find his file faster," Dumah responded.

"But Sam's right," I said. "What if one of you stays here going through the files, and I go with the other angel to places Alastor would be at."

"We're not splitting up," Dumah growled. "Not after the big deal you made coming along with me. We're going to stick together."

"I don't have much time left!" I snapped, holding my watch up. Ninety-seven hours were left.

"In four days and one hour, I have to be back at Processing," I teared up. "Under 100 hours. I can't afford to waste any more time. I'm not staying cooped up at nighttime because you think something bad will happen to me. I'm already dead! I'm not staying here and looking through piles of paper. Both of you can go a lot faster than me anyway."

I sighed.

"I'm not wasting any more time arguing either. One of you can come with me, or both of you can stay here and go through the paperwork. Just give me an address to meet everyone later."

Dumah and Sam looked at me, not saying anything.

"So, who's coming with me?" I asked. "Or am I going by myself?"

"I'll go," Sam said.

"Absolutely not," Dumah growled.

"Look," Sam scoffed. "This is my very best friend. I'm her guardian angel. I know I *look* like a kid, but I'm smart. I have skills."

"You don't know your way around here," Dumah argued. "I think it would be best for you to stay here and review the files."

"I'm going," I said. "When you guys figure it out, come find me."

"She doesn't trust you!" Sam yelled. "Why would she want to go anywhere with you? She trusts *me*."

"Dumah," I sighed. "Can you give Sam the address we're supposed to meet Barry and Sekhmet at later?"

"What?" Sam said.

"Dumah's right," I explained to her. "You don't know your way around. If you stay here, you can go through the files quickly while Dumah and I can cover some ground. Maybe get some leads."

"Are you serious?" Sam sounded offended.

"Don't take it personally," I smiled as Dumah wrote something on paper. "We'll see you after a while, okay?"

Sam slowly took the paper from Dumah and nodded, giving him a dirty look.

"You better not let anything happen to her," Sam said to Dumah.

"Meet us around six," Dumah responded before turning to me. "Let's go."

I waved to Sam and left with Dumah. Once we were back outside, my anxiety flared up again.

"Most of these people won't mess with you," Dumah said. "They're just here trying to make the best of a bad situation. It's the demons you have to watch out for. They'll do anything to get you or *me* to stay here."

"Can they do that to you?" I asked. "Even though you're an angel?"

"Ah, angels fall though, don't they?" he explained. "Since Lucifer became ruler of this realm, he and God have had an ongoing turf war with humans. Lucifer has the upper hand because God doesn't interfere with human endeavors. Sure, angels can influence, but free will makes it impossible to persuade humans to be good. Lucifer and his demons can do whatever they want to convince humans that *his* way of living *is* the fun way. The happy way. Money, sex, food, power...why do you think all of those things make you feel good? Because the devil will tell you, God is trying to keep all good stuff away from you. He can't enjoy worldly desires, so He treats them as sins. Lucifer treats them as well-deserved rewards. Lucifer is excellent at making you feel shameless about your actions. Sexual deviance? Lucifer will tell you that if sex were bad, it wouldn't feel so good. Becoming rich? Lucifer would say that money was manufactured and God has no say in something that humans need for literally everything. You murder someone, and Lucifer would ask you, 'well, what did the other guy do to deserve it?' It's all trickery and mind games with the devil. And his favorite is suicide. Your life is the only thing you didn't choose. You didn't ask to be born. It's this huge burden that you're stuck with, for decades usually, until you slowly decay away by disease or die suddenly from something horrific like a car wreck or gunshot wound or an animal attack. Existing is the only choice you don't get to make. Then, if you don't want to exist anymore, God punishes you for it. I can't say I ever really agreed with that logic."

And that's when it hit me. I looked at Dumah.

"Yes," he sighed. "That's why I was originally sent here, and that's why I felt....compelled to help you. I understand why you and your boyfriend wanted to carry out your plan. Three thousand years ago, smallpox raged through what is now called 'ancient Egypt.' The woman I was in love with got very sick with it. She begged me not to come to see her, but I wouldn't listen. I didn't care if I got ill. I just wanted to be with her. At first, she was warm with fever and vomiting. She only had a few mouth sores, so we were hopeful it wasn't what is known as smallpox. But soon, her whole body was covered in blisters. She would cry out in pain and beg to die. Watching her suffer was devastating. So we talked one night after smallpox took away her sight, and she sincerely asked me to end her life. She didn't want to suffer anymore. So I poisoned her and myself, crawled into bed with her, and held each other until we passed. We didn't end up in the same place, obviously. At first, I was so angry with the gods...God. I had done right by her. I ended her suffering, and all we wanted was to be together forever.

Eventually, my anger subsided, and once I found out there was a way to get back to her, I did everything I could to make sure that happened. I got off easy with a 'mercy kill,' but suicide was what I was being punished for. When I was eventually welcomed into Paradise, after serving my sentence, she had forgotten all about me. She was in love with someone before me, and they had a daughter they had lost during childbirth. The three of them were obliviously happy together, and I didn't want to spoil that. I suppose that's why she was so eager to die. She wanted to be with them. But it worked out well for me. I didn't have to spend an eternity in Hell and became an angel. I didn't get to be a pretty one, but it sure beats the alternative. So, now you know my story. I don't want any sympathy. Just know that I understand why you two wanted to do what you did. And I admire you wanting to make things right with him. If he has committed suicide, the only way out of Hell is becoming a death angel, after being here a couple thousand years."

I wanted to hug him and tell him how sorry I was, but I knew he meant it when he said he didn't want my sympathy.

"So your whole existence revolves around death?" I asked. "No fun?"

"No. No fun."

"I have a question."

Dumah didn't respond.

"When I met you, you were at a military base."

"What's your question?"

"What were you doing there?"

"My job."

"Someone died there the day I met you?" I asked.

"A sergeant had a heart attack in his office. No one found him for quite some time."

"That's sad," I muttered.

"He slaughtered innocent women and children while deployed because he could get away with it. He's walking around here I'm sure."

We didn't talk the rest of the walk. I wanted to ask where we were going but decided it was better to trust him without questioning anything. Despite Sam's feelings about him, he hadn't given me a reason not to trust him. Even though he came off as cold and grumpy, Dumah made me feel safe. We stopped in front of a worn-down building made of stone. There was a sign in front that said, "Eclipse."

"What is this place?" I asked.

"Sort of an exclusive club."

"Will this help us find Alastor?"

"It will hopefully help us find some answers."

We walked up to the door, where a large man greeted us.

"Holy shit, Dumah!" he said, sounding surprised. "Haven't seen you around here in a long time."

"Been busy," Dumah muttered.

"Too busy to visit your old stomping grounds?" the man chuckled. "I mean, I know you work for the other side now, but you can't forget where you started from."

I looked at Dumah. His wing feathers seemed ruffled by this remark.

"Is he here?" Dumah asked.

"Yeah, he's here. I don't know if he'll be pleased to see you, though."

"He doesn't need to be happy. He just needs to talk."

"Fine," the large man moved aside. "But don't cause any problems in there. You might not be one of the pretty boys, but you're still an angel."

"I'm aware," Dumah replied before turning to me. "Let's go."

I followed closely behind Dumah. The man who greeted us stared at me until we were inside the building. And even when I couldn't see him anymore, it felt like he was still watching me.

18

We walked inside, and I immediately smelled cigars. I vaguely remembered my dad's dad and how he always smoked cigars. He died when I was very young, and my dad wasn't close to him at all, but the cigar smell was a powerful memory I had of him. The inside looked like a large banquet hall with about two dozen round tables in the middle and rows of booths on either side. Each booth had curtains for extra privacy, and I noticed that three of the booths had the curtains drawn. As we walked past the tables, I saw a few people sitting at them staring at us.

"Eyes forward," Dumah mumbled. "Act as if you belong here."

I attempted to relax, and my eager walk turned more into a strut. We approached a large red curtain, and Dumah drew it back for me to go through. Behind the curtain was a black door. Dumah knocked on it, and it opened, with no one on the other side. I stayed close behind Dumah as we went through the door, and it shut on its own behind us.

"Dumah," I heard a voice say.

The room we were in was very dimly lit. On the side of us, a figure sat behind a desk with glowing red eyes.

"Ah Puch," Dumah replied. "You mind if we talk? Preferably with the lights up."

The lights in the room got brighter, and I gasped. The figure sitting at the desk looked like a burn victim, with shiny gray skin that was deeply scarred. The skin around his giant maw was pulled back tight and showed jagged yellow teeth. There was no hair on his head but two bull-like horns, one above each ear. He was wearing a black suit jacket with nothing under it so that you could see his bare pale chest. His collarbone and sternum were sticking out as if they would puncture his paper-thin skin. There was a robust earthy smell coming from him.

"You have got to be the ugliest angel I have ever seen," Ah Puch said in high-pitched laughter.

"You're the last one who should be commenting on who is ugly," Dumah responded dryly. This only made Ah Puch laugh even more.

"You should have stayed down here," Ah Puch shook his head. "You'd be free to do whatever you want. Instead, you're just another one of God's bitch-boys. You could still come back to our side. Word on the street is that God's lost his touch. He doesn't have as many followers as he used to. Our side is winning. You don't want to play for the losing team, do you?"

"I think we have very different opinions of what is considered *losing*," Dumah growled. "I'd say eternal damnation is the very definition of losing. But that's not why I'm here."

"Then why *are* you here?" Ah Puch asked, putting his elbow on his desk and leaning his cheek into his balled-up fist. He swiveled in his chair while pretending to pout.

"We're looking for someone," Dumah said.

"If this is a bounty hunter gimmick, I want no part in it," Ah Puch wagged his finger and looked at me. "I'm many things, but I'm not a snitch."

"We're trying to find someone we think might be here. If he happens to be working for you, you could point us in the right direction."

"Who are *you*?" he asked me suddenly. Dumah stood in front of me.

"She's my...accomplice."

"She's your accomplice?" Ah Puch repeated and laughed. "What, is she not allowed to speak for herself?"

"My name is Emma," I found myself saying with a shaky voice. Ah Puch stood up slowly, revealing his black matching dress pants. He moved swiftly, gliding towards me, until he was directly in front of my face. Along with the earthy smell, he smelled faintly of rotting meat up close. He put my face in his hand and looked me over. Then, ever so gently, he leaned in and smelled me.

"You don't belong down here," he breathed.

"We're looking for my boyfriend," I said.

Ah Puch lifted his other hand and ran his thumb across my forehead. Dumah glared at him.

"These silly fucking talismans you think will protect you here," Ah Puch laughed before slowly licking the ashes off his thumb. "Hoaxes and gimmicks to make you feel safe. Not even Dumah can protect you here."

I glanced at Dumah, who still wasn't moving.

"Oh, did he not tell you? Your valiant hero can die here."

"Are you threatening me, Ah Puch?" Dumah asked.

Ah Puch laughed again.

"Wouldn't dream of it, *compa*," he continued. "We have too much of a history. As much as I hate you, I still like you. Can't say the same for other demons in charge here though. You just rub people the wrong way."

Ah Puch let go of my face and I started slowly stepping towards Dumah.

"Would you like to stay here?" Ah Puch asked me. "You could live with no rules for eternity."

"Cut it out, Ah Puch," Dumah got in between us. "She's not yours to recruit."

Dumah looked at me before glancing back at Ah Puch.

"I'll come back later when you're not so distracted, and we can talk one-on-one."

Ah Puch suddenly grabbed me and put his arms around me from behind. I tried wiggling free, but he was much stronger than I was. Dumah put his hand on his sword.

"Ah ah ah," Ah Puch tutted. "We don't need to do that and cause a scene. Leave her here with me, and you can be on your way."

Suddenly, I heard a sizzling sound and Ah Puch gasped and let me go. The front of his suit had charred.

"Seems as though you two have the cat bitch helping you as well," Ah Puch scoffed as he wiped at his clothes. "Not all of your talismans are hoaxes after all."

"She's not yours to take," Dumah drew his sword. "Hell gets almost 100,000 new people every day. You can let this one go. She's here with me and under my protection. Now, will you waste more time or answer some questions for us?"

"Why should I?" Ah Puch walked back to his seat. "Why should I help you at all? You left me high and dry to go to Heaven. And how did that work out for you? Was your lady waiting with open arms for you? Nope! She had forgotten all about you. You did her a favor, put her out of her misery, and she didn't give a shit about you."

"It doesn't matter," Dumah muttered.

"Of course it does!" Ah Puch laughed. "Don't you get it? Being nice and doing favors for people will never get you anywhere. Making other people happy doesn't make you happy. You have to look out for number one!"

"So then, why are you so upset that I left?" Dumah asked. "You seem to be doing well. I left two thousand years ago."

"We were supposed to be a team!" Ah Puch slammed his fist down on the desk. The sudden, loud noise made me jump. "You and I had a great thing going on here. You were my most trusted partner. My right-hand man. And then to find out you were going behind my back to get out of here, to get up there...."

Ah Puch slowly pointed up and then violently spit on the ground.

"It makes me sick," Ah Puch continued. "I took you under my wing and got you a good job here. You could have moved up quickly and had so much power. And you chose to become a death angel. An outcast. You'd rather be a reject on their side than come back here."

Ah Puch rubbed his brow and sighed.

"What's the name?" he asked.

"Alastor King," I said softly.

"Name doesn't ring a bell. I could get in touch with a few others and see what I can find. Do you have a place you're staying at?"

"Yes," Dumah said, sheathing his sword and pulling out a small piece of paper. "We're going to be hiding out with Sekhmet and Baraqiel. Here's the phone number to reach me at."

"I'll get in touch with you if I find anything," Ah Puch took the paper.

"We need to go," Dumah said to me.

"It was nice to meet you, Emma," Ah Puch smiled. "I hope to see you again very soon."

I nodded at him and turned back to Dumah.

"Oh and Dumah," Ah Puch added. "Grata domum."

Dumah paused for a brief moment before gesturing for me to leave. Once we were outside of the building, I sighed heavily.

"That was so scary," I said. "And we're not any closer than we were when we got here."

"Yes, but now we have someone networking on the inside to get us to your boyfriend faster," Dumah explained. "If Alastor has already been assigned somewhere, Ah Puch will find out quickly. And who knows? Maybe Sam has already found his file and has it waiting for us at the rendezvous."

"I've always hated that word," I said, picking up speed to keep pace with Dumah. "It looks like ren-dez-vows, but you pronounce it ron-day-voo. French has always irritated me. Nothing looks like it sounds. Of course, you could probably say the same about the English language. Although I read somewhere that Mandarin is the hardest language to learn. I wonder if English is even in the top ten hardest languages to learn. How many languages do you know?"

I looked at Dumah; he had stopped several feet behind, looking around.

"Dumah?" I asked.

Dumah was slowly drawing his sword. I looked around and noticed we were the only ones on the streets. The sun had set, and the streetlights were the only light besides Dumah's flaming sword. Without saying a word, we got closer standing back to back. The streetlights around us started flickering, and suddenly, a small hoard of demons closed in on us. They were all bald with shiny, scarred skin and wore torn, dirty rags for clothes that hung on their thin frames. As they got closer, I could see their sharp teeth as they snarled at us. They also had large sockets that housed their small, beady black eyes. Dumah raised his sword above his head. I froze, not knowing what to do.

"Grenade!" Dumah yelled at me. I grabbed one of my vials of blood and threw it. Just like a grenade, there was a small explosion. Several demons blew to pieces while a few more were instantly set on fire. They made horrible, animalistic screams that made the hair on the back of my neck stand. I watched the ones on fire stumble around blindly, arms flailing. Dumah charged at the two demons closest to him. He swung his sword, cutting one in half and decapitating the other. I still couldn't bring myself to move.

"Don't just stand there!" Dumah roared at me. "Do something!"

I fumbled around and grabbed what I thought was another blood grenade, but when I threw it at the demons closest to me, I realized it was just holy water. Their skin burned and steamed, making them scream at me. I started to back up as one of them lunged at me, sending me backward onto the ground.

"Oof!"

The demon pinning me down had its hands around my throat and chomped at my face. I used one hand to hold its neck back and my other hand to grab my dagger as I tried to catch my breath. The demon's hands were burning as it tried to choke me, and I could smell that same rotting odor I smelled from Ah Puch. I raised my dagger and drove it up through the demon's throat, into its skull. The demon went limp on top of me, and I wiggled out from under it. Dumah had taken out five more demons by himself, and another was running at me. I swung my dagger at it and missed. The demon grabbed me by the front of my shirt and raised me off my feet. I swung my dagger again, and it went into the side of its temple. It let go of me and dropped to the ground.

I pulled my dagger out of its head and grabbed a blood grenade, making sure it was indeed a grenade this time. I threw it at a group of demons closing in on me. It exploded, and I held my arm up to block body parts from hitting me in the face. I checked in on Dumah, and a demon had him pinned up to a wall, his sword on the ground. I grabbed a handful of crushed cabbage palms and ran over.

"Hey!" I yelled at the demon. It looked over at me. I blew the handful into its face, and it released Dumah, howling in pain. Dumah grabbed his sword and swung it hard, slicing the demon diagonally. The couple of demons that were left scurried away. Dumah looked at me and put his sword away.

"Not bad," he said.

"You're welcome," I scoffed. "I just saved your ass."

"I had it," he replied.

"Sure," I rolled my eyes.

"We must get to our safe spot before more come back."

"Why did they randomly attack us?" I asked, rubbing my sore neck.

"I'm an angel," Dumah chuckled. "I'm not welcomed here. Demons like to pick fights with angels, especially if their only backup is a human."

"I think I did a pretty good job considering it was my first demon fight!"

"Yeah," Dumah responded. "Not too bad."

We hurried down more open, populated streets until we reached an alleyway. Dumah looked around before going into the shadows. I followed behind, keeping my hand on my dagger. Dumah stopped at a street-level window that led to the building on our right. He pushed in and gestured for me to go in.

"Are you fucking kidding me?" I asked seriously.

"It's safe. I promise."

I moved slowly to the window, looking around the alley. I sat down and slid under Dumah's hand, which held the window open. I landed unsteadily on my feet inside. Dumah jumped in after me. Everything was dark and quiet. Dumah moved ahead of me through the building, which looked like an abandoned department store. Racks and cases were everywhere like they once held clothes and jewelry. Mannequins lay broken on the floor. We made our way down an escalator that no longer moved, and Dumah pointed over at a light coming from a back corner of the store. We moved closer, and I saw Sekhmet and Baraqiel standing in defensive poses. They eased when they saw us.

"Oh, thank the gods," Sekhmet sighed. "We were starting to think you had been ambushed or something."

"Oh, we were!" I exclaimed.

"What?" Baraqiel asked. "How did you get away?"

"Emma helped me fight them off," Dumah said, holding his side and collapsing on the floor next to the lanterns they had lit.

"Are you all right?" Sekhmet asked, sitting down next to Dumah.

"I'm fine," Dumah groaned. "Just some bruises. Nothing to worry about."

"Is Sam here?" I asked.

"We thought she was with you two," Sekhmet answered.

"We separated earlier today," Dumah said. "I gave her this address, so she knows how to find us."

"What if she's attacked like we were?" I asked. "What if those things attacked her?"

"She'll be fine," Dumah sighed. "Maybe she's running behind because she found some information on Alastor. That'd be great. Then we could be done with this place."

"Emma, You look faint," Sekhmet said. "Have you drank any wine since you arrived?"

I shook my head and grabbed my pouch from my belt. I took a sip of wine. It was like drinking an energy drink. I felt more awake, more energetic, and just healthier. I drank the whole pouch in three gulps, and Sekhmet handed me hers. I replaced my empty one with the new full one on my belt.

"That's better, huh?" Sekhmet smiled.

"Barry, you've been quiet," I said. "What's up?"

"He has a bad feeling," Sekhmet said sarcastically. "I almost couldn't get him to come with me."

I walked over to Baraqiel, and he looked at me.

"What's going on?" I asked softly, putting my hand on his shoulder.

"I don't know," he said, not looking at me. "I feel like something bigger than us is pulling all the strings. I can't quite put my finger on it, but something just doesn't feel right. You two were attacked, and now Sam is missing."

"She's not missing," Dumah sighed. "She'll be here."

"Did you find out anything from Ah Puch?" Sekhmet asked Dumah.

"No, he didn't recognize the name but said he'd be contacting me if he heard anything."

"I bet anything that's who sent those demons after you," Sekhmet growled. "He's held a grudge against you for leaving. It only makes sense."

"He's mad at me," Dumah replied. "But I think he would still help me when asked. Besides, he knows I can take on a couple of dozen runts on my own. It was just a little easier having Emma there."

"Runts?" I asked.

"It's what many of us call the type of demons you faced," Sekhmet smirked. "They're weaker demons, like pawns. Big in numbers but can be taken out easily. Tanks, on the other hand, are a lot harder to take down."

"They're huge and can take a lot of damage," Baraqiel said. "But they're also slow and stupid."

"There's also Wasps, which are the bat shit crazy ones," Sekhmet added. "And Guards, which is pretty obvious. They guard the higher-ranked demons. The higher ranked ones have special jobs like influencing humans, seeing over wars, murders, and other violent crimes, and are constantly fighting for the right-hand seat of the Devil. It's all about power here. Everyone craves it and wants to take it away from other demons. There have been battles that have lasted centuries because some demons wanted more authority over others. It's ridiculous."

"Do you guys hear that?" Baraqiel hushed us. We all looked around.

Dumah drew his sword, and Sekhmet got on all fours, baring her sharp feline teeth. I put my hand on my dagger and slowly stood up. Out of the shadows, Sam appeared with her bow drawn. As soon as she saw me, she lowered the bow and sighed. I ran over and hugged her.

"You're okay!" I said, pulling back and looking at her. "*Are* you okay?"

Sam looked a little worn down. Her face and clothes were dirty, and the look on her face was a concerned one.

"I'm fine," she sighed again. "Going through the files took longer than I thought since I was the only one doing it. Did you guys find anything?"

"No," Dumah responded before I could. "But my source is looking into it for me."

"Source?" Sam repeated. "Who?"

"*My source*," Dumah muttered, looking at me. I nodded at Sam slowly.

"Well, I wasn't able to find anything either," Sam scoffed. "Emma, are you even sure he's here?"

"Yes, I'm sure!" I snapped. "He's here. He's not on Earth, and he's not on his way to Heaven. He's here."

I looked down at my watch.

"I have 93 hours left. We need to make a game plan for what's next."

"Because obviously none of Dumah's plans are working so far," Sam sneered.

"And what plans have you come up with?" he asked her. She looked away without answering.

"When people get sent here, what happens after they're sentenced?" I asked.

"Usually, they get put into some sort of job as soon as possible," Sekhmet replied. "Sometimes it can take a little bit to find someone a job, so they kind of just get some free time to roam around, taking in how miserable it is here."

"What do people do for free time here?" Sam asked.

"Pretty much anything they enjoyed doing in life," Sekhmet answered. "Gambling, drugs, sex, sports, eating, watching tv, or reading. This isn't as bad as Hell can get. It's more annoying than anything. Books have pages missing. Movies get cut off before the end. I'm surprised they even started letting people watch movies here! Or if you order a pizza, it will most likely be overcooked, undercooked, cold, or not the kind you ordered. If you want to go to a driving range, every golf club will be different from the one you need. Want to play basketball? All of the balls are slightly deflated. It is not so much physical torture as it is psychological torture. It's boring and sad."

"The worst part is the family rule," Baraqiel chimed in. "If you have family here, like a mother or father, none of you recognize each other. Husbands and wives walk right past each other without knowing they were madly in love and married for twenty years. You can't even be miserable in Hell with loved ones. Because this place thrives on sorrow and pain."

"I'd much rather be stuck here than the other places," Sekhmet said. "Here, at least you're not being ripped apart over and over for eternity."

"Or being eaten alive by various bugs and animals," Baraqiel added. "Or being burned alive."

Suddenly, a loud ringing sound made us all jump. Dumah hurried over to the phone mounted on the wall and answered it.

"Hello?" he said. "Yes. Do you? Uh, I can. All right. All right. That's fine. Okay, I'll see you soon."

Dumah hung up and turned to us.

"That was Ah Puch," he said to me. "He thinks he has a lead on Alastor."

19

My heart started racing.

"I'm coming with you," I said.

"No," Dumah shook his head. "It's too dangerous for you to go out right now. Let me talk to him, and I'll come back for you in the morning."

"I'll be fine!" I argued. "I was able to help you earlier!"

"NO!" Dumah snapped at me. "Let me talk to him first. I promise I'll let you know as soon as I find out something. Just let me handle this alone, and trust me."

I looked at Sekhmet, Baraqiel, and Sam. None of them sided with me.

"It's safer for you to stay here with us," Sam explained. "Just sit tight until daylight, and we'll venture out, okay?"

I looked back at Dumah.

"I'll be back as soon as possible," he said, placing a hand on my shoulder. "I promise."

I threw my arms around Dumah and hugged him. He cleared his throat and patted my back before pulling away quickly.

"I'll be in touch," Dumah glanced at Baraqiel, who nodded at him.

Dumah disappeared into the darkness, and I sat down next to Sam.

"Don't worry," Sam smiled weakly. "I have a good feeling about this. I bet Dumah's source has a good lead on Alastor."

I returned a smile and stared out the window, waiting for daylight. Sekhmet and Baraqiel did most of the talking for the rest of the night. Sekhmet shared stories of ancient Egypt and her family. Sam and I listened to them silently. Finally, I could spot the tiniest bit of orange coming from the windows. I peeked out one of them and noticed that more people were on the streets again.

"We should head out," Sam suggested.

"What if Dumah comes back?" I asked. "Shouldn't we stay?"

"And waste more daytime?" Sam argued. "We should keep searching. Sekhmet and Baraqiel can stay here and wait for Dumah."

"I'll stay," Sekhmet replied. "Baraqiel, I want you to go with them. Just to ease my mind that they're well guarded."

"I agree," Baraqiel nodded his head.

"I think we'll be fine," Sam snorted. "We don't need a bodyguard."

"After what I saw last night, I think it's a good idea," I said to Sam. "You haven't seen any demons yet. And if the ones we ran into last night are some of the weaker ones, we'll probably be safer if there's more of us."

"Fine," Sam huffed. "Let's get going then."

"We'll be back by nightfall," Baraqiel said to Sekhmet. "You stay here in case Dumah returns."

"Be safe," Sekhmet purred. "All of you."

"We will," I assured her.

The three of us left through the window Dumah and I came in from. Back on the street, I noticed Baraqiel shifting his glance at everyone around us. He seemed suspicious of everyone and moved in small, jerky motions. Sam seemed more brooding than usual, but I figured it was her acting protective of me. We decided to go from place to place, asking every employee who worked in every building if they knew Alastor. I would go inside one building while Sam went to the building next door and Baraqiel to the one next to Sam. That way, we were able to cover three places at a time. Although it didn't matter. We were getting nowhere. No one had heard of him or seen him. All I could think about was Dumah, and I wondered if he had already found Alastor by now. I struggled with going to food places because it all smelled so wonderful, even after Sekhmet told me how terrible the food was here. I took sips from my pouch of wine after leaving every restaurant. By midday, I was feeling fatigued and hopeless.

"We should head back and see if Dumah found out anything," I suggested.

"What?" Sam said. "We're getting a lot of ground covered today. We'll turn back once the sun starts setting."

"Sam!" I snapped. "This isn't working! I'm sorry, but you have no idea what you're doing or where you're going. It's like the blind leading the blind. I know you want to help and protect me, but we need to come up with another plan."

"You're right," Sam sighed. "I'm sorry I haven't been more of a team player. I have difficulty trusting people, especially when it involves your well-being. We can go back to the hideout and see if Dumah has made it back yet."

I looked at Baraqiel, and he shrugged.

"We could probably hit up a couple more blocks before turning back for the day," he said. "But we'll have to move quickly."

"Okay," I replied. "Let's work on this for a little longer and then head back."

We split up and went to more places, asking if they had seen Alastor. I went inside one building and noticed it was a candle shop. I thought, well, this seems like a *quaint business in Hell.* I walked around a bit, looking at the different scents. Nothing had labels on them; however, all the candles were different colors. Some came in tall, slender glass holders, while others came in shorter, wider ones.

"Can I help you?" asked a woman from across the shop.

She was much older than me, maybe in her forties, but still beautiful. Her long graying hair was pulled into a braid that hung over one shoulder. Wrapped around her waist and shoulders was a boa constrictor. She only wore a sheer black skirt that swept the floor as she walked. The snake slowly slithered around her exposed breasts.

"Oh, yes," I smiled weakly. "I was wondering if you knew an Alastor King?"

"No, honey," the woman said. "I'm sorry."

"That's all right," I smiled again. "Thank you."

"Would you like to look around the shop a little longer?" she asked.

"I have to get going," I explained. "Sorry."

"Please," the woman asked, smiling. I could see two rows on top and bottom of razor-sharp teeth. "Come smell my candles."

She grabbed my arm tightly and pulled me deeper into the shop.

"Hey!" I yelled, trying to pull away. "Let go of me!"

The woman yanked me past shelves of candles until she stopped in front of one.

"Here!" she said excitedly. "Smell this one!"

"No!" I cried.

"Just smell it," she grinned.

I inhaled hesitantly. I instantly smelled my grandmother's house. The combination of coffee, Irish Spring soap, mint, and a slight mildew smell filled my nostrils. I looked at the woman, and she grinned another fang-filled grin.

"Smell this one," she said, handing me another candle: oil, Old Spice aftershave, sweat, and laundry detergent.

"That smells exactly like my dad," my eyes teared up. I slowly fell to the floor and breathed in the candle that smelled like him. Until that moment, it was almost as if I had forgotten about my family. *I had a mom and dad, a grandma, and....a brother? Yes, a brother.* I held my head in one hand and started feeling dizzy. The woman kneeled in front of me, cradling a set of keys.

"Would you like to see your family again?" she whispered, leaning so close to my face that I thought her lips would touch my cheek. The boa constrictor started to move from the woman to me. "I could take you to go see your family. They would be able to see you as well. Would you like that?"

The woman softly ran her fingers through my hair as the snake started wrapping around me.

"Would you like to see your family?" the woman asked again, taking my face in her hand and turning it. I looked at a large metal door on the back wall. It had some sort of runes carved all over it.

"That door can take you straight to them," the woman whispered in my ear. Her breasts rubbed against my arm, and I found myself getting aroused.

"Do you like that?" she asked before licking my neck. My eyes closed, and I let out a moan. The woman took the candle out of my hand and straddled me. I couldn't move or speak. The woman took my hand and pushed it under her skirt. It was wet, and she started moaning as she moved my hand around. She started kissing my neck and lifted my shirt with her free hand. She started sucking on my nipple before I felt her bite down. I looked and saw blood coming from her mouth. I pulled my hand away from her skirt, which was also covered in blood. The woman started laughing softly at first, turning into shrill laughter.

"EMMA!" I heard a voice scream.

I came to, and the woman was standing across the room from me. She was a rotting old woman, her skin covered in open, oozing sores. She was primarily bald except for some strands of wiry white hair. There was no blood anywhere, but the giant boa constrictor was wrapped around me and squeezing me. I looked towards the door where Sam and Baraqiel were standing. Sam had her bow drawn and aimed it right at me.

"Don't move," she said before releasing the arrow. She hit the huge snake right in the head. It writhed around a moment before going limp. The old woman screamed.

"You little bitch!" she shrieked and charged at Sam. I flinched as bolts of lightning shot from Baraqiel's raised hands and struck the old woman. She howled as she seized up. Sam ran over to me and tried to help me up. I still felt dizzy and unbalanced. Sam put most of my weight on her shoulders.

"Come on, Emma," she grunted. "You have to try and walk."

I shifted one foot in front of the other and sighed.

"I'm....s-sorry," I stammered.

"Stop it," Sam said, wrapping her arm around my waist. "That's Hecate. She's known as the 'goddess' of witchcraft, but she's really just a demon bitch. She's excellent at tricking souls into getting stuck on Earth as ghosts for eternity."

The lightning from Baraqiel's hands ceased, and Hecate fell to the floor in a smoky, charred pile. Baraqiel took me from Sam and carried me in both arms. Sam opened the door to the candle shop, and I noticed that the sun was almost entirely set. She closed the door and looked at Baraqiel.

"Can we make it?" Sam asked. Baraqiel shook his head and slowly sat me back down on the floor.

"We can't just stay here!" Sam exclaimed. "It's not safe to stay here."

"It's not safe for us to go out there," Baraqiel explained. "Especially with Emma as weak as she is."

Sam pulled something from her back pocket and brought it over to me.

342

"Almost forgot I had this," she smiled. "Here."

She held a pouch of wine up to my mouth, and I took a drink.

"I feel better already," I said softly. "I think that has to be about the grossest thing that's ever happened to me, dead or alive."

Sam chuckled.

"Don't worry," she said. "Whatever you saw didn't happen. She's a trickster. She can make people see what she wants them to. Hecate is the sorceress of all sorceresses. Don't feel bad that you couldn't see past it."

"How do you know all of that?" Baraqiel asked. "I thought you said you've never been here before."

I looked at Sam.

"One of the places I went to, asking about Alastor, mentioned it."

Baraqiel locked the door to the shop and barricaded it with a large shelf. I looked around the shop at the dead snake and Hecate's burned body. I was not looking forward to spending all night there. Sam and Baraqiel blew out most of the torches that lit up the place. We moved to the far back of the store, where it was safe to talk without being heard from the outside but where Baraqiel could still keep an eye on the door. I crawled over, picked up the candle Hecate had given me and smelled it. I couldn't smell anything.

"Hey," I said, handing Sam the candle. "What does that smell like to you?"

She sniffed it and shrugged.

"Nothing," she said.

I slowly stood and picked up another one and smelled it. Nothing. I tried several more, and none of them smelled.

"None of them smell," I scoffed, looking at the body on the floor. "Fucking hag."

"Let's just hope the sun rises before she returns," Baraqiel muttered.

"What?" I asked. "What do you mean? She's not dead?"

"Not really," Baraqiel explained. "You can't kill something that's not living. Especially something that powerful."

"Dumah and I destroyed all of those demons, though."

"She's an elite like Sekhmet and I, though," Baraqiel said. "Only extraordinary weapons can kill elites, like the sword Dumah carries."

"He's probably so worried about us," I said. "I hope he and Sekhmet are safe."

"Try not to worry too much about them," Sam smiled. "Why don't you try and rest a little? I'll wake you when it's time to leave."

I laid down, but I couldn't fall asleep. I kept hearing screaming and other terrible noises from outside.

"Why is it so dangerous at nighttime?" I asked.

"Every night when the sun goes down, the demons are let loose to torture people," Baraqiel sighed. "People here still need sleep and one of the ways they're punished is to be kept up at night by the demons. No one sleeps here. They stay hidden during the day. Everyone knows to stay indoors at night. But there's always the souls who....weren't the best people. They go out at night to do terrible things. So the demons have their fun with them."

"Where do they hide during the day?" I ask.

"I don't know," he shook his head. "And I hope I never find out."

"Okay," Sam hushed. "Try and get some rest. Can't have a weary soul on the journey back to the hideout tomorrow."

I laid my head down and tried to think about every good thought I could. I thought of my family and friends. However, I couldn't remember the names and faces of my friends. I know I had two terrific friends, but I couldn't remember what they looked like. I started thinking about Alastor and was able to fall asleep.

"Emma!" Sam shook me. I jolted awake. "Get up."

"We have to go now!" I heard Baraqiel yell.

I sat up and looked around, confused. There was a loud boom that came from the back of the shop.

"Come on," Sam helped me up. "It's almost daylight, but a tank found us. I think it was trying to get to Hecate, but it heard us, and now it's trying to get in."

"Impossible," said Baraqiel. "We weren't making any noise. I don't know how it found us!"

I got to my feet and grabbed my dagger. Sam put her hand on mine.

"That's not going to do you any good," she said before handing me more wine. "Here. Drink this. And get ready to run."

I chugged the rest of the pouch and watched Baraqiel move the shelf away from the door. The booms were getting faster and faster.

"As soon as it breaks through the back door, make a run for the front door," Baraqiel said. "Then our best bet is to run as hard as we can for the hideout before the sun comes out, which should hopefully be soon."

The burnt body of Hecate started to move on the floor slowly.

"Oh, perfect," Sam said sarcastically.

There was a deafening sound as the back door broke, and in walked an 8-foot monster. It had the face of a vampire bat and was the length of a small car, with shoulders the size of tires. It stopped, looked right at us, and roared.

"GET THEM!" Hecate screamed as she slowly stood up and pointed at us.

"RUUUUUUUN!" Baraqiel yelled.

We ran through the door, out into the darkness. Because I didn't know where exactly I was going, I stayed as close to Baraqiel as possible. The tank burst through the shop door after us, roaring.

"It won't be able to catch up to us," Baraqiel breathed. "Tanks are too slow. He'll chase us until he has us cornered or gives up."

The tank roared again behind us, and I covered my ears.

"Or it calls for backup," Sam panted.

"Wait," I said, slowing down. Sam and Baraqiel looked too. "It stopped chasing us."

The tank let out another roar and stared at us from down the street. Suddenly, a group of skeletal beings ran out from behind it.

"WASPS!" Sam screamed. "EMMA, RUN!"

We all started sprinting at full speed; however, the wasps caught up to us quickly. Sam began to shoot some with her arrows, but there were too many. I grabbed another one of my blood grenades and threw it at the wasps. Several of them blew up instantly, while others kept running while on fire.

"Throw another one!" Sam yelled.

I threw another grenade into the mob of demons, blowing more up. I looked on either side of us, and more wasps came at us from the other streets. Baraqiel stopped running.

347

"What are you doing?" I asked, stopping too.

"I can buy you some time and distract them until the sun comes up," he said.

"Those wasps will tear you to shreds," Sam said. "You won't survive."

"I don't have to," Baraqiel said before turning to me. "But you do. Go. You must make it back to the hideout and meet up with Dumah. You're running out of time."

"Baraqiel..."I started.

"GO!" he yelled.

"Come on, Emma!" Sam said, grabbing me. We started running again as the wasps got closer.

Baraqiel shot lightning from his whole body, screaming as he did so. I watched all of the wasps as they drew their attention to him. As they got closer, Baraqiel electrocuted some of them, but was quickly overtaken as a large group tackled him. His body glowed brightly before disappearing under the pile of wasps. Suddenly, there was a loud electrical boom, like a transformer exploding. I stopped to look for Baraqiel.

"Keep going!" Sam breathed heavily. "Don't look back. He's gone."

Ahead of us, I could see the first light of daybreak. A now much smaller group of wasps was chasing us again. The street we were on looked familiar. We were almost back to the hideout. I grabbed another grenade, but it slipped through my hands and fell to the ground. I didn't dare stop to pick up since the wasps were so close to us now. Sam drew an arrow and shot it at the vial, making it explode.

"Nice!" I exclaimed.

"Look!" Sam pointed. The sun was coming up.

Sam slowed down to a jog and then turned around and stopped. We watched as a group of about twenty wasps turned around and dashed in the opposite direction. Soon, people were coming back out onto the streets again.

"I'm out of blood grenades," I told Sam.

"Hopefully, we won't be needing anymore," she chuckled. "That was nuts."

"Oh my god, when you shot that grenade I dropped! That was awesome."

Sam handed me her pouch of wine, and I took a drink.

"Wait," I said, handing it back to her. "Where did you get this one? I drank all of yours already."

"Baraqiel gave me his pouch in case he didn't make it," she explained.

"Do you think Dumah is back by now?" I asked.

"Let's find out," Sam said.

We crept into the alleyway and through the window where we had been before.

"Dumah?" I shouted. "Sekhmet?"

It was quiet.

"Dumah?" I said again.

We reached the room we had been staying in, and I gasped, covering my mouth with my hand. Sekhmet's body was hanging upside down in the middle of the room by her feet. Her throat had been slit and there was a large pool of blood on the floor underneath her body. Sam slowly walked ahead of me with her bow drawn, looking around. She examined something stuck to Sekhmet's body and pulled it off.

"What is that?" I asked.

"A note," Sam said, handing it to me.

"Alastor can be found in the Abyss," I read out loud. "Come alone."

I looked at Sam.

"What does that mean?" I asked. "What's the Abyss?"

"I don't know, but you're not going alone," Sam said.

"You're not coming with me," I said. "I've already gotten Sekhmet and Baraqiel killed. And who knows what happened to Dumah."

"Dumah is probably the one who killed Sekhmet!" Sam exclaimed.

"No," I shook my head. "They were friends. There was no reason for him to kill her."

"I've had my suspicions about him from the beginning," Sam said. "Something has always seemed off about him. I feel like he's behind whatever is going on with Alastor."

"But why?" I asked. "What would Alastor have to do with Dumah?"

"I don't know, but you only have 58 hours left, Emma."

I looked down at my watch. She was right. I was running out of time.

"So what are you going to do?" she asked.

"I'm going to find out what and where the Abyss is," I said.

Sam nodded and followed me back out through the window. I stood on the sidewalk outside the alley, looking around. Now I not only had to find Alastor, but I also had to figure out what had happened to Dumah. I had about two and a half days left. I could make it.

"So, who do we ask?" Sam exhaled.

"I'm not sure," I replied. A woman was walking toward us on the sidewalk.

"Excuse me?" I smiled at her. She kept walking without looking at us.

"Rude," Sam scoffed. "Here, let's ask this guy."

Sam walked in front of an older man.

"Excuse me, sir?" Sam said in her sweet little girl voice. He stopped and looked at her.

"Do you by chance know where the Abyss is?" she asked.

"The what?" he asked.

"The Abyss," Sam repeated.

"No, never heard of it," he answered.

"Okay, thank you," Sam grinned at the man before turning to me and sighing.

"At least you got him to stop and respond to you," I laughed.

"Did I hear you say something about the Abyss?" another man stopped and asked us.

"Yeah," I said. "Do you know where it is?"

"I don't know exactly how to get to it, but I know how you can find out," he replied.

"If you go to the Sentencing office, there are maps you can look at on the Information floor. They'll have something there that will help you out."

"Thank you!" I said, motioning for Sam to follow me. "Thank you so much!"

"No problem, and good luck!" called the man.

We ran to Sentencing, back to the start of our journey. Once inside, we made our way to the elevators and found the Information floor.

"I hope we get some answers," I said on the elevator.

"Me too," Sam sighed. "Me too."

We got off the elevator and walked up to the desk where a very small, old man was sitting. He looked up at us and smiled.

"How can I help you?" he asked.

"We were wondering if you have any maps that could show us how to get to the Abyss?" I inquired.

"Sure!" the man chirped. He got up from his seat, and we followed him along the shelves of books and papers. He stopped at a ladder, climbed it, and grabbed a giant book from a higher shelf.

"Ah, here we are!" he called, bringing the book down. "Be careful. It's a bit cumbersome."

I took the old man's book as he slowly climbed back down.

"Thank you," I smiled.

"Of course," he replied. "Take all the time you need with it."

"Can we, by chance, take this?" Sam asked.

"Absolutely not," the man responded. "Nothing leaves the room."

"Do you have a copy machine or some way we can print the map?" I asked, taking the book over to the nearest table.

"I'm afraid not," he grinned. "But like I said, take all the time you need."

"Thanks," Sam said sarcastically.

"If you girls have more questions, just let me know."

We waited for him to walk away before opening the book. It was filled with different maps of Hell. Sam was able to find where we were located on the main map.

"I'm trying to see if I can find which page has anything about an Abyss on it," Sam said, flipping the pages quickly. "Oh! Here it is!"

She pointed to a page. Holding her hand between the pages, she flipped back to the main map and the map of the Abyss.

"Okay, so if we're here...." she thought out loud, "then the Abyss should be here."

She pointed to a spot on the map before flipping back and forth a couple more times.

"I need a piece of paper and something to write with," Sam said.

"I'll ask the front desk guy," I responded hurriedly. I got up and made my way back to the front desk.

"Excuse me, but do you have a pen and paper I could use?" I asked.

"Sure!" said the man.

"We're good," Sam said out of nowhere. "I have a pretty good memory. I've got it."

"Are you sure?" I asked her.

"Yup," she replied, pulling on my arm. "Come on, let's go. We have quite a ways to go."

"Okay," I said reluctantly before turning back to the old man. "Well, thank you anyway."

"You're quite welcome!" he called as we got back on the elevator.

"What the hell was that about?" I asked as the elevator door closed. I went to push the button for the lobby, but Sam quickly pushed the bottom button.

"Why did you do that?"

"We're going to the parking garage," Sam responded nervously.

"Why?"

She didn't answer.

The elevator door opened, and she stepped out quickly, pulling on my arm again.

"Sam, what are we doing?" I asked.

"Just be quiet and trust me," she gritted her teeth.

Sam pulled a set of keys from her pocket and ran to the closest car.

"Where did those come from?" I asked.

Sam didn't answer me as she tried the next car.

"Sam?" I repeated.

She ignored me as she tried two more cars.

"Sam!" I yelled.

"Just hold on!" she yelled back at me. She reached the next car, which had a cracked windshield and peeled paint, and unlocked it.

"Come on!" Sam screeched as she got in, threw her bow and quiver into the back, and reached over to unlock the passenger side. I noticed the front passenger hubcap was missing and the interior looked as if an animal had chewed on it.

I got in and watched her try to start the car. She turned the key several times but the engine wouldn't start. She was shaking as she kept trying.

"Start, damn it!"

I stared, not know what to say or do. Finally the car started and Sam reversed quickly. The tires squealed, and I braced myself as we sped off. The car was loud and smelled heavily of exhaust. Sam weaved in and out of traffic and breathed heavily. She was craning her neck to see over the dashboard and I noticed she was on tiptoes trying to reach the pedals.

"Sam," I muttered. "Did you steal this car?"

"Look, I'm doing what I must to get you to Alastor before your time runs out. The Abyss is far away, and we *have* to get there before nightfall."

"Can we make it before then?" I asked.

"I'm going to try my absolute hardest."

"Do you know where you're going?"

"Yeah, I wasn't lying when I said I remembered how to get to the Abyss."

"So, what, you needed me to distract the old guy with the paper and pen question so you could steal his car keys?"

"Something like that," Sam said dryly.

"Oh my god, Sam," I scoffed.

"Look," Sam snapped, "Maybe it would be better if we just don't talk for a while, okay? I'm already freaking out and can hardly reach the damn pedals and need some peace and quiet."

"Fine."

We sat in silence as we drove through the city. I watched buildings and people pass in a blur. Eventually, there were fewer buildings until we were finally out of the city. I watched the skyline in my side mirror until I could no longer see it. We followed a highway, nothing in front of us but an open road. I occasionally checked my watch, looking at the hours count down. At 53 hours, Sam finally spoke.

"I need to pull over for gas," she said, more to herself than to me. I didn't respond. "It won't take too long, and then we can be back on the road."

We pulled off the highway to a gas station. We circled the pumps and saw that they were either occupied or out of order. Sam eventually pulled up to a pump once it became available and got out. I saw a couple walk out of the convenience store laughing. I watched the man wrap his arm around the woman's shoulder. I found it interesting to see people so happy here and was a little envious of them. The man handed the woman a small wad of cash, and they went around to the side of the building. The woman got on her knees and pulled the man's pants down. I quickly looked down as Sam got back in the car. She looked at me.

"I know," she said. "I'm sorry we had to stop here. I won't need to stop again before we get to the Abyss."

357

The car took a few tries before starting again. It made a screeching sound and I looked at Sam. She didn't acknowledge me or the car and slowly left the gas station. We got back on the road, and Sam rolled down her window before speeding up.

"We're on the outskirts of the city, so we're getting close. Probably only a few more miles or so. The Abyss is what connects to the rest of Hell."

"You got all of that from a map?" I asked. Sam didn't respond.

We drove in silence until the car started getting louder.

"What is that?" I asked.

"I don't know!" Sam replied. "It sounds like a plane taking off!"

I covered my ears and realized the car was veering off the road.

"Sam!" I yelled.

"I can't steer it! Something's wrong!"

"Brakes, Sam! Hit the brakes!"

The car screeched to a stop on the shoulder.

"Holy shit!" I exclaimed. "Are you okay?"

"I couldn't get the steering wheel under control," she said. "And now the car's off."

Sam tried starting the car. Nothing. She tried again. Nothing.

"No," she whispered.

"No, no, no, no! NO!"

"Sam-"

"No!" she yelled at me. "This is bad! This is so very bad, Emma! We're so close!"

"Can we walk the rest of the way?" I asked. "Like, would we be safe to walk out here?"

"Emma, if we don't get there before nightfall, I don't think I can protect us."

I sat there for a moment and thought.

"Okay," I said. "We try to make it on foot. If it starts getting dark, we abandon the whole thing."

"You mean go back to Processing?" Sam asked.

"It's not worth getting another angel killed," I explained. "Especially you."

Sam contemplated this for a minute before opening her door.

"Come on," she sighed. "Grab my stuff, will ya?"

I snatched the bow and quiver from the back of the musty car and hopped out,

"Luckily, it's just a straight shot from here, so if we stay on the road, we'll find it."

We walked quickly until my legs began to tire. Sam never slowed down though.

"Come on!" she snapped at me.

"I'm trying!" I said. "I'm getting tired."

"No, you're not. You're dead, Emma. Fight through the tiredness and keep going. Your body isn't going to quit. We have to get there."

"Do you have any more wine?"

Sam pulled the pouch out of her pocket and handed it to me.

"The closer we get to Hell, the wine will be less effective. So you might as well drink the rest now."

I drank the remaining wine and immediately felt better.

"You good now?" she asked. I nodded.

I picked up my pace again and started jogging, which seemed to keep Sam off my back for a while. I was scared by how scared she now seemed. After some time though, I started slowing down again. My clothes became drenched with sweat and I was starting to get a cramp in my left calf.

"Sam..." I finally said.

"No!" she barked. "Quit talking and save your breath. We're almost there!"

I stopped talking and kept going, massaging my calf every once in a while. I noticed the sun beginning to set against an orange sky. I looked at my watch. 46 hours. I had less than two days. As it began to get darker, I started getting more nervous. We had been a little more safe in the car. But out here, we were completely exposed. I realized there was a faint whooshing sound, like waves. Up ahead, I saw a light blinking in the sky.

"What is that?" I asked.

"The entrance," Sam said quietly. "We're here."

We were approaching a lighthouse, and as we got closer, I noticed a shore.

"Wait, are we back to where we started?" I asked.

"No," Sam explained. "We're miles from where Dumah docked the boat."

The sky was no longer orange but a bluish-purple color. Sam walked ahead of me, getting closer to the lighthouse. At the base of it, I saw a vast opening into what looked like a cave.

"Are we going into that?" I asked.

"That's the entrance into the Abyss," Sam pointed to the opening before putting her bow over her shoulder.

"Is it safe?"

"Safe enough. Don't worry, Emma. Nothing down there will hurt us."

I reluctantly followed Sam up to the opening. The wind howled around us as Sam walked in. There were torches along either side of the cave. Sam grabbed one off the wall and motioned for me to follow her. I kept one hand on my dagger and cautiously walked behind Sam. We walked further into the cave until I could no longer see the opening. I had so many questions, but I was too afraid to speak. We could hear something move occasionally; however, I couldn't tell if it was coming from ahead or behind us. As we went further down, the torches on the wall began to space out more and more from each other until there were none at all except the one Sam carried. We were in total darkness.

I could tell we were going downhill because of the steep path, and I had to almost walk on tiptoes. Sam suddenly held her arm out in front of me. At first, I didn't see anything ahead. Then, I could barely see *something*. Finally, I could make out the figures in front of us. We stepped down onto a flat landing of dirt. A large circular room lay before us, crowded with Runts. I slowly pulled my dagger out of its sheath, although none of the Runts even seemed to notice us. I held a shaky hand up, holding the blade out. We carefully walked right through the Runts as they all seemed dormant, like they were sleeping standing up. Sam held her finger up to her lips and I nodded. We made our way through the Runts, careful not to bump into them. This must be where they go during the day. One of them stirred, which caused a few more to move a little. Sam gestured for me to move quickly and we reached the other side of the dwelling. There was a doorway and we quietly slipped through. I let out a sigh and wiped my sweaty forehead.

"Watch your step," Sam mouthed silently. I nodded.

I looked down and immediately hugged the wall on my right. We walked down a giant stone spiral staircase with a large, deep opening in the middle of the stairs. Sam almost glided down the stairs. However, I took my time and put one foot carefully in front of the other. It took us nearly 40 minutes to reach the bottom of the stairs.

We approached a large stone archway, much like the one we had entered with Dumah a few days prior. This one also had something carved into it.

"Kur," Sam whispered. "It's Sumerian."

"What is Kur?" I asked quietly.

"Hell," Sam responded. "We're entering the true Hell now."

"I thought the note said Alastor was back in the Abyss."

"Emma, we have to keep moving."

Sam moved forward while I stayed put. She turned and looked at me. This felt wrong. I wanted to turn back.

"What is it?" Sam asked.

I turned towards the staircase and looked up.

"No, something's wrong," I said, stepping up. "We need to-"

I felt a sudden blow to the head before everything went black.

20

I slowly opened my eyes. I was lying on the ground, a cold stone floor underneath me. Movement was all around me, but I couldn't focus on anything at first.

"Emma," I heard. I blinked hard and sat up. Alastor was standing in front of me.

"Alastor?" I said, confused.

"Hey, Emma," he said, not moving.

Alastor didn't look any different from the last time I saw him, except he wore a very nice suit and tie. I had never seen him in such lovely clothes. Looking around, I saw four large figures in black armor standing in the room's corners. I moved and felt a tightness around my wrists. My hands were cuffed and chained to the floor. I also noticed that my watch was gone.

"What's going on?" I asked. Alastor paced around the room, not making eye contact with me.

"Alastor," I said sternly. "Tell me what's going on."

Alastor stopped and sighed.

"I'm trying to figure out where to start," he chuckled. "I guess I should start from the very beginning. My real name is Ankou. I was the firstborn child of Adam and Eve. I killed my brother, Barachiel, after an argument we had gotten into. My parents told me that I was not only banished from our family but from God's family too. That I would never go to Paradise for the sin I had committed. Out of grief or anger, I should say, I went into the woods and hung myself. When I died, I was greeted by Barachiel. He said he had become God's first supreme archangel. God needed to protect His precious Paradise after the Devil had gotten to Adam and Eve. It's funny because God creates man in *His* image and is shocked when man immediately sins. 'Here, have some free will. But if you use it in a way I don't like, you can't get into my exclusive club.' What a fucking joke. Anyway, Barachiel explained to me that I couldn't enter Paradise. So, I turned to the only person who *would* take me. Lucifer made me his first demon. He gave my existence purpose. Soon after Barachiel and I died, my mother, Eve, bore two more sons. Cain murdered Abel, and God punished him to wander the lands. He begged to be murdered himself, but God would not allow it. Instead, He protected Cain so he could suffer a life of guilt and torture.

"God saw that people were inherently evil no matter how hard He tried. Over and over, He tried to convince them that if they were good, they would be rewarded with Paradise. But one by one, they would sin and be sent to Hell. Eventually, God eased up on punishing those who sinned. I guess Paradise got a little lonely since hardly anyone lived perfect lives. Once God decided that people could earn their way out of Hell, Lucifer was pissed. Rightfully so too. He had his own kingdom to rule. So God sent Barachiel, and the Devil sent me to come up with an agreement. Angels and demons could persuade humans in their name. Persuade but not directly interfere. God appointed more and more angels, and Lucifer tried to get as many demons to help him as possible, but once God sent Himself down in human form, the game was over for a while. Hell was only getting about a third of what we were before 'Jesus' showed up.

"But then something crazy happened. Christianity happened, and it made people worse! People were killed in the name of God, armies battled other armies, people burned 'witches,' and Christians invaded Natives and either slaughtered them or converted them. A lot of the people who go to Hell are people who spent their entire lives claiming to be Christians. Do you know how many priests, preachers, youth pastors, and ministers we have down here? The Crusades lasted 200 years. The amount of bloodshed from both sides in the name of religion? Fucking bonkers. And almost all of them ended up here. Over the years, God got increasingly more lenient on whom He allowed into Paradise so that Lucifer wouldn't become more powerful than Him. The biggest joke is that Paradise is more or less of a trap. You can't do whatever you want like you can here. You can't have sex in Paradise. You can't have any power or control over anything. There are no animals in Paradise. There's not much to do because 'there's no need for wants.' Paradise, or Heaven, as many call it, is a scam. The Bible warns people over and over that all you do all day and night for all eternity is sit and worship God, whether you believe in Him or not. 'All nations and people will worship Jesus.' Revelation 7:9-10. 'Heaven will be filled with peace, joy, and praise.' Revelations 7:15-17. 'Precious gemstones will adorn Heaven.' Revelations 21:9-11. Do you know what that means? Gemstones are human souls that God has been collecting since the beginning of man just to sit on a shelf and collect dust! God is a selfish child who collects fireflies in a jar because He thinks their little lights are pretty and then never sets them free. They sit in the jar and suffocate slowly."

He stopped pacing the floor and looked at me. I was utterly speechless, so I let him continue without speaking.

"So," he continued, "Where does this leave you? How did you get wooed by a demon, and why are you here in Hell now? Well, I am a demon who specializes in suicides. I thought you were an easy target because of how sad and lonely your life seemed. Of course, you died before I could get you to kill yourself. But, here you are still! And it's all thanks to your sweet angel friend!"

"Du-Dumah," I whispered. "Dumah was lying to me?"

The voice that came out of my mouth did not sound like me. It sounded like a weak, wounded child—someone who was devastated and hurting. Alastor- I mean, *Ankou* laughed at me.

"Dumah?" he asked. "No, not him! Oh, speaking of...."

Ankou snapped his fingers, and two of the armored figures left the room, closing the door behind them. Ankou knelt in front of me and put my chin in his hand.

"Oh, Emma," he smirked. "You really are a silly girl; you know that. I will say, out of the hundreds- no, maybe thousands of women and men I've fucked, you have truly been one of the most boring ones."

"I-I loved you," I stammered, tears rolling down my cheeks. Ankou recoiled from me. "I thought you loved me."

"Why?" He scoffed. "Because I said I did, and you were naive enough to believe me?"

"I trusted you!" I cried.

"AND WHO'S FAULT IS THAT?" Ankou yelled back. Suddenly, the door opened behind him. The two guards returned, dragging Dumah by each arm. I gasped, seeing that both of his wings had been cut off. There were two bloody stumps where the beautiful black wings had been. The guards tossed Dumah onto the floor beside me.

One of them handed Dumah's sword to Ankou. I knelt next to Dumah and turned him over to face me.

"Dumah," I wept. "I'm so, so sorry. I didn't know."

"It's....okay," Dumah murmured. "Not...your fault."

I put his head in my lap and leaned in to hug him. He shifted his foot, and I felt something roll from his boot to my knee. He looked into my eyes and moved the small sphere under my shirt. I maneuvered my hands over it and quickly moved it to my back pocket before glimpsing at it. It was a Christ-blood grenade.

"Should have stayed here while you had the chance, angel," Ankou said as his guards grabbed Dumah by the arms. "Instead, you earned your precious wings and, what? Became God's servant! Just to end up back here to be killed."

Dumah was on his knees, his head lolling, while the guards held his wrists. "I'd rather...be...God's servant..." Dumah groaned. "...than...Lucifer's...puppet."

Ankou glared at Dumah before violently piercing him through the chest with his own sword. There was so much force that the sword came out through Dumah's back. The glare on Ankou's face turned into a sinister smile. He pulled the sword back out and threw it onto the floor.

"No!" I screamed. Dumah went limp, and I started sobbing again. Ankou snapped his fingers, and the two guards grabbed Dumah's feet, dragging him out of the room.

"WHAT THE FUCK IS WRONG WITH YOU?" I screamed. "HE DIDN'T DO ANYTHING TO YOU!"

"Calm down," Ankou rubbed his forehead. "You don't need to yell so loudly. He found out who I was and was going to tell you before taking you back to Processing. You wanted to see me, so I did you a favor."

"I can't believe this," I cried.

"Oh, but it gets so much better," Ankou grinned. "Ready to meet your traitor?"

"Please...don't."

"Come on in!" Ankou called. The moment I saw a flash of red hair, my heart shattered.

"Sam," I breathed.

Sam walked up, her head hanging low. She stood beside Ankou, not saying a word or looking at me.

"You knew?" I asked, hurt. "You knew Alastor was a demon, and you tricked me?"

"Sam has been a wonderful addition to our little...operation we have going on," Ankou roughly threw his arm around Sam's neck. "Haven't you, Sam?"

Sam didn't respond.

"Oh, you're not being shy, are you?" Ankou asked. "After all, aren't you two like best friends?"

"She's not my friend," I said, lip quivering. "I don't even know who she is."

"Sam is one of the angels secretly working with us!" Ankou explained. "We have a handful of them helping lure humans here in various, creative ways."

"You're cheating," I found myself abruptly saying. Sam and Ankou looked at me.

"You're not getting as many people in and losing many of the ones you did have, so you're cheating to get people here and trapping them. And if my time runs out while I'm here, I'm stuck here."

I looked back down at my wrist.

"Where's my watch?" I asked. "How much time do I have left?"

"Emma," Sam said. "Listen, you'll be better off here. Paradise is so....boring. You- you're better off here."

"I can't believe you did this to me," I said to her. "Why? What's in it for you?"

I watched as Ankou squeezed Sam's shoulders tightly.

"Hell is...preparing to overthrow..."

"Heaven?" I asked.

"Earth," she answered. "Angels and demons can walk on Earth, but angels don't spend as much time on Earth as they used to."

"So demons are just bullying humans into being bad?" I asked.

"Demons are letting humans do what humans always do," Ankou threw his hands up. "Humans are inherently bad. Always have been and always will be. Demons honestly don't have to work that hard. Angels do, however. Humans aren't even as creative as they used to be. There was a time when people spent all of their free time reading, writing, sculpting, and painting. Now they just have their faces constantly in their phones. There are so many different kinds of drugs and alcohol, and weapons. Gangs, war, human trafficking, school shootings, and domestic violence. The more evolved humans become, the eviler they become. Hell is already on Earth. We're expanding more and more every day."

I thought back to Elijah telling me the angels were low-staffed, and everything started getting pieced together. Angels could enter all realms. Demons could enter all but Paradise. Human souls either stayed in Paradise, stayed in Hell, or could go from Hell to Paradise under certain circumstances. If Paradise *was* indeed the best place to end up, why would angels be smuggling human souls out of Processing and trying to get them to Hell? I looked at Sam, and she mouthed, "I'm so sorry," at me. I glared at her.

"So what should I do if I'm stuck down here for eternity?" I asked.

"Well, you could do what most people do and have never-ending fun," Ankou explained. "Or, you could get lucky and get a job working for a demon. Help us out like your friend, Sam, here."

"It just doesn't make sense," I said, shaking my head. "Everything we're ever taught about religion cycles back to one common theme: love. Christianity, Islam, and Judaism all teach that there is a loving connection between their God and themselves and other people. Buddhists believe that love nourishes spiritual freedom. Wiccans even have love spells that they believe in. Hindus have six different types of love. I don't think God created us just for the sole purpose of collecting us. He made us because He loves us."

Ankou frowned at me as I continued.

"I think you're lying, just like you have been since I met you."

I then turned to Sam.

"Sam, this isn't you. You know that humans are worth saving. You know there's more good than bad. Think about the sandwich I bought from you. You never forgot about it because it was an act of generosity. I never expected anything in return and that's what made our friendship so special. So much so that you became my guardian angel. You care about me, and all of the other humans you watch over."

"It's too late," Sam whimpered. "He knows I've already betrayed Him."

"And He will forgive you," I pleaded. "You have a chance to make things right."

Sam grabbed Dumah's sword and walked over to me. She put the point of the blade into my cheek.

"Stop talking, Emma," she said through gritted teeth. "I can't be forgiven for what I've done."

"Please, Sam," I cried. "You're the girl who held the alligator. You're brave enough to do what's right."

Suddenly, Sam swung the sword at me. I winced and felt a tug on my arms. There was a loud *clang!* My chain broke, and I stood up. Sam charged across the room with Dumah's sword, which was now blazing with fire. She ran right at the guards and sliced one of them in half at the waist.

"Emma, get out!" Sam yelled. "Call out for help and get out while you can!"

Sam turned to Ankou and sprinted at him. As she thrust the sword at him, Ankou grabbed her by the wrist and kneed her in the stomach. Sam gasped as she fell to the ground. Ankou took the sword from her and smiled at me before swinging. Her head flew across the room and landed near my feet. A soft shriek escaped from my mouth as I stared at Sam's face looking up at me.

"It would have been so much easier if she hadn't known you as a human," Ankou sighed. "She wasn't evil or trying to hurt you in any way. But she's a newborn angel. Just so easily swayed to help me out. And she was doing *so* well! But I guess she just couldn't fully commit. Because of you."

Ankou wiped Sam's blood off of the sword on his leg.

"Hm," he chuckled. "You are a terrible judge of character. You know that?"

I snarled, grabbing the blood grenade from my back pocket and launching it towards Ankou and the remaining guards. It exploded as Ankou dove out the way, making him drop Dumah's sword. I ran to grab it as Ankou stood up and charged me. I slid to my knees and grabbed the sword, turning towards Ankou. The blade pierced the right side of his chest, and his hands were wrapped around my throat. I glanced at the doorway, which had been caved in from the grenade explosion.

"Oh no," Ankou sputtered, "We're going down together, just like we promised each other."

I couldn't speak, and I was getting tunnel vision. Ankou's grip tightened as I fell backward onto the floor, the sword sticking out of his back. I remembered what Sam said about calling out for help. I didn't know who to call, but I closed my eyes and whispered in prayer, "help me."

Ankou's grip started to weaken. I could breathe again. The room suddenly flooded with a bright light coming from my body, and an abrupt force pushed Ankou off of me. I felt myself begin to lift slowly off the ground.

"No," Ankou panted. "She's mine!'

He crawled on all fours towards my levitating body and gripped my foot. With all my remaining strength, I grabbed the sword's hilt with both hands and pushed Ankou's chest with my free foot, sending him backwards.

"NOOOOOOOO!" he screamed.

I pulled Dumah's sword onto my stomach and tightly held the hilt over my chest. I closed my eyes and waited for whatever came next. What I wasn't expecting was the sound of Hannah's voice.

"With two minutes to spare," I heard her say. I opened my eyes and saw Hannah and Elijah staring down at me.

"You are one lucky young lady," Hannah sighed. "Good thing I'm always early to my last appointments with clients and found Elijah! He told me what you and Dumah have been up to, and I have to say I am incredibly disappointed in him. Where is he?"

I slowly sat up, not letting go of his sword. I was in the lobby of the Processing building.

"Dumah...didn't make it," I stammered. "Ankou killed him."

"Ankou?" Elijah exclaimed. "What on earth were you doing with Ankou?"

I quickly tried to explain through sobs that my boyfriend, Alastor, was actually the demon Ankou and how Sam had helped trick me into going to Hell to him.

"Oh my goodness," Hannah sighed. "What a mess this is. I'll have so much paperwork to fill out. Elijah, thank you so much for helping sort this out quickly. Emma, there's someone who wants to speak with you."

"Who?" I asked.

"Someone who heard your call for help," she smiled.

I followed Hannah to my room, holding on tightly to Dumah's sword. She opened the door to my room, and the light coming from inside was so intense that I had to shield my eyes.

"Tone it down with the light show, Barachiel!" Hannah spat. "You're blinding the poor thing!"

The brightness of the light seemed to dim, and standing at the end of my bed was a huge angel with enormous white wings. He was by far the most beautiful creature I had ever seen. He had black, curly hair and eyes the color of honey.

"Hello, Emma," he smiled down at me. "I am very pleased to meet you. Sounds like you've had quite the adventure."

"You're Barachiel?" I asked. "Ankou's brother?"

"I am," Barachiel nodded. "I am an archangel interested in hearing about your time with my brother. Let's start from the beginning."

I sat down on the bed, never letting go of Dumah's sword, and retold my story of meeting Ankou (Alastor). Barachiel stood as still as a statue while I told him my story, living and dead. I finished with the part about my body levitating and ending up back at Processing. I stopped speaking and stared at Barachiel, waiting for him to say something.

"As you figured, my brother lied to you about Paradise. He's deep with the Devil and has desperately done everything he can to get souls trapped in Hell. Fortunately, you saw past his tricks and got yourself out of there, with my help, of course."

"You....heard me?" I asked.

"Being an archangel has its perks," he grinned. "You asked for help, God told me to save you, and I did."

"Why?" I asked. "Why did God want you to save me?"

"I have a proposition for you. But first, I want you to weigh all of your options."

Barachiel stretched his hand towards me.

"I want to show you something."

I took his hand with one of my own, gripping Dumah's sword with the other still. Barachiel wrapped his wings around me, and I felt a strong *whoosh!* We landed, and his wings opened. I looked around, and everything seemed magically unreal. There were flowers everywhere and, in the distance, a vast waterfall. I saw a herd of zebras running in a field near us.

"Is this Paradise?" I asked.

"This is what *you* imagined as Paradise," Barachiel explained. "Paradise can be whatever you want it to be with whomever you want in it."

"But only if they're dead too, right?"

"Not necessarily. God wants you to spend eternity with as much love and happiness as you can imagine. Nothing is out of the question."

I stood there for a moment, thinking about my family.

"Emma!" I heard.

I turned around and saw my brother, Simon, racing towards me through the field of flowers. I exhaled and dropped the sword. My mom and dad were behind him.

"Are they real?" I asked.

"In your Paradise, yes," Barachiel answered.

Simon got closer, and I reached my arms out to him. He embraced me so tightly that I thought we would fall over.

"I've missed you so much!" Simon cried happily.

"Simon," I smiled, tears running down both cheeks.

My mom and dad wrapped their arms around both of us.

"It's okay," my mother hushed, brushing my hair with her hand. "We're all together again. Nothing can hurt you now, Emma."

I looked over at Barachiel, and my smile slightly faded.

"Emma, what's wrong?" Simon asked.

"I'm not really with them, though," I said to Barachiel. "They're all still alive. And they'll be in their own version of Paradise when they die. If Simon gets married and has kids, they'll be in his version, and I won't ever know they exist."

Simon, my mom, and my dad stood back from me and looked at Barachiel.

"Yes, that's all true," he answered. "I told you, you have options."

"What's my other option?" I asked.

"This is one of three. Your second choice is to return to Earth."

"As a ghost?"

"As a new human."

"Like reincarnation?"

Barachiel nodded.

"Would I get a choice in going back as a boy or girl at least? Or which part of the world I would be born into."

"No, you don't get to specify anything," he said. "You only get to decide to return."

I stood there momentarily and looked at my family, who were all smiling at me.

"And the third option?" I asked.

"Become an angel," he said quickly. "Take Dumah's place as a death angel and guide humans in their final moments. We've lost two angels because of your actions, and we think it would be a fitting choice."

"*We*?" I asked. "Who is *we*?"

"Hannah, Elijah, the other archangels, and myself."

I looked around, and my eyes landed back on the zebras.

"Do animals go to Paradise?" I asked. "Or are they only here because I choose to have them here."

"Animals cannot make moral decisions," Barachiel said. I sighed.

"So this is all just an illusion to make me obliviously happy forever."

"Once you choose to stay here, you won't know it's only an illusion. Paradise will become your new reality."

"And if I return to Earth as a baby, I could wind up sick again or have an even worse life than my previous one."

A large part of me was sad that I had died so young. However, I had done more living since I died. I had seen my favorite animals up close. I had sailed a sea. I had fought demons alongside angels. I knew in my heart that moving on to Paradise wasn't where I really belonged. Not now that I had seen so much.

"Or you could end up having a much better one. A long life full of love and happiness and good health. You could end up going to a nice college, getting married, having children, growing old, and one day, dying peacefully in your sleep."

"Or I could have the tedious job that Dumah had and serve God as an angel for eternity. Unless a demon like your brother kills me."

Barachiel didn't say a word.

"What happens when an angel or demon dies? What happened to Dumah, Sekhmet, and Baraqiel? What happens to Sam and Ankou?"

"Ankou is right where you left him. Sam has become a lost soul so she will spend eternity in the The Sea of Anathema. Sekhmet and Baraqiel did not succumb to their injuries. It will take some time, but they will be okay. Dumah, unfortunately, has no choice but to return to Earth and try again as a human."

"Will he get to become an angel again?" I asked.

"That's completely up to him. But only time will tell."

"Wait, what do you mean Ankou is where I left him?" I asked. "I killed him!"

"No, you severely injured him. But he is very much still alive."

"What!" I snapped. "How is he still alive?"

"He's a powerful demon and a very old one. He's not easy to kill. And unfortunately, demons are slightly harder to kill than angels, which is one of the many reasons why there's so few of us anymore."

I picked up Dumah's sword, which lit up with fire. I knew now what my purpose was and had made my decision.

Epilogue

A woman by the name of Johanna lay motionless in her tub. Music played through a speaker that sat on her bathroom counter. She could hear traffic outside her apartment in Dresden, Germany, and a dog barking in the distance. The tub was filled with water, which was now a dark red. Her hands were slumped to each side somewhere under the bloody surface. Johanna could feel her heartbeat and her labored breath slowing down. Suddenly, she couldn't hear the traffic or the dog anymore. Johanna couldn't hear anything. There was no sound of the dark, hooded figure approaching her. The woman wearing all black with giant wings like a crow crouched next to the tub, and Johanna could see that the winged woman had white eyes. She leaned in close to Johanna and started whispering in German.

"Through this holy anointing, may the Lord in His love and mercy help you with the grace of the Holy Spirit," the death angel said softly. "May the Lord who frees you from sin save you and raise you."

Johanna smiled and closed her eyes, her head lowering onto her chest. The death angel strolled around the apartment, the smell of demon still strong. Emma tried to remember things she used to like as a human, such as music, food, and going to the movies with her friends. Now, she spends her downtime in the hut that once belonged to an angel named Dumah, on the beach or out on the sea in her boat. Some nights she stays on the ship past sundown and waits for things in the water to start moving around. Every once in a while, she catches a glimpse of a redheaded little girl floating under the water's surface. She can't talk to her or help her. But she still doesn't want her to feel alone.

Emma looked out of the apartment window, down onto the busy street. A young man with ashy blonde hair crossed the road adjacent to the building. Once across the street, the young man turned around and looked up, right at Emma. She could see his hazel eyes squint as he smiled at her, his teeth so white that they almost blinded her. She had only been an angel for about 40 years, but she spent every day thinking about him. She tried to be there for suicide deaths to give people their last rites, hoping to save as many souls as possible. Ankou, the demon who had been tormenting her for decades, disappeared into the crowd. Emma put her hand on the hilt of her sword, which was softly glowing red with flames.

Author's Note

Content Warning: This fictional piece of literature may contain content disturbing or offensive to some readers. This is not my intent. It is simply a work of fiction that started with a nightmare I had five years ago and has since then become the inspiration for the fantasy world I've created. This book contains material for readers who may be sensitive to subjects such as self-harm/suicide, dark religious themes, violence and death, sexual abuse, and homophobia. Please note that it is not the author's intent to cause distress to any reader, but if you find any of these subjects triggering, please take note and proceed with caution. Remember to practice self-care before, during, and after reading. For more information, please go to: @vanessakramerauthor on Instagram

*If you or someone you know is in crisis and needs immediate help, Call or text 988 to connect with the 988 Suicide & Crisis Lifeline . The Lifeline provides 24-hour, confidential support to anyone in suicidal crisis or emotional distress.

Made in the USA
Columbia, SC
07 February 2025

52731138R10231